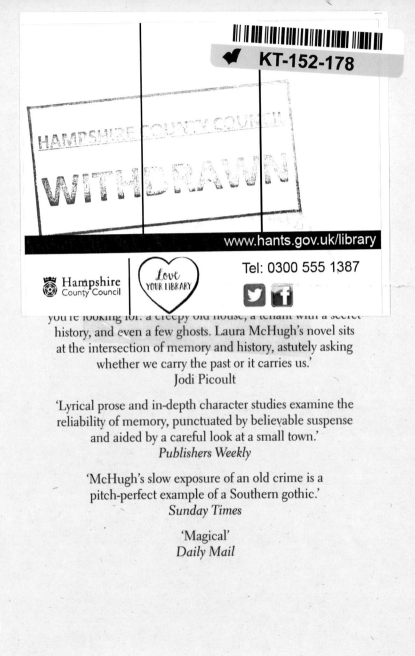

you're looking for: a creepy old house, a tenant with a secret history, and even a few ghosts. Laura McHugh's novel sits at the intersection of memory and history, astutely asking whether we carry the past or it carries us.'
Jodi Picoult

'Lyrical prose and in-depth character studies examine the reliability of memory, punctuated by believable suspense and aided by a careful look at a small town.'
Publishers Weekly

'McHugh's slow exposure of an old crime is a pitch-perfect example of a Southern gothic.'
Sunday Times

'Magical'
Daily Mail

Also available by Laura McHugh

The Weight of Blood

Arrowood

Laura McHugh

arrow books

3 5 7 9 10 8 6 4 2

Arrow Books
20 Vauxhall Bridge Road
London SW1V 2SA

Arrow Books is part of the Penguin Random House group of companies
whose addresses can be found at global.penguinrandomhouse.com.

Penguin
Random House
UK

Copyright © Laura McHugh 2016

Laura McHugh has asserted her right to be identified as the author of this
Work in accordance with the Copyright, Designs and Patents Act 1988.

First published by Century in 2016
(First published in the USA by Spiegel & Grau in 2016)
First published in paperback by Arrow Books in 2017

www.penguin.co.uk

A CIP catalogue record for this book is available from the British Library.

ISBN 9780099588351

Printed and bound in Great Britain by Clays Ltd, St Ives Plc

In memory of Floyd and Telka Silvers and the little white house on South Fourteenth Street

Do not stand at my grave and weep.
I am not there; I do not sleep.
I am a thousand winds that blow.
I am the diamond glints on snow.
I am the sunlight on ripened grain.
I am the gentle autumn rain.
When you awaken in the morning's hush,
I am the swift uplifting rush
Of quiet birds in circled flight.
I am the soft stars that shine at night.
Do not stand at my grave and cry.
I am not there; I did not die.

— Mary Elizabeth Frye,
    "Do Not Stand at My Grave and Weep"

Arrowood

CHAPTER 1

I used to play a game where I imagined that someone had abandoned me in a strange, unknown place and I had to find my way back home. There were various scenarios, but I was always incapacitated in some way—tied up, mute, missing a limb. I thought that I could do it blind, the same way a lost dog might trek a thousand miles to return to its owner, relying on some mysterious instinct that drew the heart back to where it belonged. Sometimes, in the towns where I'd lived after Keokuk, in a bedroom or classroom or while walking alone down a gravel road, I'd pause and orient myself to Arrowood, the Mississippi

River, home. *It's there*, I'd think, knowing, turning toward it like a needle on a compass.

Now, as I crossed the flat farmland of Kansas and northern Missouri, endless acres of wheat and corn blurring in the dense heat, I felt the road pulling me toward Iowa, as though I would end up there no matter which way I turned the wheel. I squinted into the bright afternoon sky, my sunglasses lost somewhere among the hastily packed bags and boxes I'd crammed into the back of my elderly Nissan. It was late September, the Midwestern air still stifling, unlike the cool sunshine I'd left behind in Colorado, where the aspens had just begun to turn.

Back in February, when I was still on track to finish my master's degree, my recently remarried mother had called to let me know that my dad, Eddie, had keeled over dead on a blackjack table at the Mark Twain Casino in LaGrange. I hadn't heard from my dad in the months leading up to his death, and hadn't seen him in more than a year, so I had a hard time placing my feelings when I learned that he was gone. I had already lost him, in a way, long ago, in the wake of my sisters' disappearance, and while I'd spent years mourning that first loss of him, the second loss left me oddly numb.

Still, I'd wept like a paid mourner at his funeral. The service was held in Illinois, where he'd been living, and most of the people in attendance, members of the Catholic parish he'd recently joined, barely knew him. I hated how funerals dredged up every shred of grief I'd ever felt, for the deceased or otherwise, each verse of "Amazing Grace" cutting into me and tearing out tiny bits of my insides. The priest wore a black cape over his cassock, and when he raised his arms to pray, it spread out dramatically, revealing a blood-red lining. He droned on at length, reminding us how much we had in common with the dead: We all had dreams, regrets, accomplishments, people we'd loved and disappointed, and at some point, for each of us, those earthly concerns would fall away, our lives replaced in an instant by darkness or—if you believed—light. Sometimes death came too soon, sometimes not soon enough, and only for certain sinners did it come at a time of one's choosing.

When he spoke of those who had preceded my father in death, he didn't mention Violet and Tabitha. Nor did he name them as survivors. My little sisters were neither alive nor dead, hovering somewhere in between, in the hazy purgatory of the missing. I had been the sole witness to their kidnapping when I was eight years old, and I had spent my childhood wondering if the man who took them might come back for me. He was never arrested, and no bodies were ever found.

Dad was buried in Keokuk, at the Catholic cemetery—despite the rift between them, Granddad hadn't gone so far as to kick him out of the Arrowood family plot—but I didn't attend the interment. No graveside service had been included in his prepaid burial plan, and my father was lowered into the earth without any last words.

Months later, a lawyer for the family trust called to inform me that Arrowood, the namesake house my great-great-grandfather had built on the Mississippi River bluff, the house we had left not long after my sisters' abduction, was mine. It had sat empty for seventeen years, maintained by the trust, purposely kept out of my father's reach to prevent him from selling it. Now I was finally going home.

It hadn't been a difficult choice to make. Even before I had given up on what was supposed to be my last semester of school, there hadn't been much tying me to Colorado. I was twenty-five years old, working as a graduate assistant in the history department, and renting an illegal basement apartment, the kind with tiny windows near the ceiling that would be difficult to escape from in a fire. The college fund Nana and Granddad had left for me was close to running out. I sat alone in my room at night staring at blank pages on my laptop, my fingers motionless on the keys, waiting for words that wouldn't come, the title of my unfinished thesis stark on the glowing screen: "The Effects of Nostalgia on Historical Narratives." Colorado had never felt like home. I had thought at first that the mountains could be a substitute for the river, something to anchor me, but I was wrong.

With the loss of my dad, the number of people in the world who knew both parts of me—the one that existed before my sisters were taken, and the one that remained after—had dwindled to a terrifying low. I worried that the old me would vanish if there was no one left to confirm her existence. When the lawyer said that Arrowood was mine, my first thoughts had nothing to do with the logistics or implications of moving back to Keokuk and living in the old house alone. I didn't wonder if the man who had haunted my dreams was still there. I thought of my sisters playing in the shade of the mimosa tree in the front yard, of my childhood bedroom with the rose-colored wallpaper and ruffled curtains. And I thought of Ben, who knew the old me best of all. A sense of urgency flared inside me, electricity tingling through my limbs, and I was dumping dresser drawers onto the bed, pulling everything out of the closet before I had even hung up the phone.

THE PEOPLE OF IOWA WELCOME YOU: FIELDS OF OPPORTUNITIES. As I passed over the Des Moines River and saw that sign, my breath came easier, like I'd removed an invisible corset. I had been born at the confluence of two rivers, the Des Moines and the Mississippi, and an astrologer once explained that because I was a Pisces, my life was defined by water. I was slippery, mutable, elusive; like a river, I was always moving and never getting anywhere.

It was strange, crossing into Iowa, that I could feel different on one side of the bridge than the other, yet it was true. Each familiar sight helped ease a bone-deep longing: the railroad trestle, the cottonwoods crowding the riverbank, the irrigation rigs stretching across the fields like metal spines, the little rock shop with freshly cracked geodes glinting on the windowsills. I rolled down the window and breathed the Keokuk air, a distinct mix of earthy floodplain and factory exhaust.

The Mississippi lay to my right, and even though I couldn't yet see it beyond the fields, I could sense it there, deep and constant.

I followed the highway into town, which, according to the welcome sign, had shrunk by a third, to ten thousand people, since I'd moved away. A hundred years before, when riverboat trade thrived on the Mississippi, Keokuk had been hailed as the next Chicago, at one point boasting an opera house, a medical college, and a major league baseball team. A dam and hydroelectric plant were constructed to harness the river, and at the time of their completion in 1913, they were the largest in the world. Later, factories cropped up along the highway, but many had since shuttered their doors, the jobs disappearing with them. What remained as Keokuk faded was a mix of grandeur and decay: crumbling turn-of-the-century architecture, a sprawling canopy of old trees that had begun to lose their limbs, broad streets and walkways that had fallen into disrepair.

The houses grew older and larger and more elaborate as I passed through the modest outskirts and into the heart of town. Block after block of beautiful hundred-year-old homes, no two alike, some well preserved, some badly neglected, others abandoned and rotting into the ground, traces of their former elegance still evident in the ruins.

I crossed over Main Street to the east side, where the road turned to brick and rattled the loose change in my cup holder, reading the familiar street signs aloud as I passed them. Though I'd never driven here on my own, I didn't need signs to find my way. I turned left onto Grand Avenue, the last street before the river. It had always been the most coveted address in town, and the fine homes were owned by people who could afford their upkeep: doctors like my late granddad, bank presidents, plant managers who had never worked a day on the line.

There were Romanesque Victorians, Queen Annes, Gothic Revivals, Jacobethans, Neoclassicals, Italianates, each house two stories or three, with towers and cupolas and columns. They sat on deep, tree-lined lots, the ones on the east side backing to a bluff two hundred feet above the Mississippi. Illinois forests and farmland stretched into the distance across the river, the occasional church steeple or water tower punctuating an expanse of green.

Two blocks down, I pulled into the driveway at Arrowood and stopped the car, taking in my first view of the house in nearly a decade. I had expected it to seem smaller now that I was grown, the way most things from childhood shrink over time. But Arrowood, built in the heavily ornamented Second Empire style, was as imposing as ever, three stories plus a central tower rising up between two ancient oak trees. Scrolled iron cresting topped the distinctive mansard roof, the tower hiding the widow's walk at the back of the house where my ancestors had once watched for barges coming down the river. Embedded in the corner of the lawn was a small plaque acknowledging the house as a national historic property and a stop on the Underground Railroad. I pulled forward to park in the porte cochere and got out to wait for the caretaker, who would be showing up to give me the keys.

A bank of dusky clouds had pushed in from the north, the soupy air making me feel as though I had gotten dressed straight out of the bath, my tank top and shorts sticking uncomfortably to my skin. I followed the mossy brick path alongside the house, marveling at the fact that Arrowood appeared not to have aged in my absence; while the flower beds at the side of the house were now empty, and the hydrangeas that once bordered the front porch were gone, I couldn't tell by looking at the house itself that any time had passed. The wraparound porch was freshly painted, the white spindles and fretwork bright against the dark gray clapboard. The mimosa tree still stretched its impossibly long limbs across the front yard, and I could picture the twins running through the grass, the gold car speeding away. I took a breath, and it was there: the lingering pain of a phantom wound inflicted long ago.

My mother had warned me that it was a mistake to come back, that Arrowood was best left in the past, and if I was smart I'd pray for an electrical fire and a swift insurance payout. I had set foot inside the house only once since we left, and for all the years I'd been away, I'd felt a nagging sense of dislocation. Nostalgia had always fascinated me, the bittersweet longing for a time and place left behind. I'd studied the phenomenon extensively for my thesis, not surprised to learn that nostalgia was once thought to be a mental illness or a physical affliction; to me, it was both. I had loved this house beyond reason, had felt its absence like the ache of a poorly set bone.

From the time we moved away up until I was fifteen years old, I had returned to Keokuk every summer to visit Grammy (my mother's mother) and my great-aunt Alice at the Sister House a few blocks to the south. I would haunt the sidewalk outside of Arrowood, peeking into the dark windows with my friend Ben Ferris whenever we thought no one would catch us, wishing that I could go inside. Nana gave me a copy of *Legendary Keokuk Homes*, published by the Lee County historical society, and I had immersed myself in the histories of all the old houses, especially Arrowood. I wasn't sure anymore how much of what I remembered about the house was actual memory and how much had leached into me from the book and Nana's stories. Now that I was allowed back in, I was afraid it wouldn't match the vision in my head, that it would all look wrong. The one time Ben and I had managed to sneak inside — the summer we were fifteen — it had been too dark and we were distracted by more pressing things.

I glanced over at the Ferris house next door, a cream-colored Gothic Revival with steep gables and narrow lancet windows and a handsome brick carriage house beside the drive. Maybe Ben was over there now, close enough to hear me if I called his name. I didn't know what I would say if I saw him, how I would explain the years of silence.

The breeze picked up, fluttering the delicate fernlike leaves of the mimosa, and a few raindrops specked the front walk as a four-door Dodge truck lumbered into the drive and parked behind my car. The caretaker climbed out, a man about my dad's age whose copper-colored hair had retreated halfway up his skull, revealing a broad, shiny forehead. His features crowded together at the center of his face, a bit too close to each other, as though they didn't realize they had room to spread out. He wore tan Carhartt pants and work boots and a navy-blue shirt with the sleeves rolled up to accommodate his thick forearms.

"Miss Arrowood?" He had a raspy voice and a cordial smile. "I'm Dick Heaney. Sorry to keep you waiting."

"You didn't, really," I said. "I just got here."

"It's such a pleasure to finally meet you," he said. "I don't know if your mother ever told you, but we were good friends back in the day. I knew your dad, too. He was a few years above me in school."

I nodded, wanting to be polite, though I'd never heard either of my parents mention him. I hadn't even known Heaney's name until I spoke to the lawyer.

"I was so sorry to hear about Eddie. I can't imagine how hard that must've been for you."

I looked away, uncomfortable with his sympathy. I didn't want to talk to Heaney about my dad. I didn't want to talk about anything. I wished that he would give me the keys and drive away, leaving me alone with the house.

"Well, I've got everything set up for you, I believe," he said. "All the utilities are up and running. Internet, too. And the cleaning crew was here not too long ago, so everything should be in good shape."

"I appreciate it."

"Here you go." He dug a key ring out of his pocket. "They're marked, one for the front door and one for the back, off the laundry. The doors to the porches still have the skeleton keys in their locks, though most of them don't open anymore." He craned his neck toward my car. "You got a moving truck coming?"

"No."

"Oh, okay. If you want to pop your trunk open, I'll start carrying things in. We're fixing to get soaked here in a minute."

"You don't have to do that," I said. "There's not much to carry."

"I'm happy to help."

"That's so nice of you. I can take care of it on my own, though."

He stuck his hands into his pockets. "Well, if you change your mind, let me know. You've got my number. I'll be by to cut the grass in a day or two, but if you need anything before then, give me a holler. My workload's pretty light at the moment, so I'm available whenever you need me."

I hoped I hadn't offended him by turning down his offer to help carry my things. He'd been working at Arrowood for ten years, since the original caretaker retired, and the house had been vacant the entire time. I wondered if it would be difficult for him to adjust to my being here. There would be less work for him now, since I could handle daily upkeep on my own, but there would still be things for him to do. He would keep making repairs as long as the trust had money to pay for them.

Heaney was halfway to his truck when he turned around. "I can see a bit of your mother in you," he said. "Welcome back, Miss Arrowood."

It was unusual for someone to compare me to my mother. I didn't resemble her, and I hated to think that we were anything alike, yet he seemed to intend it as a compliment. Maybe she was different back when he knew her, before she'd had children and lost them.

Once Heaney had backed out of the drive, I approached the wide front steps. A wren eyed me from the porch railing, and when I got closer, it chirped and flew up into the mimosa tree. The front door was comically large and elaborately detailed, like something out of a fairy tale, and I wondered where you would find another one like it if it had to be replaced.

I turned the key in the lock and pushed. The door didn't give easily, seeming to lean into me as I leaned against it, but I managed to get it open far enough to step inside. Darkness closed in as I shut it behind me. All the curtains were drawn, the only light filtering in through the stained-glass window above the second-floor landing. The air was heavy with the antique smell of old books and wood polish and moth-balls, and I could feel it pressing against me from all sides as I stood, feeling exposed, in the cavernous center hall. My breath seemed to echo, bouncing off the black walnut floors, the old-fashioned wallpa-per, the lofty plaster ceiling, to whisper in my ears.

To the left was a parlor with sliding pocket doors that led to the din-ing room, with its pressed-tin ceiling and venetian-glass chandelier, and the kitchen beyond it. To the right was Granddad's office and a music room with a 1960s Sears console stereo and a Mathushek square grand piano that I had never heard anyone play. I followed the hall past the curved walnut staircase to the drawing room at the back of the house, my sandals ticking on the hardwood. It was brighter here, the curtains thin and gauzy. Sheets covered the furniture, though I could make out the familiar shapes beneath: the ancient leather sofa and chairs, worn slick by a hundred years of legs and elbows; the inlaid mahogany coffee table that my mother had ruined when she spilled a bottle of neon-pink fingernail polish on it. Triple-hung windows looked out over the flagstone terrace and down to the river. The window glass was old and imperfect, marked with bubbles and whorls. It seemed unlikely that the windows had remained intact all these years, and I wondered if the caretaker would have gone to the trouble of reglazing broken ones with antique glass or if the trust that provided for Arro-wood went so far as to stipulate such a thing.

Outside, a decorative wrought-iron fence marked the back of the yard, the only thing keeping someone from walking off the edge of the bluff and tumbling to the water below. A stone table and bench sat out on the terrace, along with two large urns that used to overflow with petunias and sweet potato vines. There was the crab apple tree, minus the sandbox my granddad had built beneath it for me and my sisters, and the pole that had once held a martin birdhouse modeled after Ar-rowood. It was like one of those children's games where you compare two pictures to find the differences; the view was deceptively similar to the one in my memory, except that certain pieces were missing.

I passed the hall that led to the laundry room and the porte cochere and returned to the main staircase, the heat and humidity growing more oppressive as I ascended to the second floor. I peeled my shirt away from my skin to fan myself. My parents' bedroom was down the hallway to the left, and while it was the largest of the bedrooms, with a sitting room attached, I had no desire to make it my own. I turned to the right, past the narrow stairwell that led to the third floor and the widow's walk, and paused, swallowing the bitter lump that rose in my throat as I neared the last three doors. They were identical to all the others: four-paneled, dark walnut stain, faceted glass knobs, transom windows above that didn't open but let light bleed through.

The doors were closed, and I pictured the rooms as they had been when my sisters were here. Matching yellow cribs nestled end to end under the bright windows of their bedroom—old cribs that my mother groused about because the slats were spaced just right for the twins to get their arms and legs stuck; two child-size rocking chairs along the wall, one scarred with tiny tooth marks where Violet had gnawed on it; Madeline books and plastic stacking rings scattered on the braided rug, along with two of every stuffed animal, a Noah's ark of Elmos and Barneys and Winnie-the-Poohs, to keep covetous tears to a minimum. Next to Violet and Tabitha's room was the bathroom we shared, with the silver striped wallpaper and cold marble floor and old-fashioned claw-foot tub. My room, on the opposite side of the hall: white sleigh bed that had belonged to another Arden Arrowood, who had died of pneumonia at ten years old; a shelf of antique dolls that I was not allowed to touch; ruffled pink curtains Grammy had sewn for my sixth birthday.

I left the twins' door closed and stepped into my old room, my stomach knotting up as I removed the draped sheets from the furniture. My bed was still there, and the matching dresser, and the rolltop desk, where I'd kept markers and crayons and a collection of geodes that my dad had cracked open with a hammer. We had left all the furniture behind in the move, because Granddad didn't want us taking a single thing that belonged to Arrowood. I'd often thought of this room, of my abandoned belongings awaiting my return, and now I inhaled as deeply as I could, filling my chest until it burned, imagining that the stale air was preserved from my childhood, that breathing it in could somehow take me back to that Saturday seventeen years ago when I had last seen my sisters, before anything bad had happened.

CHAPTER 2

The storm held off, the clouds grumbling and spitting but not willing to commit. I unloaded my car, stacking boxes of history books at the foot of the staircase to carry up later, and took my travel mug into the kitchen to dump out the last of the burnt coffee I'd bought at a truck stop outside Kansas City. I pressed my hands against the cool marble countertop. There was still a large grayish stain near the sink where I had once spilled a pitcher of grape juice. I'd thought my mother would yell at me, but she had merely snorted. *Who cares? That counter's old and ugly like everything else in this house.* She had wanted to replace it with shiny new laminate, something Nana never would have allowed.

It was past dinnertime. My stomach hadn't felt right all day, but now, standing in the empty kitchen, I was starving. I checked the refrigerator out of habit, though of course there was nothing inside. I was irrationally panicked by the thought of leaving Arrowood so soon after I'd returned to it, like it might disappear in my absence, but I needed to get something to eat. "I'll be right back," I said, patting the front door as I locked it.

I drove slowly down Grand, relieved to see that all the houses I remembered were still there, and then cut over toward Main Street to get to the A&W Drive-In, where Grammy and I used to go in the summer for Coney Dogs and root beer floats. As I approached the restaurant, expecting to see the familiar orange and brown sign, I noticed that all of the outdoor order stations had been removed. I pulled in under the awning and saw that the building was empty. Industrious wasps had lined the window frames with papery honeycomb nests.

Disappointed, I got back on the road and kept driving, trying to think of someplace else to eat. I passed the old Kmart and saw that its sign was missing, too. The store had been transformed into an Assembly of God church, a banner with hand-lettered worship times strung above the automatic doors. Toward the end of Main, where it turned back into the highway, a Walmart had been built at the edge of town, its massive blacktop parking lot sprawling over what had once been a soybean field. A new strip mall huddled nearby, filled with standard small-town shops like Dollar Tree and Payless, and next to that was a Sonic Drive-In, its neon sign obscenely bright against the overcast sky.

Sonic held none of the nostalgia of A&W, where the root beer had been served in frosted glass mugs, but it was a drive-in, and that had to count for something. I ordered a corn dog, which arrived limp and greasy, and a limeade, which was served in a sweating Styrofoam cup. I didn't want to sit in my car staring at the Walmart as I ate, so I drove to Rand Park to sit on a bench in the muggy evening air and watch the river roll by.

The Mississippi was just as I remembered it, wide and gray beneath the dull clouds, its calm surface swirled here and there with eddies. I knew all of its variations: muddy and swollen in late spring, bearing dead trees with the bark skinned away, smooth as bone; deep blue in the summer sun, the shallows choked with water lilies; ice-sheathed in winter and dotted with duck blinds. When I was little, there had been a rock wall between the park and the water, but it had washed away in the flood of '93, the year before we moved. I used to come to the park with Grammy and Grampy, my mother's parents, and in one of my few clear memories of him, Grampy had climbed over the wall to scoop a baby turtle out of the river for me. It had been no bigger than a quarter.

After I finished eating, I pulled out my cellphone to call my mother and let her know I'd made it to Keokuk. She was living in Minnesota with her new husband, Gary. Technically he wasn't "new," since they'd been married for nearly five years, but I was still getting used to the idea of him. Gary presided over the congregation of an evangelical megachurch, one of the largest in a regional franchise. I didn't believe Mom at first, when she explained that churches could be franchised, the same as a Kentucky Fried Chicken.

I attended a service with her once when I was visiting, and found the Passage to be the complete opposite of the Catholic churches I'd attended growing up. I was used to kneeling on a wooden rail and re-citing rote prayers with a gruesome, life-size figure of the crucified Christ hanging over the altar. The Passage had a coffee shop in the lobby that sold DVDs of Gary's sermons, and a bright yellow play-ground slide that funneled children downstairs to Sunday school. A Christian rock band played onstage, complete with a concert-quality light show, and on the back of each lushly cushioned pew, instead of a little shelf holding hymnals or missals, there was a cup holder for your latte. It didn't feel like a church, and I supposed maybe that was the point.

I was glad to see Mom doing well—she had been despondent for so long after what happened to the twins—but she seemed to have become a different person. She had stopped taking the pills she'd depended on for as long as I could remember, the ones to ease her anxiety and manage her depression and help her sleep at night. She was always quoting televangelist Joel Osteen, or starting sentences with "Gary says . . ." instead of speaking for herself. She shopped at Chico's now, and Coldwater Creek, and wore a flashy diamond ring, which she constantly reminded me was 1.2 carats, as if that meant anything to me.

My mother thought that Gary had come into her life through divine intervention, the hand of God pushing them together. She and Dad had been separated for some time, though not divorced, and purposefully or not Dad had drifted closer to Keokuk, tightening his orbit around the place he'd been set on leaving. I had gone away to college, leaving Mom alone for the first time in her life, in a shabby duplex in Rochester. My mother, who had ignored Grammy's deathbed pleas that she return to church, claimed that the Holy Spirit came to her one morning and dragged her out from under the covers. According to Mom, the Spirit guided her as she showered, curled her hair, dressed in her nicest suit (the navy polyester one that she wore to funerals), and drove until she reached a church. The Arrowoods were Catholic, and my mother's family was Methodist, but Mom wasn't concerned with denominations. She recognized the Passage from a commercial she had seen on television. When Pastor Gary shook my mother's hand that day, she felt peace flowing into her after years of emptiness, filling up all the dark, dusty cracks in her soul.

A romance blossomed during their weekly Bible study meetings. They married soon after my parents' divorce was final and moved into a spacious new ranch house—so new they got sick breathing fumes from the carpet and paint. I'd never known my mother to be religious, but she claimed that she had been born again, and she played the part of pastor's wife with the convincing zeal of a pre-scandal Tammy Faye Bakker.

Mom answered just as the machine was picking up. "It's me," I said. "I made it."

"Arden, I still think this is a mistake," Mom said. I could hear a TV news show in the background, the kind where everybody talks over each other until one of them starts yelling, and then they see who can yell the loudest. "What about school? I know it can't be easy, not after the mess you got yourself into, but Gary says if you don't finish now, it'll get harder and harder to go back."

"I didn't call to talk about that, Mom. I just wanted to let you know I got here okay."

"I'm only thinking of your best interests. It's hard enough to get a job these days." She said it like she knew from experience, which she didn't. She hadn't worked in a long time, unless you counted being Gary's wife. "And you know it didn't go so well when you were staying up here with us, so that's not really an option if things don't pan out."

"Yeah, well, that's one thing I don't have to worry about now, a place to stay."

She sighed heavily and I imagined her eyes rolling, her pale lashes made spidery with multiple coats of black mascara. "Gary and I are praying for you, that you'll get yourself back on track. We're praying real hard."

I pictured her and Gary praying for me while they drank their lattes and swayed to the Christian rock band that played onstage at the Passage, Mom wearing a brightly printed Chico's tunic and matching acrylic nails, and Gary with his hair shellacked into a gravity-defying pompadour. They were praying that I would get myself together, that they would never again receive a late-night phone call requiring them to come to my aid.

"Hey," I said, wanting to change the subject. "I didn't realize the caretaker was an old friend of yours and Dad's."

"What?"

"Dick Heaney, the caretaker. He said he knew you back in school?"

"Maybe," she said. I could sense her disinterested shrug over the phone. I'd been dismissed by it plenty of times myself. "It's a small town."

After I hung up, I sat watching the river awhile longer, the surface changing color, chameleon-like, as the sun lowered down behind the clouds. Gnats and river moths flitted around my face, landing on my sweating skin, catching in my hair. My muscles were stiff from the long drive, and my head was beginning to ache, a red drumbeat at the base of my skull. I drove back to the house (*my house*, I whispered as I opened the door) and headed upstairs to take a bath.

The bathroom was exactly as I remembered it, with the same striped wallpaper and veined marble floor and framed print of Raphael's "Sistine Madonna," which had faded into sepia tones. The old claw-foot tub was still there, each scaly foot clutching a silver ball. The twins and I had taken baths together, always begging our mother to dump in more Mr. Bubble, which she usually refused to do. She'd sit on the toilet seat with her ratty copy of *Fear of Flying* splayed between her fingers, shaking her head without looking up from the pages. I opened the cabinet under the sink, half-expecting to see the same pink bottle of bubble bath seventeen years later, or maybe even *Fear of Flying*, which never seemed to leave the bathroom, though of course I found neither. A family of silverfish scuttled under a rusted toilet brush, disturbed by the light.

I twisted the handles to run water in the bathtub and flinched at the high-pitched shriek that cut through the quiet room. I had nearly forgotten how it was in an old house, all the ghostly sounds: the way the floors creaked and settled as night fell, the radiators knocked and hissed, doors slammed shut when the wind took a deep breath through the chimneys. I'd forgotten how water laboring through ancient pipes could trick you into hearing voices in the walls. I had thought once, when I was little, that I heard someone in the hallway whispering my name. Instead of calming me with logical explanations, my mother had suggested that the other Ardens were calling to me, the ones who had died in the house long before I was born. I had nightmares about them crawling into my bed in filmy white nightgowns: Arden Blythe, who had succumbed to pneumonia in the third-floor bedroom, her skin burning with fever and her lungs filling up; Arden Jane, who had fallen from the landing and broken her neck; Arden Amelia, who went into anaphylactic shock, stung by a bee that had entered the kitchen in a bouquet of peonies. None of them had lived past childhood.

I stripped off my clothes and sank into the water, leaning back and stretching out as far as I could. Even then, my toes couldn't reach the opposite end of the tub—it was grand in scale, the same as the rest of the house. When I closed my eyes, I could smell the sweet candy scent of Mr. Bubble, and I wished it could be that simple, to shut my eyes and move back in time, erasing everything that had gone wrong in the years between. I traced the scars on the inside of my arm, jagged pink lines spanning wrist to armpit, reminders that I could not undo anything, that I could not go back to Colorado.

The old rubber stopper I'd put in the drain was shrunken and cracked, and the bathwater seeped out before it had a chance to turn cold. I nearly fell stepping out of the tub onto the slick marble floor, where a large puddle had spread out across the tiles. Either I'd splashed water over the side without realizing it, or the tub was leaking. I'd be more careful next time, and if there was a leak, I could call Heaney to come and fix it.

Back in my room, I unpacked my sheets and made the bed, then parted the long ruffled curtains, the ones Grammy had made for me. After years in the sun, they had faded from bubble-gum pink to the color of jaundiced flesh, and dust sifted down to the floor as I moved them. My skin felt clammy after the bath, refusing to dry, and I wanted to open the windows, let in the night air. After a few minutes of struggling, I gave up. The wooden sashes had settled into place after years of inertia. On the other side of the glass, the moon was obscured by clouds, and it was too dark to see the river, but no matter. I sensed it there, a living thing, an artery pulsing. I'd never felt right being away from it. In the dismal towns where we'd drifted after Keokuk, I'd look out my window at scrub brush or empty fields or a parking lot and find nothing large enough or strong enough to anchor me. Nothing outside but miles between me and the river and home.

I was too hot, my skin too slippery, to consider putting on a nightgown, so I loosened my towel and lay down on top of the sheets, thinking about my sisters' room. Were the cribs still there? The little rocking chairs? My mother hadn't taken any of their things when we moved, and I wondered if their dresses still hung in the closet, cloaked in spiderwebs, if their dolls and books remained strewn across the floor beneath a shroud of dust. I wasn't ready to find out.

I had read recently of a kidnapping that took place in a small Midwestern town not unlike Keokuk. A girl was playing in the park with her big sister when a man they recognized from their neighborhood called them over to his car. The younger sister turned her head to scan the playground, and when she turned back, her sister was climbing into the passenger seat. She heard the man say to the older girl, *I'm going to tell you a secret*. When he was found less than an hour later, the girl's body had already been dumped in a grove of hickory trees. I wondered what secret he had told her, once they were alone. *I'm the last thing you will ever see.*

I knew how she felt, the sister who didn't get into the car. I had been right there with Violet and Tabitha, had left them for only a minute. I wished that I had been taken, too, so they wouldn't have been alone. Instead, I was left behind and they went on without me, their lives from that moment a whispered secret that would never reach my ears.

CHAPTER 3

As I surfaced from sleep, the bed felt uncomfortably crowded, like someone was pressed up against me, but when I rolled over and opened my eyes, I was alone, the sun blazing through the windows, roasting me like a rotisserie chicken. It was disorienting to wake up in my childhood room, and I lay there for a minute, admiring all the little details that I had missed for so many years. The fleur-de-lis medallion on the ceiling, the intricate molding around the windows, the swirling patterns that emerged if you stared long enough at the rose-colored wallpaper, the hazy view of the Illinois riverbank through blistered glass.

I slid my phone off the nightstand to check my email, ignoring the little bubble that showed the number of unread messages, which had recently topped ten thousand. I'd long ago given up on opening or deleting all the unwanted mail: advertisements from Old Navy and Target, credit card offers, blog posts and newsletters I couldn't remember signing up for, notices for appointments I'd missed, bank statements I preferred to avoid. I scrolled through the most recent messages, still unable to break the habit of seeking out my adviser's name amid the junk. There was nothing from Dr. Endicott, or my fellow graduate assistants at the university—there hadn't been in months—though one name stood out, familiar and unwelcome: Josh Kyle, the founder of a website called Midwest Mysteries.

I had first heard from Mr. Kyle more than a year before. He'd tracked down my email address in the online student directory and wrote to introduce himself and request an interview. He called himself a "mystery buff" and was quick to distance himself from the more sensational sites that his site was often lumped in with, like CrimePhile and Haunted Heartland ("I am NOT one of those ghost hunters or gore freaks"). In that first email, Kyle had sounded like a twelve-year-old blogger who took himself too seriously. I wondered if he was, in fact, twelve years old, so I had pulled up Midwest Mysteries and clicked on the Contact page. Kyle's picture had been enhanced with a brooding black-and-white filter. His ball cap was pulled low over his sunglasses, leaving his face in shadow, his body hidden beneath a shapeless windbreaker.

When I read the feature he'd written on Midwest Mysteries about the twins' disappearance, I was surprised to find it more in-depth and insightful than other Internet articles I'd come across, most of which copied liberally from the "Arrowood Kidnapping" page on Wikipedia. He also mentioned a personal connection to the case: He was from nearby Fort Madison and remembered hearing about the twins on the news when he was a kid.

Why exactly do you want to interview me? I'd asked. I was all for bringing attention to the case if it could spark a new lead, but I didn't see how interviewing me would accomplish that. I didn't have anything new to add.

I'm writing a book, he'd replied. *About famous unsolved Iowa crimes. The three big ones are the Villisca ax murders, the* Des Moines Register *paperboy kidnappings, and the disappearance of your sisters. I want to add more personal details to bring the cases to life. It would be helpful if you could share some family stories, that sort of thing.*

So you're hoping to profit from this? I'd asked.

It's possible, he'd written, *that I could make some money, though I rarely make much from my writing. My other books have yet to break even. I'm not doing this to get rich. My ultimate goal is to reexamine cold cases, draw attention to them, in hopes that they might get solved.*

I wasn't completely sure that I believed him. Professional investigators had failed, and I had no reason to believe that an amateur one, a "mystery buff," would fare better. Was it even possible to solve a crime like the Villisca ax murders, when everyone involved was long dead? My sisters' case was nearly two decades old, and the paperboy kidnappings even older. It didn't seem likely that publishing personal details about the families would help anyone except for Josh Kyle, if it helped him to sell more books. I couldn't stop him from writing about my family, but I didn't have to assist him.

After that first encounter, I had blocked any emails from Kyle and tried to forget about him and his book. Then, the day my father's obituary hit the Keokuk paper, there was Mr. Kyle's name in my in-box again. He'd switched email accounts.

The subject line read, *Sorry for your loss.* In the body of the email, Kyle had sent his condolences and apologized for possibly offending me, noting that he'd sent several emails after our last exchange with no response and had taken the risk of emailing me from a different address in case I had blocked him. I didn't write back.

Today, though, his subject line froze my finger midscroll: *Harold Singer.*

There had been one man in town with a gold car like the one I'd seen drive away with my sisters inside, a factory worker named Harold Singer. The police had dogged him to the point that he lost his job at Union Carbide and was practically run out of town. Singer claimed that he had parked along Grand Avenue earlier in the day, that he liked to sit there looking at the nice houses while he ate lunch in his car. He claimed that he had not seen me or my sisters in the yard on the day in question.

My parents never discussed the case in front of me, and I didn't learn the details until I was a few years older, when Grammy allowed me to read through her scrapbook of newspaper clippings. I had heard snippets of gossip from kids at my new school, once they realized who I was, but I didn't know which parts were true until I saw it all in print. Regardless of Singer's claims, police obtained a search warrant for his house and car. Hidden in a crawl space beneath his home they uncovered shoe boxes containing dozens of rolls of undeveloped film. Yes, he admitted, he was an amateur photographer. That wasn't a crime. When the film was developed, investigators discovered that the photographs featured several houses around town, and that many of the pictures included children—playing in front yards, biking down the sidewalk, swinging on swing sets.

When Singer was questioned, he said that the children were incidental to the photos; he had been taking pictures of the houses to case them for potential robberies. Singer never wavered in his assertion that the timeline was all wrong, that he'd been at Arrowood around one o'clock that afternoon and then went home to sleep after finishing his lunch. No one believed him, because two witnesses (myself and my friend Ben Ferris, who lived next door) placed his car there closer to four. Ben had seen it from his bedroom window, and he knew what time it was because he was supposed to be practicing his violin. No one could confirm Singer's alibi; however, several interrogations, searches of his property, and the impounding of his car had not revealed any evidence that he'd taken the twins.

I had always believed that Singer was the one who had abducted them, because I saw my sisters in the gold car as it sped away. It was the only solid lead we had. The car wasn't located and searched until four days after the kidnapping. I knew how quickly Singer could have killed and disposed of Violet and Tabitha, or handed them off to someone else. In four days' time, he could have erased all evidence of the crime.

I opened Josh Kyle's email. *I'm sorry to bother you,* he wrote. *First of all, I heard that you've returned to Keokuk. (I'm sorry, by the way, if you were hoping to keep that quiet—the caretaker told someone at the utilities office as he was preparing for your arrival, and word spread, as you can imagine.) Anyhow, I wanted to welcome you back. Second, I gather from your lack of response that you're not interested in helping with the book, but I feel it's only fair to inform you that I'm no longer including the Villisca and Des Moines cases in this volume—the book will focus solely on your sisters' disappearance. I've done some investigating on my own and interviewed others involved in your case, including Harold Singer. Based on what I've learned, I believe your eyewitness account to be incorrect. I'd like to speak with you about what you claimed to see the day your sisters disappeared. I know how painful this must be, but if it were me, I'd want to know the truth.*

I wasn't sure what to think. Whatever truth Josh Kyle thought he'd unearthed, he must not have shared it with anyone officially associated with the case. No one had called me with any updates. There hadn't been any updates in years. And his accusation stung—that I was wrong about what I saw. How would he know? He wasn't there. What I saw that day was etched into a movie reel in my brain, and no matter how badly I wanted to forget what had happened, I couldn't. It played on an endless loop.

The twins were taken on a bright September afternoon. I had started second grade the week before, but this was a Saturday, Labor Day weekend, and it still felt like summer. My mother was somewhere inside the house, sleeping or reading a Danielle Steel novel or staring at a pile of laundry, the outside world muffled by thick plaster walls and heavy silk drapes and all the layers of black walnut woodwork. My father was away from the house, supposedly working. At the time, I couldn't have told you what he did or why he was working on a holiday weekend, though I'd once heard Granddad call him a snake-oil salesman. I had promised my mother I'd keep an eye on the twins for a little while, and I was happy to do it. As firstborn, I was naturally bossy, and at the age of eight, the only people I could boss around were Violet and Tabitha, who were not quite two years old.

I'd been up late the night before with an upset stomach, vomiting in the bathroom I shared with my sisters on our side of the second floor. I had crossed to the other side of the house in the dark to wake my mother and tell her that I was sick. She was alone in bed, a slight lump under the down duvet, Dad probably still awake somewhere downstairs, watching TV or listening to his records. Prescription bottles lined Mom's nightstand. She asked if I had a fever, and I said I wasn't sure. I wanted her to press her palm to my forehead, burn her hand, cry out for my father. I imagined her turning on all the lights, calling Granddad in a panic to ask him what to do. Instead she felt around for her sleeping pills, swallowed one dry, and sent me back to my room.

I was tired and light-headed when I woke up in the morning, though my stomach felt better, and if whatever I had was contagious, the twins hadn't yet come down with it by afternoon. We were playing Girl Scouts on the expansive front lawn, and I was the long-suffering troop leader. I wasn't supposed to take them outside, but it wasn't nearly as fun to play Scouts indoors. The twins were easily distracted and didn't pay any attention as I lectured them about their imaginary badges for making s'mores and identifying birds. They weren't old enough, really, for games with rules, and I wished that Mom would play, too. She hadn't played Girl Scouts with me in a long time. When she was pregnant with the twins, we had spent whole afternoons stretched out on her bed playing Candy Land. She would nod off sometimes in between turns, and I would stare at her stomach where her shirt had ridden up, the skin stretched so tight that it was tearing apart, jagged pink fissures spiraling out from her protruding belly button. The bigger her stomach got, the less patience she had for games. *Playing with children is hard*, she had told me, spreading her swollen fingers across the mound of her belly and pushing back against the pointy elbows and knees that gouged her from the inside. *Once your sisters are born, you'll have someone to play with you all the time*.

The twins lolled on the blanket I'd spread in the shade of the mimosa tree, where the afternoon sun couldn't reach us. We were close to the house, close enough that I thought Mom wouldn't yell at me if she found out we'd gone outside. None of our neighbors were out enjoying the nice weather. Mrs. Crutchfield, who lived in the Neoclassical to our left, had a diabetic foot and rarely left the house. Across the street, the Brubakers' Queen Anne sat empty, surrounded by scaffolding so that it could be painted and repaired while Mr. and Mrs. Brubaker were on vacation in the Wisconsin Dells. I glanced at Ben's house and considered asking for a third time if he could come out to play. The first time I'd knocked, his mother said he couldn't leave his room until he finished practicing his violin. He'd only recently started lessons and was still struggling with the first and simplest exercise, "Mississippi Hot Dog," which didn't even count as a song. Ben hadn't wanted to play violin. He had wanted to take an art class at the Y, but his mother hadn't given him a choice. The second time I knocked, Mrs. Ferris hadn't even bothered to answer the door.

Workers from the landscaping company were making a racket in the Ferrises' yard, at work on an all-day project to prepare their lawn, shrubs, sprinklers, and flower beds for fall. Two of the Tru-Lawn trucks were parked at the curb in front of our house, and an unfamiliar gold-colored car sat behind them. It was getting to be naptime for the twins, and I knew that I should take them inside before my mother came looking for them.

I remember holding Violet's soft, sweaty hand, admiring the clover crowns I'd strung together and placed on her and Tabby's identical white-blond heads in lieu of Girl Scout beanies. They were beautiful children, with my mother's pale hair and skin. Most people had trouble telling them apart. Even our father would sometimes call the twins by the wrong names when he scooped them up to kiss them good night. But I could always tell the difference. There were subtle clues that anyone could have noticed—Vi had a way of tilting her head when she smiled or laughed, and Tabby was the shyer of the two—but beyond that, I'd always had a sense of who was who. Violet was Violet and Tabitha was Tabitha, and anyone who loved them like I did could have told them apart in the dark.

The twins were fighting sleep and so was I, but then Tabby reached up and grabbed the dandelion I'd tucked behind my ear and said, "Mine." Violet snatched it out of her hand and screamed, "No! Mine-mine-mine!" and Tabby let out a supernatural howl.

"It's okay," I said, grabbing Tabby and kissing her sticky cheek. Both girls had grape juice stains on their faces that Mom hadn't bothered to wash off, and purple blotches all over the white blouses Grammy had sewn for them, the ones with bright yellow buttons shaped like ducks. "There are lots of dandelions. I'll run get some for you. For *both* of you."

I squeezed Violet's hand, told the twins to stay put, and ran around the side of the house toward the backyard, where dandelions had spread through the grass. There were thick patches of clover, too, and poison ivy vines climbing the iron fence. It had been that way since Tru-Lawn had stopped coming to our house early in the summer. I'd heard my mother complaining to my father about it, urging him to pay the bill or start tending to the lawn himself. I looked back over my shoulder once before turning the corner, to see Violet and Tabby chasing each other across the yard. I loved the way they ran, their arms flapping and their chubby little legs stuttering. They were smiling, their fight already forgotten.

I pulled the hem of my shirt up to form a pouch and filled it with dandelions, counting twice to make sure I had an even number so that they could be divided equally between the twins. Next door, mowers and hedge trimmers and Weed Eaters buzzed around the Ferrises' backyard. My head pulsed uncomfortably, a remnant of the previous night's illness. When I approached the front lawn, the twins were not under the tree.

I thought that they must be on the other side of the yard, just out of sight, or up on the porch, or that maybe my mother had taken them into the house. Then I heard a door slam. I turned to see the gold car peel away from the curb and, inside the passenger window, a flash of my sisters' white hair.

I stared after the car for a moment, confused, and then gasped at a visceral pain, like I had been stabbed through the chest with an icicle—as though my heart knew what my head hadn't yet grasped. I had been holding the dandelions in my shirt, and my hands dropped to my sides as I began to run, the yellow flowers falling at my feet as I sprinted across the lawn and down the sidewalk. The gold car was nearly out of sight. It turned toward Main, which could take it any number of places—across the river into Illinois, south to Missouri, north to the highway. I ran until I wheezed, looking down cross streets, but the car was gone.

I clicked Reply on Josh Kyle's email. *Let's meet*, I typed. *I'd love to hear why you think I'm wrong.*

I'd barely hit Send when his name popped up again at the top of my heap of new messages. *Thank you for agreeing to speak with me*, he said. *Friday at noon? We could meet at the roadside park on the river road, if that's all right with you—it's a good halfway point between us. I have something to show you.*

Yes, I replied. *See you in two days.*

CHAPTER 4

I tried to put the meeting with Josh Kyle out of my mind and focus on settling in. I went to get groceries at Hy-Vee, where Grammy had always shopped, and without realizing what I was doing, I'd filled the cart almost exclusively with my favorite childhood foods: blueberry Pop-Tarts, powdered doughnuts, SpaghettiOs, tomato soup, Cap'n Crunch cereal, Coca-Cola in little glass bottles. I bought some cheap wine, too, the kind that comes in a box with a spigot, and picked up a copy of the *Daily Gate City* so I could check job listings in the classifieds.

I didn't feel like unpacking after eating lunch, so I decided to take a tour through town to see if the rest of my old haunts had fared as poorly as the A&W Drive-In. I started with the Keosippi Mall, where Ben, his little sister, Lauren, and I had hung out on weekends in the summer. The parking lot was nearly empty when I pulled in, and all the store signs had been removed from the front of the building, leaving behind vague outlines that I still recognized as JCPenney, Woolworth's, RadioShack, and Montgomery Ward. Instead of movies, the weather-beaten theater marquee advertised a bingo night and service times for New Life Evangelical Bible Church. It appeared to be a trend in Keokuk, and maybe in all the other small, dying towns across the heartland: churches taking over abandoned retail space. Jobs trickled out and God seeped in to fill the void.

The public tennis courts where Ben and I had played were fractured and glittering with broken glass, the nets gone, the chain-link enclosure sagging halfway to the ground. The elementary school we had attended sat inexplicably empty, plywood over the windows, holes in the crumbling asphalt where the playground equipment had been torn out. I guessed that there were no longer enough students to fill two schools and they were all bused across town to the newer one.

On Main Street, Keasling's Pharmacy & Gifts, where Grammy had replenished her constant supply of Brach's Chocolate Stars, had been torn down, and a brand-new Walgreens perched directly across from the gaping space. The hardware store was gone, and the doughnut shop, and the deli. Many of the buildings on Main were unoccupied, their cracked plate-glass windows patched with cardboard and duct tape. One storefront had burned, its charred remains grown over with trumpet vines as it awaited demolition.

Since Main Street was also Highway 136, with the only bridge across the river for miles, light traffic flowed constantly in both directions, but the sidewalks were mostly empty: a teenage boy clacking by on a skateboard, his cheeks welted with acne, his unlaced shoes held together with black electrical tape; an emaciated woman in a tube top smoking a cigarette as she pushed a battered stroller; a pair of men in cheap suits drinking gas station coffees in front of the Keokuk Savings Bank.

I drove up and down the numbered streets starting with First, just west of the bridge, losing count of the abandoned houses. The yards were overgrown, paint weathered away, wood rotted out. It took me a while to realize that not all of the houses that looked abandoned were empty. I spied toys in the tall grass, televisions glowing inside broken windows, people going about their lives while their houses decomposed around them.

I knew it might be a bad idea, but I needed to see Grammy's house, the Sister House, where I had spent my summers, the house where my mother had grown up. The Sister House was a pink Victorian with a wraparound porch, surrounded by drooping evergreens that kept the front yard in perpetual shadow. It was known as the Sister House because it was built as a father's wedding gift to his two daughters, who were so close that they married a pair of brothers in a joint ceremony and refused to live apart. The upstairs and downstairs living spaces were identical, and a speaking tube connected the two floors so the sisters could talk to each other whenever they pleased.

My grandparents bought the house when my mother was small, renting out the upstairs apartment to pay the mortgage. After Grampy died, Grammy's sister, Alice, had moved in upstairs. The house became a Sister House again, though instead of newlyweds the sisters were widows. When Grammy and Aunt Alice passed away, Mom had moved their things to a storage unit and then sold the house at auction. We had needed the money.

I dropped my car off at Arrowood and walked south to Orleans Avenue, where gnarled elms hung over the sidewalk. Their roots had burrowed beneath the concrete slabs, heaving them up at odd angles and breaking them into pieces. In my mind, the Sister House sat on a hill, though now, as I approached it, the ground was barely sloped. I saw the drooping evergreens that shaded the yard, and then the house came into view. I stopped, a pinching sensation in my chest, as though someone were stitching it up: a needle punching through, thread pulling tight. It was hard to reconcile what I was seeing with the picture in my head. The porch had been removed, leaving a thick scar where it had been torn away, and the original carved wooden door had been replaced with one made of cheap fiberglass. The tall windows at the front of the house had been exchanged for squat vinyl ones, the gaps between old and new filled with chipboard. I couldn't tell anything else about the condition of the house, because it was covered in vines. Virginia creeper had swarmed over the yard, scaled the walls, and worked its way through a missing window on the second floor. The Sister House looked utterly abandoned, draped in a leafy shroud.

Without thinking, I entered the yard and made my way through the vines to the front door. A broken lockbox lay on the top step, the kind realtors use to store keys, but there was nothing inside. The crimping in my chest was unbearable, my legs wobbling as though my bones had gone limp. I reached out and tested the knob, which twisted easily in my hand. There was no traffic, no one walking by, the street barely visible through the trees. I slipped into the house and shut the door behind me.

I stood motionless, my skin prickling in the heat, and listened. The house was silent but didn't quite feel empty. The air was stifling and reeked of smoke—not just cigarettes, but other burnt things, as though someone had lit a bonfire indoors. A pile of ruptured trash bags lay just inside the entry, beer cans and fast food wrappers spilling out. A black puddle had seeped across the foyer and dried on the hardwood.

I edged around the trash bags into the living room, where the windows were covered with newspaper. Dead flies and mouse droppings peppered the floor, and the wood-paneled walls had been painted a deep purplish red, like raw liver. My pulse drummed in my ears. Gone were the green plaid couch, the knobby rug, the sagging bookcase, the framed photos of distant relatives on dusty farms. I knew that even if I dragged those things back from wherever my mother had stored them and arranged them exactly as they appeared in my memory, the room wouldn't feel the same. It looked like someone had been squatting here at some point. There were clothes piled in the corner and a mattress with a large brown stain spreading out from the center in concentric circles, as though someone had wet the bed over and over again.

The built-in china cabinets in the dining room, the ones Grampy had made, had been hacked apart, the splintered pieces piled on the floor like kindling. The tiny kitchen, where Grammy, Aunt Alice, and I had eaten hundreds of breakfasts at the Formica table, now appeared too small to have ever held furniture. How had all the knickknacks fit? I cataloged missing pieces: the white enamel trash can that opened with a foot pedal; the monolithic Westinghouse fridge; the squirrel-shaped nutcracker that had fallen on and broken Alice's toe; the coffee percolator; the aluminum canisters labeled FLOUR, SUGAR, and GREASE; the Coca-Cola bottle opener that had been attached to the edge of the counter; the ancient radio that gave the farm report every noon; the red metal step stool for reaching the highest cabinets. Stripped of those things, it was no longer my grandmother's kitchen. It was a room completely foreign to me. A room I did not want to be in.

I tried the switch in the hallway, but there was no power. The door to Grammy's bedroom at the end of the hall was missing, and a weak rectangle of light spilled from the opening. As I took a step forward, a shadow moved across the doorway, and I froze. I had always felt safe in this house, and now, looking down the hall where a shadow blocked the light, I was scared to breathe. Someone was in my grandmother's room.

The floor creaked, and I was running back toward the front of the house, passing the staircase without glancing up the stairs, the pinching in my chest like fingers reaching through my ribs to probe my heart. I flew through the front door and out to the street. Aunt Alice and my grandparents had been dead a long time, and now the Sister House was gone, too. It had been a mistake to go inside. I didn't want what I had seen to take root in my head, to ruin the carefully curated pictures in my memory. I jogged back toward Arrowood—fully understanding, for the first time, why Nana and Granddad had gone to such extreme measures to keep the house in the family and to ensure that it stayed exactly the same.

Back at Arrowood, I set to work unpacking and making the place feel lived in. Whomever Heaney had sent to clean hadn't done a very good job, and my first priority was to tackle some of the dust and cobwebs. I dug around in the laundry room cabinets looking for cleaning supplies. This back part of the house had once been servants' quarters, and there was a separate stairwell that led up to the second-floor hallway so that the help didn't have to use the main stairs. The laundry was a bright, serene space with tall windows on two sides to let in the sun. The plank floors and cabinets were painted a glossy white, the walls papered a soft dreamy blue, my great-grandmother's enormous French serpentine armoire the only dark piece in the room. A musty odor lingered in the air, like wet laundry left to mildew, though I doubted anyone had done laundry here in a good long while.

I found a can of furniture polish and some rags and carried them to the entryway. It was one of the few parts of the house that was not wallpapered. Growing up in a house rich with nineteenth-century character, my mother had longed for shag carpeting and beige drywall and popcorn ceilings. Arrowood was even more ornate and old-fashioned than the Sister House, and as soon as Nana and Granddad retired to Florida, leaving my parents and me alone in the house, Mom set out to update the décor. She vowed to peel off every shred of wallpaper, starting with the entry. It didn't take her long to give up once she realized how difficult it was to remove the glue—she grumbled that the

Arrowoods had probably boiled a horse in the front yard to make it—and the plaster walls were mottled gray and brown, like damp stone, where she'd angrily scraped them bare. *Looks like the inside of a crypt*, Mom had said. When Mrs. Ferris from next door saw it, she thought my mother had hired someone to apply a faux finish and asked how much it had cost.

I sprayed Old English on a rag and smoothed it over the wainscoting and the banister, moving on to the study to wipe down the bookshelves, which were still filled with Granddad's anatomy and physiology texts, medical journals, and leather-bound encyclopedias. My mother used to cram her paperback romance novels into the empty spaces, though none of her books remained. After a moment of uncertainty, I retrieved one of my boxes of books from the foot of the staircase and placed the volumes one by one next to Granddad's. *Lee County, Iowa: A Pictorial History; Keokuk and the Great Dam; Indian Chief: The Story of Keokuk; The River We Have Wrought: A History of the Upper Mississippi; Legendary Keokuk Homes.*

Among my history books was *The Illustrated Book of Saints*, which Nana had given to me as I prepared for my First Communion. Nana knew which saint to pray to in every situation. Saint Erasmus for abdominal pains. Saint Jude for lost causes. Saint Agatha to protect you from fire. I had been fascinated by the gruesome stories and pictures. Agatha, who had been assaulted and tortured, was depicted with her severed breasts on a plate. Saint Apollonia's teeth were broken and knocked out before she was burned to death. Saint Florian was sentenced to be burned alive, though when he proclaimed that he would ascend to heaven on the flames, he was drowned.

I had noticed, despite the many references to fire, that only a handful of saints were drawn with flames in their hands or hearts or atop their heads. Nana explained that the flame represented a deep religious fervor, and I decided that the burning saints were the best and most powerful, the closest to God. While I no longer believed that the saints were watching over me, I still invoked them absentmindedly from time to time, much as I could still recite the Nicene Creed or work a rosary in my sleep, though I had long since stopped going to church.

After I finished with the books, I pulled the sheets off the armchairs and the desk and slid the heavy drapes aside to let in some light. The room looked so much better that I decided to do the same throughout the first floor. When I was done, I dragged all the sheets down the hall to the laundry room and kicked them into a pile in the corner.

As I turned to go, I heard the muted trickle of water running. Back in Colorado, in my basement apartment, I had heard that sound every time someone upstairs took a shower or flushed the toilet, but here I was alone in the house. I imagined corroded plumbing leaking inside the walls, rotting the joists and softening the bones of the house, one of the many potential problems I'd hoped to avoid, right up there with fires from the remaining bits of knob-and-tube wiring. If Nana were here, she'd be praying to the patron saint of plumbing, whose name I couldn't recall. I couldn't quite tell where the sound was coming from, so I pressed my ear to the blue wallpaper to listen.

The doorbell rang then, a series of deep melodic gongs, startling me. Mom had chipped through a plaster wall with a hammer to disconnect the bell years ago, after cursing out the two young Mormons who had unintentionally woken the twins from a nap. It must have been reconnected after we'd moved away. I hurried back to the entry and peeked through the sidelight. I was slightly disappointed to see Heaney. I considered not answering the door, but my car was parked outside, so he knew I was home.

"Hi, Miss Arrowood." His lips lost their color as they stretched into a smile, as though the blood had been pressed out of them. "Sorry to bother you," Heaney said. "I wanted to let you know I was here before I gave you a scare creeping around the yard."

"Oh, thanks."

"You getting settled in?"

"Yeah."

Heaney's gaze drifted over my shoulder, into the house. "Anything you need me to take care of inside today?" I shook my head. "All right, then. Thought I'd check." He took a couple of steps back.

"Oh, wait, there is one thing—were you watering the grass out there a minute ago? Or using the hose for something?"

"No. Did you want me to? Water the lawn? Or . . . ?"

I shook my head, and after waiting fruitlessly for me to explain why I'd asked about the hose, Heaney edged closer. He was only a few inches taller than me, our eyes almost level, his breath bracingly antiseptic, like he had just rinsed his mouth with Listerine. I tried to imagine him hanging out with my mom and dad in their high school days. How well had he known them? Aside from Mrs. Ferris, I didn't know any of my parents' childhood friends.

"Whatever you need, I'm here for you," Heaney said. "Don't be afraid to ask. I want you to think of me as family."

It was a nice sentiment, though it didn't strike me the way he'd likely intended. *Think of me as family*. Even at my lowest point in Colorado, I had refused to call my mother for help. I was still angry that someone else had called her for me. I watched Heaney go down the steps and into the yard, wondering if it had been hard for him to ring the bell after years of letting himself in; if he had felt, in a way, that the house belonged to him, the same as I had, all those years it wasn't mine. I listened again for the sound of running water, but wherever it was coming from, it had stopped. The house was too quiet, holding its breath.

I had been disappointed that it was Heaney at the door, though I wasn't sure whom I'd expected. Ben? Even if he hadn't heard people gossiping about my return, his parents still lived next door to Arrowood and had surely noticed the car outside, seen me coming and going. They would have told him I was back. Did it mean anything, that Ben hadn't yet come by? It had only been two days, and there were a dozen logical reasons for his absence, the most likely being that he didn't live here anymore. He and his sister, Lauren, would have moved away for college, and maybe they'd never returned. Ben had always wanted to illustrate comic books when he grew up, or work in animation. It would make sense that he had started a new life someplace else. I knew there was also a chance that Ben was here and didn't want to see me, though I didn't want to think about that.

I wouldn't have admitted to anyone that when the doorbell rang, a tiny spark flickered through the circuitry of my brain, the tenuous hope that the twins might magically show up on the doorstep now that I was home.

Josh Kyle's email had been nagging at me all day, a splinter needling its way beneath my skin. What evidence could he possibly have that would change my mind about Singer? Still, I wanted to know what he had to say. The moments surrounding my sisters' disappearance were so firmly stitched into my memory that they were bright and clear after so much else had come unraveled and faded away.

After the gold car had disappeared with my sisters inside it, I'd squatted under a tree and buried my face in my Hello Kitty T-shirt, trying to catch my breath. Something dug into my hip, and I pulled a half-eaten sucker from my pocket. Violet, Tabitha, and I had been to the bank with our mother early that morning, and each of us had received a Tootsie Pop from the teller. Violet hadn't liked hers, and after a few slobbery bites, she'd managed to get it stuck in Tabitha's hair. I'd worked the sucker free and shoved it into the pocket of my shorts. It was fuzzy with lint now, though I could still make out the marks of Vi's tiny teeth and a blond hair that must have been Tabby's. I held on to the sucker, a sticky talisman, as if it might make them reappear.

I don't know how long I waited before I ran home to tell my mother.

Her face had gradually reddened at the bank that morning during a whispered conversation with the teller, and she had been in a twitchy mood all day. I was scared to tell her what had happened; I wasn't supposed to take the twins outside in the first place. It was my fault that they were gone, and in that moment, I was more upset about the fact that I had done something wrong and would get in trouble. It hadn't yet occurred to me that the twins might not come back, that I might never see my sisters again.

The rest of that first day remains jumbled and patchy in my head. I don't know exactly what I said to my mother, or what she did when I told her. I can't remember my father coming home, or Grammy picking me up to take me to the Sister House. At some point that afternoon I must have fallen asleep, because I had a vivid dream that everything was fine, that the twins were safe after all. I would sometimes immerse myself in the memory of that dream, to feel again the warm flood of relief, however fleeting.

I didn't speak to the police the first day, or the next. Grammy said I was too distraught, and sick. I'd started vomiting again, and my fever returned. My mother told them my story, the one I had told her, about the gold car that had turned toward Main. When a policeman—wiry, ruddy-cheeked Detective Eckland, who had once visited my school with McGruff the Crime Dog—finally met with me and asked me to tell him what I'd seen, my throat closed up and I began to wheeze. Hot tears gushed out and Detective Eckland fetched me tissues and cold water in a paper cup and a roll of Wild Cherry Life Savers, but nothing helped. Finally he repeated my account as relayed to him by my mother, and asked me to nod if it was correct. He had everything right except for the icy wound that lingered in my chest.

I stayed at the Sister House, where Aunt Alice closed the drapes and popped popcorn on the stove and Grammy read to me from *Anne of Green Gables* until her voice grew hoarse. The two of them sheltered me from what was happening outside. I wasn't aware, at the time, that the entire town was consumed by the kidnapping of the Arrowood twins; that bloodhounds searched the river bluffs, and that the night crew at the dam, where debris would often wash up, was put on alert for bodies. I didn't know that parents locked their children indoors, or that candlelight vigils were held in the streets, or that the Sisters of Perpetual Adoration, at their convent in Oskaloosa, had begun to pray in shifts, twenty-four hours a day, for my sisters' safe return. Our house and neighborhood were scoured for clues. The highway patrol was called in, and later, the FBI.

My father assured me in a broken voice, over the phone, that no one blamed me. I didn't believe him.

Days passed with no sign of the twins, and my parents did not come to take me home. I didn't return to school, either. Nana called from Florida and together we prayed to Saint Anthony, the patron saint of lost things, which Nana said included missing children. *Saint Anthony, Saint Anthony, please come down. Someone is lost and cannot be found.* I had said another prayer, silently, to all the burning saints, Anthony included: *May your flames light the way to bring my sisters back home.*

Grammy and Aunt Alice did everything they could to comfort me, and I pretended that the twins were back at Arrowood with Mom and Dad, and that I would see them soon. My teacher sent a fat envelope stuffed with letters from my classmates, and I dug through them to find Ben's. He had drawn two rabbits with big, sad eyes, the paper smudged where he had erased and reworked the feet to get them right. My name was at the top of the page, embellished with curlicues. Below the drawing, Ben had printed a single sentence. *When are you coming bake?* He had always struggled with the silent e, adding it in all the wrong places, but I knew what he meant. No one had talked to me yet about going back. I stuck the letter inside my pillowcase, where I could hear it crinkling every time I rolled over in Grammy's bed, unable to fall asleep.

I had moments of happiness while in limbo at the Sister House. Upstairs, in Alice's half of the house, you could see the river from her bedroom window, through a gap in the trees, and we would sit on her bed dealing hands of Old Maid or playing Chinese checkers on a wooden game board with marbles she kept in a mason jar.

She and Grammy loved to cook, and after a lifetime of feeding families and visitors and boarders, they did not seem to know how to prepare food in small quantities, so there was always too much to eat. A typical lunch would have the table laden with pork chops and fried potatoes, corn cut from the cob, boiled cabbage, sliced tomatoes, rolls, sweet pickles, and pickled peppers. Chocolate pudding for dessert, or oatmeal cookies, or homemade fudge that they had boiled on the stove and poured onto buttered plates to cool. They also shared a love of plants, and their windowsills were crowded with things growing roots in old salad dressing bottles and mayonnaise jars. There were cupboards full of treasures to explore—fossils and coins and antique postcards, and stacks of musty *Seventeen* magazines that had once belonged to my mother.

A month passed before my father came to retrieve me. I'd barely been outside in all that time. He didn't speak in the car as we drove past tree after tree tied with yellow ribbons. The house was quiet, and my mother didn't come down to greet me. She'd been frazzled before, from lack of sleep and taking care of the twins, and would occasionally set meat out to thaw and forget to cook it, or send me to school without brushing my hair, but now everything was worse. She got more prescriptions in addition to the Xanax and sleeping pills, but they didn't seem to help. She stopped doing laundry. She wouldn't go near the twins' room, which was two doors down from mine, and so I began to put myself to bed each night, sometimes not brushing my teeth or washing my face, thinking that would somehow draw her up the stairs to scold me, though it never did. I would sneak into the twins' bedroom and touch the dresses in their closet, lie on the floor near their cribs, fold their blankets under my head so I could breathe in their scent as I slept.

At school my teacher, Mrs. Wagner, seemed on the verge of tears every time she spoke to me. She put stickers on all my papers, even the ones I didn't finish. My classmates kept their distance, as though my situation might somehow be contagious, except for Ben. He played hopscotch with me at recess, ignoring the boys who made fun of him. I knew by then that a man had been found in possession of a gold car like the one I'd described taking the twins. His name was Harold Singer.

The twins' second birthday came in December, and Grammy made a cake with pink frosting, which no one ate. It sat on the kitchen table, untouched, until it grew mold and someone threw it away. My mother couldn't bear to celebrate Christmas at Arrowood without Violet and Tabitha, so I was sent back to the Sister House for the holiday break. Aunt Alice put up her aluminum tree and we made popcorn-and-cranberry garlands to hang. I didn't have my embroidered Christmas stocking, and there was no mantel, so I taped a gym sock to the radiator, where Grammy assured me Santa would find it. I taped up socks for my sisters as well, and in the morning, all three lay on the floor, stuffed with oranges and nuts and Freedent chewing gum, things suspiciously unlike what Santa usually left at home.

My parents came for dinner that night, and Grammy and Aunt Alice prepared a spread of baked ham with mashed potatoes and gravy, green bean casserole, Jell-O salad, and rolls and apple pie. After we finished eating, Mom and Dad announced that we would be moving to Illinois. My father was pursuing a new business venture there, and it was becoming too difficult to stay at Arrowood, surrounded by memories of the twins. They were also concerned that it might not be safe to continue living in the same town where Harold Singer roamed free.

There was a snag in Dad's plan. He knew that Arrowood would be passed down to him when his parents died, but Nana and Granddad were still living. They had grudgingly retired to Florida before the twins were born, in hopes that the balmy weather would soothe Nana's crippling arthritis, and the house was still in their names. Since they weren't planning on moving back, Dad wanted permission to sell the house right away and collect the money. Granddad wouldn't allow it. The house had been in the family for nearly one hundred and forty years, and he didn't want it sold.

They flew up to visit us for the first time in a year, and I was shocked to see that Nana was in a wheelchair. She sat crying quietly in the foyer with my mother and me while Dad and Granddad shouted at each other in the study. Mom lay slumped on the stairs, eyes closed and mouth open as though she had fallen asleep, and I stood staring at Nana's shoes, sturdy orthopedic loafers that looked at odds with her delicate pearl-buttoned sweater set and tailored slacks. I knew that she must be having trouble with her feet, because prior to that day, I had only ever seen her wear heels.

Nana motioned for me to climb up onto her lap and I did, inhaling the comforting scent of talcum powder and Prell shampoo. Her fingers were twisted at odd angles, the joints knobby and swollen despite her prayers to Saint Alphonsus, the patron saint of arthritis sufferers. She tried unsuccessfully to smooth my hair, tug the wrinkles out of my shirt. Nana had wanted to come as soon as the twins went missing, but traveling was hard on her, and she and Granddad did what they could from Florida, calling in favors and hiring a private detective, who spent most of his time tailing Singer. Nana had been diligent about keeping in touch after they moved away, calling every Sunday to speak to me and the twins, though she had only seen my sisters in the flesh a handful of times.

Don't listen to the yelling, she murmured, forcing a smile, her dry lips sticking to her dentures. Tears took an indirect route down her face, following the grooves and wrinkles, clinging to the bristly white hairs on her chin. *Everything will be fine.* Her voice wavered. She wasn't good at lying.

Granddad made it brutally clear how disappointed he was in my father, going so far as to blame the twins' disappearance on Dad's deficient parenting. He regretted coddling Eddie, who was the baby of the family and the sole remaining child, only thirteen years old when his two older brothers were killed months apart in Vietnam. Nana and Granddad had provided my father with an education and a trust fund, and that hadn't been enough. They had allowed us to live under their roof, had fed us and paid the bills while my dad dabbled in pyramid schemes and made dubious investments. If we wanted to leave Arrowood, we were free to go, but we wouldn't be welcome back. Regardless, the house would not be willed to my father, and it would not be sold. I imagined Arrowood living on without us, extraordinary measures being taken to keep it viable: foundation rebuilt, plumbing repaired, wiring replaced. It would go on, a house without a heart, like a body on life support.

Time split in two, and from there we started a new calendar, our lives forever divided into *before* and *after.* Days crept into years and *after* became the only time that seemed real, everything *before* dissipating into a lovely dream that I wasn't sure had existed. Each of us became a different person *after*, and while I couldn't say with certainty that these weren't the people we were meant to be, it seemed that the twins' disappearance had knocked us irrevocably off course. We had struck an iceberg, and though three of us survived, we were left adrift, each to find the shore on our own.

CHAPTER 5

I slept fitfully, dreams wending through my body, tightening ligaments, straining muscles, grinding teeth. In the darkness, I felt the tickle of the twins' wispy hair, their small hands tucked in mine, their breath warm on my cheek. I sang to them in the dream, whispered verses of mockingbirds and diamond rings.

I woke with a dull headache and aching jaw, my sheets clammy and my hair still damp from washing it the night before. When I went to brush my teeth, I saw that I had broken the tip off one of my canines in the night, leaving a sharp, jagged edge. It wasn't the first time. For the past several months, I'd been grinding my teeth incessantly. I'd cracked a molar in Colorado, and I was still making payments on the crown. I wanted to pretend the tooth was fine, but it drew blood when it touched my tongue. Reluctantly I got dressed and drove downtown to Ferris Family Dental—Ben's father's practice—where Grammy had taken me every summer to get my teeth cleaned, because my parents couldn't seem to remember to take me to a dentist during the school year.

I was nervous about seeing Dr. Ferris. I didn't want him to ask what had happened to me, why I had disappeared from his children's lives after so many years as close friends. I hoped, instead, that he might talk about Ben and Lauren, tell me where they lived and what they were doing and spare me the awkwardness of having to ask.

"I don't have an appointment," I told the receptionist, "but I broke a tooth, and I was wondering if Dr. Ferris could take a quick look at it."

"Are you a current patient?" she asked, winding a section of high-lighted hair around her pen. Her eyebrows had been plucked into dramatic arches that made her look like a cartoon villain.

"Former patient, I guess," I said. "I've been gone for a while and just came back. Arrowood. Arden."

She tugged the pen out of her hair, her eyes widening. "*Arrowood?*"

I nodded. It occurred to me that while people might recognize my name, hardly anyone would recognize my face. Certainly not the younger generation, who hadn't known any living Arrowoods.

The receptionist tapped on her keyboard, eyes flicking from the screen to me and back as she typed. "You're not in the new system. You'll have to fill out these forms. I'll check and see if we have time to squeeze you in today."

She handed me a clipboard and stared after me as I sat down to fill out the papers. A woman sat across from me reading an issue of *Good Housekeeping* while her little boy, maybe five years old, banged a Matchbox car against the side of Dr. Ferris's aquarium. "Fishy, fishy, fishy!" he screamed. "Stop that," the woman mumbled, not looking up from her magazine. The boy dropped the toy car and pounded the aquarium with his fists.

It didn't take long to complete the forms, because I didn't have answers for most of the questions. Insurance provider? None. Date of last cleaning? No idea. I returned the clipboard to the desk and flipped through the magazines. Nothing left but *Field & Stream* and *Golf Digest*. I walked back toward my seat, avoiding the little boy, who had thrown himself onto the floor and was swishing his arms and legs back and forth like he was making snow angels on the carpet.

"Arden?"

I turned around, and Ben Ferris stood in front of me, wearing a white lab coat. Ben. My first and best friend. He was taller than I remembered him being when we had said goodbye the last time, when he barely had to lean down to kiss me. I could tell by the way he was looking at me that he hadn't forgotten anything, and an uncomfortable buzzing sensation spread from my heart out through my limbs, like a swarm of frantic insects. Ben's wistful expression was quickly broken by a grin, and I took a halting step toward him, not sure of the appropriate greeting for someone I'd once been so close to but hadn't seen in years.

Ben didn't hesitate, though. He wrapped his arms around me. "I heard you were coming back. I can't believe you're here."

I could feel myself warming in his embrace, the heat and humidity of those long-ago summers seeping into the air-conditioned office, and I hastily stepped back, letting my arms fall to my sides.

"I can't believe you're a dentist." He used to say that he would never work with his dad, no matter how much his parents pressured him. He had wanted to be an artist. I had wanted to be a history teacher.

Ben laughed. "Yeah, well, it's a job. Come on back, I'll take a look at your tooth."

"Is your dad not here?" I asked.

"He's out playing golf," Ben said. "He probably spends half his time on the course, now that he's got me here." He gave me an amused smile. "Don't worry, I promise I'm qualified. I've pulled tons of teeth. Some human ones, even."

"Ha-ha," I said. He still had the same sense of humor. I was glad he was making this easy for me, not dredging up the past, not asking why I had shut him out.

I got situated in an exam chair and Ben leaned over me, shining a light into my mouth. I could smell his aftershave, woodsy and subtle, unlike the Axe body spray he used to coat himself with. I wondered if his mom had picked it out for him. Or a girlfriend. I glanced furtively at his left hand and was relieved not to see a wedding ring, though I chided myself for checking. I had no claim on him anymore.

He poked around my mouth with a metal pick, his gloved fingers gliding over my gums. "You grind your teeth a lot?"

"Yeah."

"I can tell. Have you been feeling stressed?" Concern showed on his face, though I couldn't be sure if it was concern for me or for my teeth. Possibly both.

"I guess. My dad, you know. And moving back."

"I'm so sorry about your dad, Arden. I would have gone to the service, but I didn't know they were having it in Quincy. Everyone thought there would be something here in town."

"It's okay," I said. "It all happened pretty fast. I didn't really have time to tell anyone."

"My mom took flowers," he said, "out to the cemetery. We were all thinking of you, worrying about you. Lauren tried to track you down. She wanted to call, but she couldn't find a current phone number."

Lauren. I hadn't spoken to her in so long.

"Thank you," I said, "for the flowers, and everything. I'm all right, though, really. Just a lot going on." I was still reclined in the chair, and it was a bit uncomfortable talking to him this way, like I was on a therapist's couch.

"Well, you might want to think about getting a mouth guard to wear at night, at least until your stress levels ease up. You don't need a crown, but I'll have to grind down the sharp edge." He pulled the instrument tray closer.

I tried to sit up. "How much will it cost?"

"Relax," he said. "This one's on me. It'll only take a few minutes."

"You don't have to do that," I said. "I can pay."

Ben smiled. "I know, but I won't let you. I have a favor to ask, and this is my way of buttering you up."

He leaned in, and it occurred to me that I hadn't been in such close proximity to a man since Dr. Endicott. I instinctively pressed my arm against my ribs, the scars from my accident hidden like squirmy things on the underside of a log. I tried to keep my eyes closed while Ben worked, though it was hard not to stare at him, to compare this version of him to the one in my memory. It was similar, in a way, to viewing age-progressed images of the twins—the disconcerting sense that I was looking at a stranger who bore a slight resemblance to someone I'd loved. Ben's hair was cut short, no longer sticking up every which way, and his face had lost its boyish softness. Dark stubble covered the acne scars along his jawline, and I remembered how badly he had wanted to grow a mustache the summer after sixth grade. We had ridden our bikes to the public pool almost every day that summer, and on the way home we would sometimes stop at an abandoned house at the edge of the woods, though I knew Grammy watched the clock and worried the entire time I was gone.

"I wish I could shave," Ben had said one afternoon. We had spread our beach towels out on the sloping back porch of the house. If we lay down flat on our stomachs, we couldn't see above the weeds.

"Why?" I asked. "It looks painful." The one time I had watched my father shave, he'd nicked himself, the razor dragging a swath of blood down his neck.

"We're gonna be in junior high. All the other guys are already shaving."

"No, they're not," I said. "If they say they are, they're probably lying."

I was already resigned to the fact that I was a late bloomer. My body refused to exhibit any of the signs of womanhood I'd been promised in the health class film that the girls had watched while the boys were sent outside to play baseball. Some of the girls in my class had been wearing training bras since fourth grade, and many had graduated to real ones. That spring, I had fretted over the hard knots of tissue that had developed beneath the skin of my flat chest. Convinced that cancerous tumors were growing inside me, I had reluctantly confided in my mother. She had rolled over to grab a bottle of muscle relaxants from her nightstand, irritated that I'd woken her. It was four in the afternoon.

It's not cancer, she'd snorted, tapping a pill into her palm. *Don't they teach you this stuff at school? Congratulations. You're becoming a woman.* The film had said we would grow breasts. It hadn't mentioned anything about stony lumps that would, for me, take years to soften and expand.

"Feel this," I had said, taking Ben's hand and placing it on my flat, twelve-year-old chest as we lay on the porch of the abandoned house. His fingers rested uncertainly on my shirt, and I pressed them into my flesh. "You think not having hair on your face is bad." His ears had turned pink, and he had smiled sheepishly, his hand lingering and then falling away.

When Ben finished working on my tooth, I ran my tongue over the smooth edge, the damage seemingly undone. "Thank you," I said. "Now, what was the favor you wanted to ask me?"

I was hoping, irrationally, that he would ask for things to go back to the way they were, that we could somehow undo the distance between us, as simply as pulling slack from a rope.

He crossed his arms over his chest. "You remember my mother."

"She's unforgettable."

Ben smirked. "Something like that. Anyway, she's heading up the visitors bureau now, and she's been up in arms over some report that named Keokuk the worst town in the state. She's working with the historical society to set up one of those holiday home tours as part of an initiative to boost tourism and revitalize the town, and she would love to include Arrowood."

"That sounds great," I said. "But I don't know about opening Arrowood up to tourists. I mean, I just got back myself."

"I know," he said. "I don't want to pressure you. She wanted me to ask you, and I was going to wait until you got settled, but then you showed up today. I was thinking about how you were always so into local history, and all the old houses. Seems like a good fit, something you might enjoy."

He was right about the old houses, though I doubted I would enjoy anything that involved his mother. "I'll think about it," I said.

He smiled. "Thanks. I'd better get back to work, but I'd love to get together and catch up soon. Want to do dinner this weekend? Maybe Saturday at the yacht club?"

My family had belonged to the yacht club *before*, in our former life, and we'd eaten dinner there dozens of times with the Ferrises. It wasn't fancy like the name implied, just a clubhouse with a restaurant and some docks. My dad had kept a ski boat there. The boat had a glitter-flecked, ruby-red hull that reminded me of Dorothy's shoes in *The Wizard of Oz*, so Dad had dubbed it the *Ruby Slipper*.

We spent a lot of time on the boat before my mother got pregnant with the twins. Dad would be in the driver's seat, his back and shoulders deeply sunburned, a can of Coors in his hand. I would sit backward, the wind whipping my hair in my face, and watch my mother slice through the wake on her skis, her pale hair flickering behind her, the river calm but for us splitting the surface, our waves diminishing as they raced toward shore.

"Sure," I said to Ben. "The club's fine."

"Great. I'll see you Saturday, then. My cell number's on there." He handed me a business card with BENJAMIN FERRIS, DDS in glossy letters, his fingers curling around mine and then sliding away. "I can pick you up around seven." My hand warmed where he'd touched me, like a match had been struck across my skin.

Back at the house, I stood at the kitchen sink and ate a Pop-Tart without toasting it. I was debating eating another one when I spotted Mrs. Ferris out in the yard near their carriage house, staring at Arrowood. I backed away from the window, watching her from the side. She tilted her head, as though looking up at the second or third story, and then she turned and disappeared into the carriage house.

I wondered how hard she would try to convince me to participate in her home tour. Maybe I should suggest that she'd have better luck organizing a tour of all the abandoned houses, for people who were into ruin porn. I was afraid, if I opened Arrowood up to strangers, that it would attract people for the wrong reasons, that they would be snapping selfies in Violet and Tabitha's bedroom and looking for ghosts.

Still, part of me was enticed by the idea of having a holiday celebration at Arrowood. My parents used to throw a Christmas party every year, up until that last year when we were packing up to move. They had a twelve-foot-tall spruce delivered from a tree farm, and Dad would haul the Arrowood family ornaments down from the storage room on the third floor. In kindergarten I made a paper angel with my handprints as wings, and Dad had placed it at the top of the tree, so high up that I could barely see it from the floor.

While I had a composite image of those holiday parties, the only one I remembered with any clarity was the one when I was seven. The house smelled of spiced cider and fragrant pine boughs my mother had draped on the windowsills, banisters, and mantels. I wore a red and green Fair Isle sweaterdress with itchy red tights, and black patent leather shoes that I had outgrown. I grew tired of trying to get my mother's attention to ask her if I could remove the uncomfortable shoes and tights, and eventually I snuck into the laundry room, peeled them off, and stuffed them into one of the closets. I put on a pair of gym socks I found in the dryer and hoped that my mother wouldn't notice.

When I came out of the laundry room I saw my father down the hall, standing under one of the sprigs of mistletoe my mother had hung for the party. He held a mug of cider in his hand, and he was kissing my mother, or so I thought. I hesitated, waiting for them to finish. Bing Crosby's *White Christmas* was playing on the stereo, and I knew every song by heart. My father had been playing that album for the entire month of December. When he pulled away from the kiss, I saw that the woman was not my mother. It was Julia Ferris, Ben's mom, her manicured fingernails gripping the lapel of my father's jacket.

I still haven't forgiven you, she said. *You have to make it up to me.* She gave his jacket a little tug, then let go and clicked down the hall in her high heels, back toward the party. Just then my dad turned and looked right at me, a pensive expression freezing on his face. He set his mug on top of Nana's curio cabinet, next to the framed portrait of him and his brothers in matching blue sport coats and ties.

"Hi, sweetie," he said, walking toward me. "Did you see the mistletoe?"

I nodded, staying right where I was. When he got close enough, Dad reached down and picked me up. He was warm and flushed from drinking, or because my mother had insisted on lighting fires in every fireplace on the first floor. His jacket smelled faintly of cigar smoke and Aqua Velva.

"Mistletoe means you have to kiss. Isn't that silly?" He grinned to show me how silly it was. He carried me over to the mistletoe and I looked up at the little bundle of leaves. My mother had tied it to a long red ribbon so that it hung just above our heads. My father kissed my cheek. His skin was smooth; Mom had made him shave before dinner. He picked up his drink and took a sip. There was a snowman on the mug, its neck wrapped in a jaunty scarf.

"Want to try it?" Dad asked. He held the mug to my lips. It was warm, the liquid inside still steaming. I took a sip, but it didn't taste like the cider my mother had given me earlier. It was bitter, and I swallowed hard to keep from spitting it out.

He looked me in the eye a moment too long and then set me down. I slid along the wood floor in my socks, back toward the laundry and up the rear stairs, my throat burning from Dad's drink. I crept into the twins' room. They were wearing matching footie pajamas, sleeping in identical positions in their separate cribs—on their tummies, with their knees tucked under and their bottoms in the air. I curled up on the floor, listening to them breathe. I couldn't hear the party beneath us at all. Thick layers of plaster and wood silenced Bing Crosby and the clinking of glasses and my mother's shrill laughter. The sturdy bones of the house absorbed it all before it could reach me.

CHAPTER 6

I arrived early for my Friday meeting with Josh Kyle. The roadside park had a swing set and picnic tables that looked out over the river, and I sat at one of the tables to wait, picking at the peeling paint and reading the graffiti that had been carved into the wood with fingernails and pocketknives. Bees swirled around the lone garbage can, McDonald's wrappers and Dairy Queen cups spilling out onto the ground and stinking in the heat. Though it was nearly October, it was eighty degrees, and sweat dripped down my neck into my bra.

Across the road from the park, Riverside Cemetery nestled at the edge of a cornfield. Grammy and Grampy and most of my mother's other relatives were buried there, though the oldest graves had been washed down the Mississippi long ago in a hundred-year flood. Grammy and I used to take a picnic lunch along when we went to pay our respects. I had always secretly hoped to be buried at Riverside instead of at the Catholic cemetery in town, because I didn't want to lie next to the three other Arden Arrowoods. Why my parents chose to give me such an ill-fated name I couldn't say, though I assumed they hadn't thought it through in the way that I did, as a little girl reading my own name on the stones and guessing at my odds.

In the Catholic cemetery, the Arrowood family plot sat on a west-facing slope in the good part of the old section, where the markers were all upright and the grass still got mowed. My ancestors had favored decorative tombstones with lambs and weeping angels, torches and doves, large stone arches and pillars topped with draped urns. Three empty spots waited for my sisters and me, prudently reserved for us by Granddad in case we died young or failed to marry. There were two small marble angels for Violet and Tabitha, but no slabs engraved with their names, because no one wanted to set in stone something that might not be true.

I'd been waiting at the picnic table for about ten minutes when a white van with tinted windows pulled into the gravel lot. It was the sort of van I always avoided parking next to, because it looked like a vehicle you might use if you wanted to kidnap someone. Though of course I knew you didn't need a van for that.

Josh Kyle emerged wearing the same hat and jacket that he wore in his website photo, both embroidered with the logo for Midwest Mysteries. It was too hot out for the jacket, and I figured maybe it was part of his investigative uniform, that he felt like he needed to wear it to look professional. He wasn't wearing the sunglasses from the picture, though. Instead he had regular glasses with thick black frames. I hadn't expected him to be so clean-cut and normal-looking, someone I might find attractive if I walked past him in a bar. He didn't appear to be much older than me, though the hair sticking out below his cap was salt-and-pepper gray.

I stood up, and he reached out to shake my hand, his grip firm and businesslike.

"It really is you," he said. His voice, too, was a surprise, low and soothing like a radio announcer's. "You look just like your pictures."

"What pictures?"

"They were posted by your school, something to do with the history department," he said. "I have a Google alert that sends me anything that comes up with your name."

"Really?"

"I promise that sounds creepier than it really is. It pulls anything with the word 'Arrowood.' Just part of the research."

"I'm sorry," I said. "It's none of my business, but—how old are you?" I didn't feel too bad asking, considering how much he already knew about me.

One corner of his mouth turned up in a lopsided grin. "Twenty-six. I graduated high school the same year as you." He took off his hat and raked his fingers through his hair. "Everybody asks. Completely gray before I turned twenty. Runs in the family."

"Oh."

"Anyway, it's great to finally meet you," he said, putting his cap back on. "I'm glad you agreed to do it."

"Yeah," I said. "I'm curious to know why you think I'm wrong."

He gestured toward the picnic table, and we sat down across from each other. He leaned forward and planted his elbows on the table. "Well, you know I interviewed Harold Singer. And I'm guessing you're familiar with that whole part of the case? With his story?"

"I know the police searched his house and found those pictures. Places he was casing to rob, supposedly. But they didn't find anything connecting him to my sisters. I think that's only because it took them so long to search his car."

"So you probably also know that he said he wasn't parked in front of your house at four. He claimed he was parked there earlier in the day, around one o'clock."

Out on the river, a barge sounded its air horn, and gulls swooped low over the water.

"That's what he said, but he had no witnesses. No alibi. Two people saw him there at four, including me."

Josh stuck his hands in his jacket pockets. "I think I found proof that he wasn't lying about the time. But I need your help to be sure. I was hoping you'd take a look at something for me."

"I don't mean to sound skeptical right from the start, but what kind of evidence could you have possibly found after all this time? That was missed by everybody else?"

"I got it from Singer," he said. "Some pictures. From that day."

"I've already seen the pictures," I said. "They're not even sure when he took them. There's no way to know."

"Not those. Not the pictures of the houses. Those were from the film police found at his place, under the floorboards. There were other rolls of film, other pictures. When he saw they were looking for a gold car, he got nervous. He bundled anything he thought might be incriminating into a garbage bag, and he buried it out in the woods. It would have been smarter to just burn everything, but he wanted to keep the photos. That's how it is with guys like him—they get a thrill out of something and they don't want to give it up, even if it might get them in trouble."

I was fairly certain I knew where the conversation was leading, but I had to ask. "What's in the pictures, then?"

"Kids."

Ice spread through my chest. "My sisters?"

"In one picture, yes."

"If he has a picture of my sisters, why didn't you go to the police as soon as you saw it?"

"Because I won't know whether the pictures mean anything until you look at them." His glasses had slid down and he pushed them back up. "Like I said, I think these images could prove his innocence. Or at least put his guilt in doubt, for you, anyway. They're not . . . pornographic, or explicit in any way. Just close-ups of kids, playing. Riding their bikes, stuff like that. Your sisters are in one of them. Some are of you."

My stomach twisted. *Some are of you.* I had always wondered why I had been left behind. Maybe he had planned to take me, too. Maybe he would have, if I hadn't run to the backyard to get the dandelions.

"And how does that prove him innocent?" I asked. "Because if anything, it makes him sound worse than before."

"If these were taken the day your sisters disappeared, I think there's a way to determine what time of day he took them. I brought them with me—they're in the van."

I studied his face. The sun glared against his glasses, so that I couldn't see his eyes. "Why did he show them to you?"

"Because I told him I wasn't convinced he was guilty, that I was trying to find out what really happened. There was no physical evidence tying him to the disappearance, and I wanted to hear his side of things. I think I was the first person who was willing to listen to him."

I glanced over at Riverside. I hadn't gone to see Grammy and Grampy and Aunt Alice since I'd moved back, hadn't checked on their graves.

"Have you told him you think these pictures can prove his innocence?"

"No. Not yet. I wanted you to see them first."

I followed him over to the van, a nervous prickling sensation crawling across my skin. When he handed me the first picture, my hands began to shake. It was me, wearing a pair of purple shorts and a Hello Kitty T-shirt. The same outfit I'd worn the day the twins disappeared, and never wore again.

"This is you, right?"

I stared at the picture. Eight-year-old me had an animated face, like I was telling a story. My sweaty bangs were stuck to my forehead. I was looking outside the frame, at the twins. I thought of Singer, taking this photo, and acid crept up my throat.

"It's me," I said. "But I can't be sure it's the same day. I wore that outfit a lot that summer. It was my favorite shirt."

He handed me the next photo. Me again, smiling wide enough so you could see that one of my front teeth was missing. The other would soon follow, and the tooth fairy would leave a worn Buffalo nickel under my pillow at the Sister House. I had been the last person in my class to lose those top teeth, and I had prayed to Saint Apollonia for them to fall out.

"I lost that tooth a few days before."

Josh nodded, visibly relieved. "So that makes it pretty likely this was the day. Here's what I was talking about." He pointed at the picture. "See how the shadows are, here? They'd be much longer at four. The sun would have been high when this was taken. It couldn't have been late afternoon."

I looked closely at the photo, trying to take in what he was saying. I couldn't have said how long shadows would be at any given time of day, except that they would be minimal near noon, as these were. He had a point, though it didn't seem like conclusive evidence.

"Just because he took pictures when he says he did doesn't mean he couldn't have come back again later," I said. "It doesn't really prove anything."

"It might. He was telling the truth about this much, at least. It introduces doubt to all the assumptions that were made."

"What was it like, when you talked to him? Did he seem . . . credible?"

Josh shrugged. "His story hasn't changed in all this time. He's adamant about his innocence."

"Do you think he would talk to me?" I had always wondered what it would be like to confront Singer face-to-face, to ask him what he'd done to my sisters. I thought I'd know, when he told me, whether or not he was lying.

"Why would you want to?"

"Maybe it would help," I said, "to talk to him in person. Maybe it would be easier to believe what you're telling me."

"I don't think that's a good idea. Talking to him isn't going to make you feel any better. He's . . ."

"The kind of guy who takes pictures of little girls. I know."

"It's not that," Josh said. "He's angry. At you, your family. He's not the most upstanding guy, and he's served some time for petty stuff, but he's maintained from day one that he was wrongly accused in the kidnapping. Whether it's true or not, he thinks you ruined his life. He's really made an effort to rehabilitate himself in the past few years, but no matter what he does, regardless of the fact that no charges were filed, people still think he's the guy who took the Arrowood twins. He's not going to be pleased to see you."

"I'm not expecting some sort of happy reunion."

"Arden, I really appreciate you looking at the pictures. Why don't we wait and discuss talking to Singer another time."

"Please."

We stared at each other. I couldn't tell whose side he was on, if he thought he was protecting me from Singer or Singer from me.

"I can call him up and ask him, but I doubt he's going to agree to it."

"Okay."

Josh sighed and rubbed the back of his neck. Then he took out his phone and walked around to the other side of the van to make the call.

He returned a minute later. "He'll do it," he said. "I can drive you, if you want. He's up near Mount Pleasant. Or you can follow me, if you'd rather do that—if you're not comfortable riding together."

"You can drive," I said. I had emailed my mother to let her know I was meeting the man from Midwest Mysteries to talk about the twins, so in the unlikely event that Josh Kyle decided to kill me and chuck my body into a ditch, she could give the police his name. She had emailed back, warning me that I shouldn't get involved, that nothing good could possibly come out of rehashing the case.

He opened the passenger door, removing a storage tub full of computer parts from the seat. "Sorry about that," he said. "Work stuff." He stowed the box in the back of the van and then got in and started the engine.

"What kind of work do you do?" I asked. "Aside from the website."

"Freelance programming, mostly. I do some computer repair on the side."

"So Midwest Mysteries is just a hobby?"

"For now," he said. "I'd like to have it the other way around—spend all my time on the website and writing my books, and only program when I want to. Hasn't happened yet."

He headed north on the highway. I could hear things rattling around in the back of the van as we swung around a curve.

"How about you?" Josh asked.

"What?"

"You're done with school? Are you working? Or looking?"

"Yeah," I said. "I'm looking. I'd like to do something at least vaguely related to history, if possible."

"There are lots of museums around here."

There were. I didn't bother to tell him that most of them ran on donations and volunteers, or that an extensive knowledge of history was not necessarily profitable in the way that an understanding of computer hardware and software might be. No one would pay me fifty dollars an hour to explain the past. History, unlike technology, was irreparable and often ignored.

I caught Josh glancing at me a few times as we drove, and each time I thought he would say something, but he didn't. We were headed away from the river, deeper into farmland, thousands of acres of corn swaying like a restless sea. Every so often, a long driveway cut through the fields, straight as a hem stitched with a sewing machine, a white farmhouse hazy in the distance.

"Why are you so concerned with proving Singer didn't do it?" I asked.

"It's not so much about him," Josh said. "I want to figure out what really happened. If he's innocent, we need to clear his name and move on. As long as everyone thinks Singer's responsible, the case might as well be closed. It'll never be solved."

"And what does it matter to you, if my sisters' case is solved?"

"It's like a riddle," he said, his long fingers wrapped tightly around the steering wheel at precisely ten and two. "I hate not knowing the answer. That's what gets me with cold cases. Nobody has the time or money to pay attention to them anymore, so they just sit there, getting colder. It's not that they're unsolvable—they all have solutions, and I can't stand not knowing what they are. It's like leaving a Rubik's Cube with the colors all mixed up."

I'd bought a Rubik's Cube at a yard sale when I was a kid. I'd never been able to solve it, though I eventually peeled off the colored stickers and rearranged them to make it look like I had.

"You said you had a picture of the twins," I said. "Can I see it?"

"Of course," he said. "I wasn't sure if you'd want to. If that would be too hard for you. I have the rest of the pictures at my office if you want to stop by there on the way back." He slowed the van and steered onto the shoulder as we neared a gravel turnoff. "Are you sure you want to do this?"

"Yes," I said. I wasn't sure I wanted to, but I felt like I needed to. If I didn't do it now, I never would.

Josh drove down the lane until we reached the end. A decrepit motor home sat amid a cluster of trees, a sagging lean-to tacked onto the side. Out front, a scrawny black dog trotted back and forth, tethered to a stake. The yard was cluttered with stacks of tires and scrap metal and hubcaps. We got out of the van, and the dog wagged its tail, parsing out strangled barks as it pulled against the chain. Panic numbed my limbs as realization set in—what I was about to do, the man I was about to see. It was too late to tell Josh that I wanted to go back, that I had changed my mind.

He knocked on the door and Singer opened it. Or, at least, I assumed it was Singer. I had never seen him in person. My memory of his appearance was based entirely on old newspaper clippings, and I barely recognized him. He was squat and balding, his puffy face splotched with rosacea and an assortment of flesh-colored moles. A cat with a shredded ear wove itself around his ankles in a figure eight, purring heartily.

Singer held the door open and we walked in, a current of fear buzzing through me as I brushed past him. The air in the motor home was stale and bitterly perfumed, air freshener trying and failing to mask the stench of cigarettes and cat piss.

"You want a beer, Mr. Kyle?" Singer asked, not looking at me. Josh said no thanks and Singer grabbed himself a Milwaukee's Best from a half-empty case on the floor.

The three of us squeezed into the built-in dinette, Josh and me on one side with Singer facing us. Junk mail and grocery store circulars were piled on the tabletop, and tacked to the wall next to us was a crinkled certificate congratulating Singer for completing one hundred hours of community service at the River City Animal Rescue. It was difficult to comprehend that I was sitting two feet away from the man long believed to have kidnapped my sisters. Singer took a draw on his beer and smacked the can down on the table.

"You want to talk to me, huh?" he asked me, baring his teeth in a fake smile. "I want to talk to you, too. You fucked up a lot of things for me when you falsely accused me of shit I didn't do."

Josh jumped in before I could respond. "Hold on, Mr. Singer. You know she didn't accuse you of anything. She never identified you as a suspect. She saw a car, is all. A gold car. Which you happened to have. So let's not go blaming anything on Miss Arrowood." Josh stared Singer down, and he backed off and took a swig of beer.

"All right, all right." He held his hands up. "She didn't say my name. Fuck me for having a gold car, I guess. Look"—he pointed at Josh—"I need a minute alone with her. That's all. There's something I gotta tell her in private."

It was obvious that Singer wasn't on his first beer of the day, maybe not even his third or fourth. I could smell his breath from across the table.

"I don't think that's necessary," Josh said. "If you don't want me to hear what you're going to say, I'll cover my ears."

I poked Josh's leg under the table, hard, and he frowned at me, shaking his head almost imperceptibly.

"It's fine," I said. "I'll be fine."

"This is a terrible idea," he muttered, pulling himself up from the table. "I'll be right outside the door." He locked eyes with Singer. "*Right* outside. Arden, yell if you need me."

Neither Singer nor I responded. My hands gripped the edge of the vinyl seat, while Singer spread his fingers out on the table between us. Grime lined his nails and the cracks of his knuckles.

"You have a watch on that day?" he asked, as soon as the door clicked shut.

I stared at him, not answering.

"Because I don't know one goddamned kid that can tell time. I know good and well they only took your word because of who you are, and how that stacked up against who I am. Old Granddaddy Arrowood was calling in favors, throwing his weight around from all the way down in Florida. I got fired from my job and couldn't get another one after everybody started saying I took those kids. I had cops up my ass for months, years. Nobody believed me. But I wasn't there when you said I was."

"Did *you* have a watch on that day?"

He sneered at me, his lips curling up over his teeth. "I know it was lunchtime because I was eating my fucking lunch."

"You took them," I said, my voice wavering. Something brushed against my leg under the table, and I jerked away, choking back the cry that rose in my throat. It was just the cat. "Your car was there, and when it left, they were gone. That's the only thing that makes any sense."

"Really?" he said. "I'm not that smart, and even I can see there's plenty of holes in that story. You're not saying it's the *only* thing that could've happened, you're saying it's the easiest thing to believe. Doesn't make it true. Maybe somebody had my car. Maybe it was a different car altogether. You didn't have a license plate number. You got zero evidence on me, that's all anybody ever had."

"What about the pictures?" I said. "He showed me."

"Oh, right." Laughter rasped in his throat. "You think you got me all figured out. I'm one of *those*, a registered sex offender, a guy that likes taking pictures of kids." He tipped his beer can back, emptied it. "You have no idea. You don't know anything about me. I had a kid of my own, did you know that? Never laid a hand on him. I would've killed anybody who did."

He leaned forward, his face inches from mine, and I shrank back involuntarily. His voice lowered to a rough whisper. "I took pictures of some kids. That was it. I never touched a one. Not a single one, ever. Doesn't make me a saint, but it's something. You even know how I got labeled an offender? Huh?" His words had begun to slur together.

"Taking a piss in public. I was drunk. Waiting around my kid's school to try and catch sight of him, because my ex got full custody and moved away after everything that happened. Didn't matter there was no proof, everybody knew what you accused me of."

I sat very still, tensing every muscle to keep from shaking. "I saw them. Through the window as you drove away."

Singer squinted at me. "You couldn't see something that wasn't there."

"I know they were in your car."

He put his elbows on the table, spreading his hands wide. "How big's that yard of yours, huh? Big fancy yard, isn't it? You couldn't see shit from that far away. I had to zoom in on my camera just to get a decent shot."

The footage of that day ran through my head. The door slamming. The car pulling away, my sisters in the window.

"Their hair," I said. "I saw their hair."

Singer stared at me, blinking. And then he started to laugh. His hand slapped the table, and I jumped, banging my knee. "The dog," he said, shaking his head. "That goddamn fucking dog. Had me one of them little white fluffy things, what do you call it, a Maltese? With all that soft hair? I was thinking it might work pretty good, lure a little girl over to the car. Never quite got up my nerve. Couldn't do it."

Frost crept through my veins, tingled across my chest. I couldn't hold myself together any longer, and I began to shiver, my jaw threatening to chatter.

"I'll be damned," Singer continued, looking dazed. "So all this time you thought you saw them, all this time I'm on the hook, and what you saw was a goddamn dog. Don't that beat all."

"Swear on your life it wasn't you," I said through gritted teeth.

"Darlin', I'll swear on whatever the hell you want, but my life's not worth much, thanks to you."

"Please."

"I didn't take your sisters. They were practically babies. I couldn't have cared less about them." His mouth curved into a twisted grin. "You're the one I was looking at."

I got up and shoved the door open, nearly knocking Josh to the ground. I pushed past him and he made no move to stop me.

"Thanks for agreeing to talk to us today, Mr. Singer," he said.

"I'll be waiting for my check," Singer called after us.

Josh didn't say anything until we were back on the main road, heading toward Fort Madison. "Are you okay?" he asked.

I didn't answer him at first, afraid of what I might say. I kept my eyes on the corn that walled us in on either side of the road, the stalks six feet high and beginning to wither. My hands lay clenched in my lap, my nails cutting into my palms. "You're paying Singer to talk to me?"

"Yeah," he said. "That's the only way he'd agree to do it. I had to pay to interview him for the book, too."

"He tried to put all the blame on me. He thinks it's my fault his son was taken away from him."

"I'm sorry, I know. I shouldn't have left you in there alone with him, but you didn't give me much choice."

Up ahead of us, a railroad crossing signal began to flash red, and the striped bar came down to block the road. Josh coasted to a stop, and we sat watching the train cars flick by.

"Did Singer have a little white dog?" I asked. "Back then?"

"Not that I know of," Josh said. "He never said anything about a dog when I interviewed him. But I can look into it. Why?"

"He said he had a dog with him, to lure kids over to his car. He thinks that's what I saw, the dog—not the twins."

"I'll see what I can find out."

The end of the train zipped past and was gone, leaving a humming in my ears. I wasn't sure Singer was telling the truth—about the dog or about my sisters. He seemed to have an answer for everything, and it was difficult for me to question the one thing I had always known to be true, that he had taken Violet and Tabitha. Was it possible that I was wrong about what I saw, that I had mistaken the white flash in the car for my sisters and saved that altered image as the truth? The implications were unsettling; Singer's life had been all but destroyed and the case left unsolved. If I was wrong, and Harold Singer hadn't taken the twins, where had they gone?

CHAPTER 7

On the way into Fort Madison, we passed the state penitentiary, a massive stone building with turrets like an ancient castle. It was older than Arrowood, the oldest prison west of the Mississippi to still be in use, beautiful in a way modern prisons never are. I had often imagined Singer locked up behind the crumbling stone wall and the loops of razor wire.

"Are you still up for looking at the rest of the pictures?" Josh asked. "I understand if you've had enough for today."

"I'm fine," I said. "I need to see them." Up ahead, past the riverfront park and the old depot museum, a familiar sign caught my eye. "Is the A&W still here?" I asked.

"Yeah," Josh said. "Are you hungry?"

I didn't know if I was hungry or not, I just wanted to eat. And while I knew, logically, that comfort food didn't fix anything, I hadn't wanted anything else since I'd returned to Iowa. I wondered what Dr. Endicott would say if I added nostalgic eating to my thesis. *The irrational belief that consuming the foods of one's childhood will take you back in time.*

After ordering Coney Dogs, onion rings, and root beers to go, Josh drove through a neighborhood of run-down Victorians and parked on the street in front of a two-story with peeling yellow paint. I had already finished my root beer and regretted not ordering the ridiculously over-size one that Josh had gotten.

"I don't know if I mentioned that my office is also my apartment," he said as we climbed the steps to the porch.

"That's all right."

"Come on in," he said. "I'm on the second floor."

The front hall of the house still had what appeared to be its original staircase, though the woodwork had been painted over multiple times and paint was chipping off the banister in layers. Rubber treads had been nailed onto the steps. Entryways that had once led to parlors and sitting rooms had been sealed up to form apartments. I hated to see grand old homes chopped up into awkward living spaces with just enough of their old charm intact to remind you of what had been lost, but it was a matter of practicality. No one had live-in help anymore, or enough kids to warrant so many bedrooms, and few people could afford to heat or cool such a big, drafty house or keep it in good repair.

I followed Josh into his apartment and set the food down on the kitchen counter while he rummaged in a cabinet for plates. If the avocado-and-gold linoleum was any indication, the kitchen had been added sometime in the 1960s.

"We can eat at the coffee table," he said, gesturing toward the adjoining room, where a large bay window jutted out from the front of the house. "I don't have a real table."

I carried my plate to the living room and moved some books off the couch so I could sit down. *Cold Case Homicides: Practical Investigative Techniques. The Encyclopedia of Serial Killers. Gray Hat Hacking: The Ethical Hacker's Handbook.* An L-shaped desk took up the opposite wall, its surface hidden beneath papers and file folders and coffee mugs. A map of Iowa hung on the wall above the desk, dotted with red thumbtacks, and next to the map was a framed movie poster for Truman Capote's *In Cold Blood.* Piled in the corner were the ravaged carcasses of a dozen desktop computers. I tried to imagine the room as it had once been, before the wood floors were obscured beneath lumpy brown carpeting and decades of grime had built up on the molding and the windowpanes. Someone's bright, airy bedroom.

Josh rattled the empty cup that I had left on the counter. "You need something else to drink? I have some Coke. And milk, I think." He stuck his head in the fridge. "Wait, no, the milk's bad."

"Water's fine."

He joined me in the living room and removed his hat and jacket for the first time all day. I was fully prepared to see signs of cutting or cigarette burns, deformed limbs, birthmarks—something he wanted to conceal badly enough to wear a jacket in the heat—but his arms were normal, unmarked, his chest and shoulders unexpectedly well defined beneath a slim black T-shirt. I reminded myself that not everyone had something to hide.

We ate in silence, and when we finished, Josh set our plates on the floor. "Ready?" he asked.

I nodded, wiping my hands clean with a napkin, and he brought me a stack of photos from a folder on his desk. I started flipping through them, stopping when I came to one of me, out of focus. I must have moved as the shutter snapped. Pins and needles spread outward from the cold spot in my chest. Off to the side were Violet and Tabitha, their little faces and their matching shirts, the ones with the buttons shaped like ducks, stained with grape juice. They were wearing the clover crowns I had made for them that day. No one else had seen the crowns. No one but me could be sure that this picture had been taken just before the twins disappeared. My sisters and I were laughing, smiling. I dropped the photos onto the table.

"Do you have anything to drink?" I asked. "Like a real drink?"

He nodded solemnly and crossed the room to the kitchen, returning a minute later with a bottle of Kraken black rum, the saucer-eyed sea monster on the label looping its tentacles around an unsuspecting ship. I poured an inch of the molasses-colored liquor into my water glass and choked half of it down.

"They're from that day," I said. "From right before."

"Hardly any shadows. Early afternoon."

I nodded. "He still could have taken the girls. He could have done it earlier than I thought." I wasn't sure of the words as I said them. I had been wrong about the time. What else had I been wrong about?

"Or it could have been someone else," Josh said.

I sipped my rum, not wanting to think about the pictures anymore. It was spicy, slightly medicinal.

"So this is your office?" I said, gesturing at his messy desk.

"Yeah. The headquarters of Midwest Mysteries. I know, it's impressive." He smiled drily.

"How did you get started with all this cold case stuff in the first place?" I asked. "What made you want to spend all your time thinking about murders and kidnappings?"

"My older brother ran away when I was eleven," he said.

I didn't know what to say. It wasn't the answer I had expected.

"Everyone's pretty sure that's what happened, anyway," he continued, adjusting his glasses. "He was seventeen, almost eighteen, and he'd been fighting with our parents. He'd gotten in with a group of guys who were selling pills at the high school. Mom and Dad wanted to send him to rehab, or to one of those tough-love lockdown schools. Then he was gone before they could follow through with it. The things he took with him—his pocketknife, tent, sleeping bag—it was pretty obvious he'd made the choice to leave. But he didn't come back, and we'd all thought he would.

"My mom got it into her head he'd been kidnapped like those paperboys in Des Moines, even though there was no reason to think that. Those kids were a lot younger, in a bigger city. My brother was pretty good at fending for himself. We all knew something bad might've happened to him after he left, but maybe not. Maybe he just wanted to be out there living on his own, and that's what he was doing. My mom couldn't take that. She was calling the police all the time, trying to get them to do something, but what could they do? It's not easy to find someone when you have no clue where they might have gone. And a teenage runaway isn't exactly a high priority when they have actual crimes to investigate."

"How long ago was that?"

"Fifteen years."

"Did they ever . . . ?"

He shook his head. "No. They haven't found him and he hasn't come back on his own. I've tried looking, of course. My cousin Randy works for the police department, and I have a few other contacts who feed me information when they can, mostly people I've met through the website. Retired cops, private investigators. Sometimes unidentified remains come up that might be a match. That's hard, though, without knowing where Paul was living or how old he would have been when he died. If he died. If he's still alive after all this time, he'd have a new identity, maybe a family of his own. No reason for him to come back, and no way for me to find him."

"I'm sorry," I said.

He shrugged. "I've always had an interest in unsolved crimes, especially the cases everybody else has given up on and forgotten about. Like I was saying earlier, it's like a puzzle with missing pieces, and I can't leave it alone. I want to keep rearranging it until it makes sense. You know how it is, though, don't you? That's partly why I wanted to talk to you." He paused, fixing his gaze on me. "You've been through the same thing. I was thinking, if someone could give me a clue, help me find out what really happened to my brother, I'd jump at it. I figured you'd feel the same way."

I did want to know. There was nothing I wanted more. But at the same time, it was hard for me to let go of Harold Singer.

"The time thing," I said. "It proves I was wrong, but it doesn't prove he's innocent. I wasn't the only one who saw the gold car. There was another witness."

"You're right," he said. "Ben Ferris. Your friend. Supposedly he saw the car from his bedroom window. I asked him for an interview and he refused. I hate to put this out there, but it's true, Arden, and you need to consider it . . . you and Ben, you were eight years old. You were *kids*. And memory's a strange thing. It's malleable. A crowd of people could all witness the same thing and each have a different recollection of what happened. Eyewitness accounts aren't reliable without evidence to back them up, because memory isn't fact—it's our interpretation of what happened, and it can change over time. Maybe you should talk to Ben about it. He'd obviously be more open to talking to you than to me. But I don't think it matters, since you already know you were wrong."

His words were harsh, unvarnished. I swirled the rum around in my glass. I didn't need Josh Kyle to explain to me how memory worked. "What's your theory?" I asked. "If Singer's innocent, then what happened?"

Josh grabbed a thick stack of folders from his desk and thumped them down in front of me. "I'm not sure yet. Since I started looking into it, I've considered everything I've come across, no matter how far-fetched. Are you familiar with a case from back in the eighties, a girl named Heather Campbell who vanished from Burlington while a traveling carnival was in town?"

"No."

"She was eleven years old. They never found her, never found a body. There was a string of unsolved disappearances along the Mississippi River Valley in the eighties and nineties that had investigators wondering if it was the work of a serial killer. They were having trouble, though, figuring out a connection. I talked to a retired detective who'd spent some time on the case, and he said each of the disappearances roughly coincided with a visit from a traveling carnival, but that nothing concrete was ever found to tie them together. It wasn't always the same carnival company, and some of the girls who went missing hadn't even gone to the carnival that day. A few of them disappeared fifteen or twenty miles away from where it was set up. And they couldn't rule out the possibility that the carnival was a coincidence. All kinds of other things happen during carnival season, too. Could have been a schoolteacher who traveled around in an RV over summer break, or somebody who worked on barges going up and down the river, or a transient riding the rails in the warm weather."

"So they never figured it out?"

"No. There weren't any new cases coming up that seemed related, and after a while they figured whoever was responsible had died or moved on or gone to prison for something else. But I thought your sisters' case might be connected. There was a carnival at the fairgrounds in Quincy that Labor Day weekend when the twins disappeared. Quincy's only about an hour away."

"You're assuming they're dead."

"What?"

"If a serial killer took them."

He shook his head, apologetic. "I spent a lot of time on it. Too much. It made for a great story, but I couldn't make the pieces fit. All the victims were older than your sisters, and all of the girls were taken at night, within a much closer range of the carnival. What I'm trying to say is, I know what it's like to be fixated on the wrong answer, like you with Singer, convincing yourself that you're right, despite all the evidence telling you otherwise. I can't rule out stranger abduction, but it's rare, and the truth is probably much simpler. I think your sisters were taken by someone who knew your family, someone who could have gone unnoticed in your neighborhood that day."

"Everyone in town knew my family. By that logic, Singer still fits."

"Except for the complete lack of evidence against him. And he didn't have any direct connection to the Arrowoods that I'm aware of." Josh leaned forward, his elbows on the coffee table, his dark eyes searching mine. "Have you ever been in Ben Ferris's bedroom?"

Heat spread across my cheeks. "Why are you asking?"

"Have you looked out his bedroom window? I haven't, but I'm wondering if he could have even seen the car from there, or if his view would have been blocked by the carriage house."

"Can you drive me back, please?" I asked. "I'd like to go home." The air in the apartment had grown unbearably close. I felt unbalanced, like I would get sometimes after a day of boating on the *Ruby Slipper*, my head unable to stop compensating for the bob and roll of the water even with my feet on dry land.

"I'm sorry," he said, reaching out his hand but stopping short of touching me, as though he suddenly remembered that we were practically strangers, that a comforting gesture might overstep certain bounds. "I get a little carried away. I didn't mean to upset you."

"It's okay. I'm just not feeling well. It's hot in here, and the greasy food . . ."

He got up from the floor, his biceps flexing as he pushed up from the table. "I could get you some water?"

"Let's just go."

He nodded and grabbed his keys.

Josh stopped next to my Nissan at the roadside park and waited for me to pull out of the lot, following me onto the river road and then turning in the opposite direction. The foundering sun caught in my mirror as I rounded a sharp curve, blinding me for an instant and then disappearing abruptly as the car swooped through a tunnel of trees. I rolled down the windows and cool evening air sluiced through, funneling into my sleeves, stirring up straw wrappers and gas station receipts from the floorboard. An endless barrage of river bugs smacked into the windshield, smearing into cloudy arcs when I ran the wipers.

I couldn't get Singer's pictures out of my head. Me with my Hello Kitty shirt and missing tooth and sweaty bangs. I'd looked happy, unaware that my life was about to change. Unaware that Harold Singer sat in his car with a camera lens focused on me, watching, waiting, working up his nerve. Wondering what it would be like to lay his hands on an eight-year-old girl. What had he been thinking today, when we were alone, crowded together at his narrow table, close enough to each other that he could have reached out and clamped his calloused hands around my throat? I shuddered, recalling the curve of his lips when he smiled at me, his mouth inches from mine. *You're the one I was looking at.*

I was supposed to be the unlucky one, branded with a tragic family name, the fourth in a line of Arden Arrowoods who had gone to early graves. What would have happened if the twins had stayed and I'd been the one to disappear? Would they have been okay without me? Maybe my family would have held together, and they could have remained at Arrowood and lived the life they were meant to. I wanted to believe that I would have done that for them, given the choice—that I would have taken the twins' place in the car.

Singer's picture had captured one of my last moments with my sisters, but it didn't provide any clues as to what had happened next. All the events leading up to their abduction were firm in my mind, though as Josh pointed out, my recollection was obviously flawed. I wondered if Ben's was any better. I would have to bring it up when we met for dinner. I'd ask him to tell me exactly what he remembered.

As much as I didn't like hearing it, what Josh said was true, that memory is a slippery thing. I had researched the mechanics of memory in relation to my master's thesis, which was supposed to explore the effects of nostalgia on historical narratives. As I got deeper into the project, I began to concentrate less on history and more on my own past. Dr. Endicott had picked up on my distraction and warned me not to lose focus. *You're treading too far into the realms of psychology and sociology,* he'd said, as though history was a discrete and separate thing, completely disentangled from other human threads.

I had worried, for a long time after the twins disappeared, that they would forget me. After we left Keokuk, I wrote letters to Violet and Tabitha and mailed them to Arrowood. I don't know what happened to the letters—if they were forwarded or returned to us, my mother never mentioned it—but I imagined them sitting in a neat stack, waiting for my sisters to walk in and find them. I kept the girls apprised of any changes to my appearance—lost teeth, haircuts, growth spurts—to make sure they would recognize me when we were reunited. I informed them of each new address, so that they could easily find us when they returned. Gradually the letters grew more intimate, like journal entries, confessions that no one would ever read.

When I got older, I thought about it more realistically; I knew, even if my sisters returned, that they likely wouldn't retain any memories of our family. They had been too young at the time of their disappearance. In my thesis research, I read about the phenomenon of childhood amnesia. Up until they're seven years old, children can vividly recall things that happened to them very early in life. Then, for unknown reasons, around the age of eight, they begin to forget. The memory clock runs down and those old memories expire, deleted by the inner workings of the mind.

There were exceptions, of course, usually when an event had a strong emotional impact on the child. Those memories were deeply embedded, and lingered into adulthood. I assumed that was why I remembered so many little details from the day the twins went missing, like the grape juice stains, and the half-eaten sucker, and the clover crowns, and why, out of the hundreds of days I'd spent with my sisters, all but a handful had faded away. I could sense the weight and warmth of those missing days, the multitude of inconsequential moments we had shared. I hoped, if Violet and Tabitha were able to recall their abduction, that they might also remember me.

I was glad to get back to Arrowood, though the moment I entered the house, I was enveloped by an oppressive dampness that clung to me like a clammy swimsuit. If fall didn't come in earnest soon, I'd have to get Heaney to chisel my bedroom windows open so that I could sleep at night without sweating through the sheets.

I climbed the stairs, my hand sticking to the banister, and stopped at the bathroom to brush my teeth. As I stood at the vanity, water seeped over the thin soles of my sandals and in between my toes. "Don't panic. It's not a big deal." I said the words out loud, trying to convince myself. There wasn't that much water, really, no worse than the first night after my bath. It was probably a slow leak in the bathroom pipes, and I could call Heaney to take care of it in the morning.

I grabbed towels from the linen closet and squatted down to wipe up the water, making my way toward the tub. The clawed feet were hollow on the back side, and I worked a towel around each one to dry it out. The towel stuck on the last one, and when I yanked it loose, something skittered across the floor and disappeared under the edge of the vanity. I jumped to my feet, momentarily startled, and then knelt down to see what it was: a grimy chunk of plastic about the size of my thumbnail. I picked it up and turned it over, nearly dropping it back onto the floor as I realized what I was holding. A tremor started in my hands and worked its way up through my bones. The piece of plastic was a cracked and timeworn button, a button shaped like a duck, just like the buttons on the blouses my sisters were wearing the day they disappeared. My vision blurred and I squeezed the button against my palm until it cut into my skin.

I slumped back against the wall, my bare legs sticking to the marble floor, my heartbeat like a door slamming shut, over and over. I traced my fingernail along the button's curved edge, the once bright yellow duck now dull and faded, the color of a stained tooth. I told myself it was possible that it had been out in the yard all these years and then tracked inside, though I knew that wasn't likely. I tried to remember whether all the buttons had been intact when the twins disappeared. There was one way to find out.

I found Josh's number in the signature line of the last email he'd sent, and I could tell when he answered that he wasn't expecting to hear from me so soon after I'd left. His low voice resonated in my ear as he said my name. "Arden?"

"Yeah, I just have a question. I hope I'm not interrupting anything."

"No, nothing important. Ask away."

"In the picture, the one with the twins, can you see how many buttons are on their shirts?"

"How many buttons?"

"Yes."

"Okay. Sure. Hold on a second, let me check." I could hear the faint whisper of his breath, and I imagined the phone cradled between his shoulder and jaw as he flipped through the photos. "Looks like . . . three buttons on one. And three on the other. How many are there supposed to be?"

I realized I wasn't sure. "It's not the number that's important, I guess. I just wanted to know if it looked like any were missing."

He was silent for moment. "Do you want to tell me why?"

"No. It's nothing."

There was a noise like he was exhaling through his teeth. As the sort of person who couldn't leave a Rubik's Cube with the colors mixed up, he was probably having a hard time not pushing for a better explanation, but he let it go. Maybe he felt like he had already pushed me enough for one day. "Well, if you change your mind and want to talk about it, feel free to call back. I'll be up late."

With Josh's goodbye fading in my ear, I tucked the button into my pocket and moved into the hallway, something completely irrational beginning to crystallize in my mind. Over the years, I had implored psychics, mediums, Ouija boards, a variety of saints, and an invisible God I wasn't sure existed; all had failed to give me what I wanted. Then, today, I had spoken to the man suspected of taking Violet and Tabitha, and I had seen the last known photo taken of them before they disappeared. Maybe that had been enough, finally, to conjure them. Maybe, somehow, through means I couldn't begin to understand, my sisters had sent me a sign. For the first time since returning to Arrowood, I stood in front of the twins' bedroom door and reached out to twist the glass knob.

The room was musty, like when the twins had colds and Mom would run the humidifier. I flipped the switch, expecting a burst of light that didn't come. The bulbs had probably burned out. I took several steps forward into the darkness and stopped. I could hear the wind outside, shuffling the leaves of the oak trees against the house. Along the far wall, under the windows, the cribs sat end to end, draped in white sheets.

I took shallow breaths and moved closer until I could reach out and touch them. The sheets were cool against my fingertips as I pulled them away and dropped them to the floor. My eyes welled up as I made out the familiar bedding with the pink-and-yellow butterflies. No one had stripped the mattresses or made the beds. The blankets in each crib still lay in twisted piles, as though the twins had just woken from a restless sleep. I leaned down to stroke the blanket in Tabitha's crib, and it felt tacky, moist. I drew back the curtains to let in some moonlight, and my arms froze in place, outstretched. The window-panes wept. Condensation trickled down and pooled on the sill, swelling the wood. I shivered as though those same drops traced down my scalp, along my spine. At the bottom edge of the glass, water beaded around smudges shaped like tiny fingerprints. I took the button from my pocket and set it on the puddled windowsill.

Violet? I whispered. *Tabitha?* I pressed my palm to the cool, wet glass as water slid down my wrist, along my scars.

CHAPTER 8

As I was getting dressed the next morning, the phone began to ring. I'd only gotten a landline because the Internet package was cheaper with it than without it, and only two people had the number: Heaney and the lawyer, and I had called Heaney on my cell barely ten minutes before to tell him about the leak, so I doubted it was him. I hurried down the stairs, though by the time I reached the kitchen, I'd missed the call. There was one new voicemail.

"Miss Arrowood? Are you there?" The message continued in silence for several seconds before cutting off, as though the man had been waiting, giving me a chance to pick up, the way people used to do with answering machines. The number was "unknown." It wasn't the lawyer. Maybe I'd already made it onto a telemarketing list.

Heaney arrived, and I waited out on the terrace, distracting myself with the classified section of the newspaper while he banged around inside the house with a giant red toolbox. I circled a few jobs that I thought I might be qualified for: night clerk at the Super 8, gas station attendant, and some sort of phone-answering position that didn't look entirely legitimate. I couldn't afford to be terribly choosy. I still had money in my college fund to keep me going for a while, but I wasn't sure how long it would last.

"I got you all fixed up," Heaney said when he finally emerged. "I think it's just that the tub hadn't been used in a while. Nothing major. And I got one of your windows open. The rest are being stubborn, but we'll try again once the weather cools off. I think all the humidity has them swollen shut."

"Thanks. One window's better than none."

"You've sure got a gorgeous view out here," Heaney said, wiping his forehead. "If I lived here, I'd eat all my meals at this table, looking right out over the river."

"We used to," I said. "In the summer, anyway. My sisters and I. Mom said it was easier to let the rain and the birds clean up after us."

Heaney pressed his lips together. "I'm sorry," he said. "About your sisters. I wanted to say something sooner, but I didn't want to upset you by bringing it up. I always wished they'd caught the guy that did it."

"Thanks," I said. "Me too."

"How's your mother getting along, anyway?" he asked. "I figured she might be planning on moving back here, now that you have the house."

"No. She seems happy where she is. She got remarried a while ago."

Heaney's posture shifted slightly, and he sucked in his lower lip. It almost looked like he was disappointed. "Well, good for her," he said.

"You tell her I said hello. I'd love to catch up when she comes for a visit."

I didn't bother to tell him that she wouldn't be coming to visit. I doubted that Mom would ever again set foot in the state of Iowa, let alone in this house. With the exception of her trip to pick me up in Colorado, she had never gone out of her way to see me.

I was surprised when Mom called not long after Heaney left. Usually I was the one who called her; she rarely reached out unless she had important news, like a death in the family, and I wondered if something had happened to Gary.

"You never emailed me back," she said. The Home Shopping Network was blaring in the background. "Don't tell me you went and talked to him."

It took me a moment to realize she was talking about Josh Kyle. "I wanted to see what he had to say."

"I don't care what he has to say, and you shouldn't, either. He wants to dig up the most terrible thing to ever happen to our family and sell it for his own benefit. I'm telling you now, I don't want you having any part in it."

"He's a decent guy," I said. "He's just looking for answers."

"Lord help me, Arden, it's closing in on twenty years. There are no answers. It's time you got that through your head."

I wished that for once she would turn down the television when she talked to me. "How can you not want to know?"

My mother sighed loudly into the phone, and the nasal voice of the woman on the Home Shopping Network was replaced by the soothing drone of the man on the Weather Channel. She was flipping channels, and I knew the conversation was over, that she was seconds away from saying goodbye. I thought of the button, sitting upstairs in the twins' room. I knew she wouldn't want to hear about it, yet part of me ached to confide in her.

She hadn't always been so closed off, so hard to talk to. I remembered sitting at the dressing table with her when I was little, after my parents had moved into Nana and Granddad's old room. Nana's talcum powder and clip-on earrings and Dresden figurines were gone, packed away to Florida, the rosewood dressing table now home to my mother's blow-dryer and curling iron and hot rollers and cans of Aqua Net hairspray. She had a purple Caboodles makeup case that looked like a tackle box, and I would watch her stroke coat after coat of Maybelline mascara over her pale lashes while she told me stories about things she had done with her friends back in high school. I had never met her old friends, who had gone off to college or gotten married and moved away. She was trying to make new ones, women from the yacht club and the neighborhood, women my father knew. Most of them were older, and a bit too reserved for my mother's taste. Sometimes Mom would make up my face with glittery eyeliner and blue shadow and a coral lipstick that she let me keep because it made her teeth look yellow. If she was in a good mood, we'd lip-synch in the mirror to a mixtape of Madonna and Cyndi Lauper songs that she only played when Dad wasn't around, because he didn't like that kind of music.

I'd never stopped hoping that that version of my mother might reemerge. She didn't have as much time for me after my sisters were born. She had been tired and distracted. And after losing the twins, she had sealed off the mothering part of herself, like cauterizing a wound.

"I almost forgot," I said before she could hang up. "Dick Heaney said to tell you hello. He wants to see you next time you come visit. He looked really disappointed when I told him you'd gotten remarried." I wanted to see if she remembered Heaney after all, if she would say anything about how she knew him.

Mom made a noise in her throat that could have been an acknowledgment or maybe just a swallow of wine that went down wrong, and then she was off the phone.

I spent the afternoon on Midwest Mysteries, reading through old posts on the Arrowood forum. I was mortified to discover that there was a separate page devoted entirely to me, which Josh Kyle hadn't mentioned. At the top was a familiar newspaper photo from *The Des Moines Register* feature titled "Still No Answers": me, looking out from a window in the twins' room, my hand pressed against the glass, shortly before we left Arrowood. The picture and story had been widely distributed, and had sparked an intense debate as to whether two uncertain shapes in the window were reflections, tricks of shadow and light, or the ghostly visages of my sisters. Critics of paranormal photography debunked the apparitions as pareidolia, the imagined perception of pattern or meaning where it does not actually exist.

Grammy had blamed the photograph for directing unwanted attention toward me, for making me known to countless strangers, some who gathered here on the Arden Arrowood page, apparently, to discuss my mental state, comment on photos, and list the questions they would ask if they met me in person. And yet the forum was not about me, exactly. They wanted to know what it was like to be in my shoes, to be part of a famous tragedy. I was a symbol to them, of mystery and suffering. My identity wasn't my own; I was the twins' surviving sister, someone wholly defined by what I was missing.

There was a picture of me with Dr. Endicott, standing outside his office in Kaufmann Hall, and I couldn't stop staring at it. I wondered if someone from the history department had posted it to the forum, or if it had been dug up elsewhere on the Internet. I stood two feet away from him in the photo, my shoulders slumped, my arms hanging awkwardly at my sides. My focus was somewhere between my professor and the person taking the picture, as though I didn't dare make eye contact with either one. Dr. Endicott smiled winningly, gazing directly at the camera.

The alarm on my phone chimed to remind me that Ben would be picking me up for dinner in fifteen minutes. I turned off my laptop and sprinted upstairs, where I hastily brushed my hair and smeared on lip gloss. I dug through my closet in search of an appropriate outfit for dinner at the club, immediately ruling out ninety-nine percent of my wardrobe, which was either ultra-casual (jeans and sweats) or pseudo-professional (bland turtlenecks and slacks from JCPenney that I had bought to wear to work in the history department). Finally I located an emerald-green maxi dress that I had scored on clearance at Target, my go-to outfit for Friday night happy hours with the other graduate assistants, when we would complain about our shrinking stipends and gossip about our professors and then go home before we got drunk enough to talk about anything too personal.

The dress was badly wrinkled from being crammed in the bottom of a box, and while I knew there must be an iron somewhere in the house, I didn't have time to look for it. The lower half of my body would be hidden by a tablecloth for most of the evening, anyway, and a cardigan would cover the top. I hurried past the ornate mirror in the hall without glancing at my reflection. I wanted to look nice for Ben, and if I didn't, it was better not to see it confirmed in the mirror. On the way down the stairs, I tucked my hair behind my ears and then untucked it and fluffed it with my fingers, knowing that it would quickly revert back to its original state regardless of what I did to it.

Grammy had generously called my hair "sandy," not "dishwater blond," which would have been more accurate. I'd never had pretty platinum hair like the twins, not even when I was a baby. I often wondered how Violet and Tabitha would have looked as they aged, if their hair would have darkened over time to match mine or stayed light like our mother's. If they were still alive, they would be nearly nineteen years old. College students. Almost everything about them would have changed by now, each tiny tooth lost and replaced with a grown-up one, smooth baby skin freckled and blemished and scarred, limbs stretched, bodies filled out, voices altered. It killed me to think that I might have passed them on the street, that it would be possible to look right at them and not recognize them, not know we were sisters. I wanted to believe that an internal device would somehow sense our shared blood and sound an alarm.

Ben was walking up to the door as I opened it, and he grinned when he saw me. He wore a suit jacket and pressed khakis with a crisp button-down shirt, and I felt sloppy and childish in my wrinkled dress. Ben looked like a real adult, which he was, and I wondered if he still had his collection of nerdy T-shirts—*The X-Files* and *Star Trek* and *Mystery Science Theater*—tucked away in a box somewhere. We climbed into his car and set off down the river road, the Mississippi restless and glittering as the evening sun angled down over the bluffs and the tops of the cottonwood trees.

The restaurant at the club was nearly empty when we arrived, and Ben and I were seated at an intimate table with a river view, though the view was rapidly diminishing as the sky dulled and dusk crept in. I could just make out the stilted cabins on the opposite bank, a darkening thicket of trees rising up behind them, headlights ghosting along a narrow road. A teenage waitress greeted us with a self-conscious smile, her chapped lips refusing to part and expose her teeth. She felt around in her apron pocket for her order pad, mumbling that she knew it was in there somewhere, and then finally gave up and wrote our orders on her hand. Ben and I sat in silence for a minute, watching the sky and river turn black. I tore open a packet of saltines from the cracker basket, spraying crumbs across the table, and then set them down without eating them.

"Sorry we didn't get much of a chance to talk the other day at the office," Ben said finally, his smile relaxing me. "Are you settling in okay?"

"Yeah," I said. "Still getting used to being back in the house."

"I hope you don't mind me asking," he said, "but what have you been doing for the past . . . *ten* years? Is that right? I can't believe it's been that long."

"Going to school, mostly. And moving. I've lived in four different states since I saw you last. I guess this makes five."

He shook his head. "That must have been hard, moving all the time."

I shrugged. I didn't know how to explain that after a while it gets harder to stay in one place. I'd grown used to the pattern my dad had set—if things weren't going well, move on to a new town that hadn't yet proved disappointing.

"Didn't you ever think about going somewhere else?"

"Sure," he said. "I thought about it, when I was in school. Things change as you get older, though, you know? Different priorities. I've lived here all my life, my family's here. It meant a lot to my dad that I came back and joined his practice."

The waitress plunked down our drinks, giving my Diet Coke to Ben and Ben's iced tea to me. Ben said thank you and then switched them after she left.

"So, are your degrees in history?" he asked, thumbing through a pile of sugar and sweetener packets.

"Yeah," I said, leaving out the fact that my master's was incomplete, that I hadn't turned in my thesis and didn't know if I ever would. I wondered what he would say if I told him about Dr. Endicott, if I laid my arm across the table and told him how I'd gotten my scars.

"I knew you'd stick with it," he said. "You were obsessed, carrying that *Legendary Keokuk Homes* book around, telling me all those boring stories over and over. I think you had the whole thing memorized."

He was teasing, but it was true. "Tell me about that thing your mom's doing, the tour," I said.

"You'll have to get the details from her, but really what they're trying to do is boost tourism here, raise some money to fix things up. I don't know if you've had a chance to look around town, but it isn't exactly thriving. It's sad, when you think about how it used to be."

The waitress delivered a basket of warm bread, and Ben pushed it toward me, along with the butter. "I guess I could at least go talk to your mom about putting Arrowood on the tour, see what all I'd have to do."

"She'll probably try to recruit you to join the historical society, too. I mean, if you're planning to stick around awhile." He tilted his head to look at me, and for a moment the grown-up Ben, the dentist who wore ironed shirts, receded, and there was my Ben, my best friend. I had missed him.

"I think so," I said. "I hope so."

"I'm glad to hear that." He kept his eyes locked on mine long enough that my pulse ratcheted upward, and then he busied himself with his drink, pouring in two sweeteners, his spoon clinking against the glass as he stirred. "Lauren's thrilled, by the way. She's in town from Iowa City for a friend's wedding and she really wants to see you, but she couldn't get away tonight. Could you maybe stop by Mom and Dad's tomorrow and say hi before she heads back to school? She hardly ever comes home, so it might be a while before you catch her again."

"I'd love to," I said. "Is she in grad school now?" His sister and I had been close once, too. Lauren was a few years older than the twins, and during each summer I spent in Keokuk it had been hard for me to look at her without imagining Violet and Tabby at her age, wondering if they were playing softball or having sleepovers or whatever else Lauren was doing.

"Would you believe dental school?"

"Are you kidding? Her too? How did that happen?"

"Well, Dad will have to retire eventually, and we'll share the practice. It's amazing how appealing dentistry starts to look when you're not good at anything else."

"But . . . do you even like it?" I asked. "You never wanted to be a dentist. And what about the comic books? You were such a good artist. I was sure you'd end up doing something creative."

He shrugged, tapping his fingers on his glass. "That was just a hobby. I was never good enough to get anywhere with it. I don't draw much anymore." He was quiet for a moment, and then his face brightened. "Right now all my creative energy is going into restoring my house. I bought a foreclosure on Orleans Avenue, just a couple blocks from the Sister House."

"Congratulations! What style?"

"Folk Victorian." He grinned. "I knew you'd ask. I hope you're very impressed that I knew the answer. I never could keep the different kinds straight like you. I'd love to have you over once I get things cleaned up a little. Right now the first floor is down to studs, and there's nowhere to sit."

"I'd love that," I said, pinching crumbs off a piece of bread. "I went to see the Sister House the other day. It looked abandoned."

"Yeah," Ben said softly. "I'm sorry you had to see it like that. It was a rental for a while, but the bank's got it now. I actually considered buying it when I was looking at foreclosures, before my place came up for sale. It's not beyond fixing."

The waitress appeared with heaped plates of breaded catfish and hush puppies and french fries, everything crispy and golden and glistening with grease. I closed my eyes and inhaled, transported back to the era when my family had come here for catfish every Friday during Lent, the powerful link between scent and memory urging my fingers to trace the sign of the cross, north-south-east-west, across my flesh.

————

The oldies station was playing Britney Spears songs from the nineties as we drove back home. We agreed that it was a sacrilege—"oldies" should refer only to music made before we were born—but it didn't stop us from singing along, trying to remember dance moves from the videos we used to watch together on MTV. Ben parked in my driveway and rolled down the windows.

"Thanks for dinner," I said. A light breeze sifted through the car, fluttering the pharmacy school graduation tassel that hung from his rearview mirror. The scent of Ben's woodsy cologne swirled around me, and I wanted to bury my face against his neck, breathe him in. His lips parted, and my mind raced ahead, placing words in his mouth. He would ask why I had stopped writing back, all those years ago, and I wouldn't know what to say. Or he would skip right over the past and ask to come inside.

"My pleasure," he said. "I hope we can do it again soon."

I smoothed my dress with my palms, watching the wrinkles flatten out and reappear. Neither of us had mentioned the twins, and I knew once I did, the night would no longer be about me and Ben. Part of me didn't want to know the answer, didn't want to raise the question.

"Can I ask you something?"

"Of course." His hands rested on the steering wheel. I remembered how his fingers used to be smudged with graphite, silver lines under his nails from constant sketching.

"The day the twins disappeared . . . you saw the gold car, too. How did you know what time you saw it?"

He didn't say anything at first; his gaze was fixed straight ahead, on his reflection in the windshield or something in the darkness beyond. He shifted in his seat, twisting to face me. "Is there a reason this is coming up now?"

"There's this guy who's writing a book about the case. He has a website that's all about unsolved crimes. He wanted to talk to me. He said he asked you for an interview, too, and you turned him down."

Ben frowned. "Josh Kyle? Yeah, I wasn't sure it was a good idea."

"I didn't think so, either, but I met him, and he seems all right."

"You sure?"

"He's a little intense, maybe, but I guess you'd have to be, to do what he does."

"Do you know about his brother?"

"Yeah. He told me he ran away and never came back. He said he's still looking for him."

"Did he tell you everybody thought he had something to do with his brother going missing?"

"No. Why would anybody think that?"

Ben sighed. "It was all over the news when it happened. He and his brother went camping up near Bonnett Lake, and two days later Josh drove home alone in the family station wagon. Well, almost home. He was what, eleven or twelve? Didn't really know how to drive. He wrecked the car on a gravel road just outside Fort Madison. All the camping gear was gone. His brother was gone. He said he'd slept in the car and woke up alone, the campsite cleared out. Their neighbors started talking about how he didn't get along with his brother. Josh was one of those awkward kids who always kept to himself. He didn't really have any friends, and his older brother picked on him mercilessly. People thought he might have snapped and done something to him out there in the woods."

It didn't seem likely to me that an eleven-year-old boy would be strong enough and smart enough to kill his much older brother and get away with it. I tried to picture Josh at that age, small and awkward, alone in the woods, not yet obsessed with the intricate puzzles of unsolved crimes.

"You can probably find the old stories online," Ben continued. "I'm just saying, you might want to know more about him before you get involved with his project."

"I'm not asking for him. I just need to know, for me. How did you know what time you saw the gold car? Did you look at a clock or something?"

The wind picked up, clacking the branches of the oaks. Ben raked his hand through his hair, an old habit from the days when it was long enough to be unruly. "I remember my mom sent me to my room to practice the violin, and told me not to come out until she came to get me. Dad was out golfing, Lauren was with our grandparents for the weekend, and the house was quiet. After a while, I thought Mom had forgotten about me, and I snuck downstairs to see what she was doing, but she wasn't there. I went back up to my room and played some videogames. Later I saw her coming out of the carriage house. She'd been spending a lot of time working on the upper level . . . she was fixing it up as a sort of guesthouse. I know I saw the car before my mom came back, but that could've been anytime."

He looked at me in a way that sent the years reeling backward, to a time when we were inseparable, when Ben was as much a part of me as my bones and my grief. He touched my hand, tentatively, with the tips of his fingers, points of heat on my cool flesh. I wondered, if he wrapped himself around me, if I might begin to thaw.

"They asked me if it could have been around four," he continued, "because that's when you saw it. I said yes. I was always on your side, and I thought if you saw it at four, I must have seen it at the same time."

My heart stuttered. I had been so sure, and it felt like a betrayal to question my own memory. But if Ben and I, the only two witnesses, were both wrong, I had to admit it was possible that some other truth existed, and that the search for my sisters had been on the wrong path from the start.

I didn't feel like going inside after Ben left, to sit alone in the empty house. Instead I sat in the wet grass beneath the mimosa tree, looking out across the dark yard to the street, where I could still picture the gold car pulling away from the curb. I hadn't known that my last day with my sisters had been preserved on film, and seeing those images in print after carrying them around for so long in my head was strangely comforting. In Singer's picture, the same as in my memory, the twins and I were happy and smiling.

After Violet and Tabitha disappeared, I started to pay close attention to photos of missing children, the ones in newspapers and on flyers and TV. When you see a picture of a missing child, it's usually a school photo or family snapshot of the kid with a huge grin and bright eyes, oblivious to their approaching demise. That child who was now likely dead, covered with leaves in a ditch or floating in a pond somewhere, or held captive in a dark basement with no hope of getting out, that little boy or girl smiled and smiled while you studied the picture and begged them to tell you where they were, what had happened. I wanted them to stop smiling. I wanted them to know that something terrible was coming, to be ready. I wanted them to fight back, or run and scream, or stay home that day, to avoid whatever had made them go missing. It was too late by then, by the time you saw their smiling faces on the posters.

The twins were no different. The image that was plastered on posters and shown constantly on the news was their eighteen-month photo, taken at the Sears portrait studio in the mall. They were wearing aqua dresses with fluffy tulle skirts, their pale hair clipped to the side with matching butterfly bows. They grinned, showing off tiny pearl teeth in their tiny pink mouths.

It was the same with pictures of me from *before*. But not *after*. In every school picture from then on, my expression was resigned, wary, grim. When the photographer urged me to smile, I stared him down, unyielding. If I went missing, the world would know that I had seen it coming, that my fate was unavoidable. No one would have to look at my smiling face and think, *It never should have happened to this one, so happy and full of life.*

CHAPTER 9

Josh called me Sunday morning while I was sitting out on the terrace in my nightgown, eating Cap'n Crunch from the box. The sky was pale and chalky, a haze over the river. The window Heaney had opened for me slid shut while I slept, and I had woken with the faint scent of mildew clinging to everything. Even now, in the open air, I could still smell it on my skin.

"Hi, Arden," Josh said. "I hope you don't mind me calling. I thought it would be easier. Do you have a few minutes to talk?"

"Yeah," I said. "I'm not doing anything."

My laptop sat on the table in front of me, a dozen tabs open in the

Web browser. I'd been reading about the disappearance of Josh's brother. Whether or not Josh's official account was truthful, he had clearly been traumatized by whatever had happened in the woods. One of the articles said that he'd been injured in the ensuing car crash, suffering bruises, abrasions, and a broken wrist, and that his parents insisted he be kept at the hospital overnight for observation, because he appeared to be in a state of shock. Someone in another article questioned whether he could have incurred those wounds in a struggle with his brother and staged the crash as a cover-up.

"I wanted to go over a few things." I thought I could hear papers shuffling. I imagined him in his apartment, wearing his windbreaker, his gray hair hidden beneath his ball cap. "First, I looked into Singer's claim that he had a white dog in the car with him. There's nothing about a dog in any of his statements. He didn't say anything about it to investigators."

"So he was lying."

"Not necessarily. He might not have thought it was relevant, and besides, if he was planning to use the dog to lure kids into his car, like he told you, he wouldn't have been eager to bring it up."

"I guess. Maybe." I swiped a cloud of gnats away from my face.

"My next step is to see if there's any evidence that he owned a white dog back then. His friends or neighbors might remember. And I can find out if dog hair was found in the car when they searched it."

"You're thorough," I said. "I didn't think you'd take the dog thing so seriously."

"I know it's important to you. If there was a dog, it might be easier for you to accept that you didn't see the twins with Singer. So I'll find out. In the meantime, I'm narrowing down the suspect list."

"Who's on it?"

"Your neighbors, the Tru-Lawn crew that was working at the Fer-rises', a FedEx driver who knew your parents and delivered a package down the street. Pretty much anybody who could have been in the area without drawing attention to themselves."

I had thought for a long time that every possible lead had already been investigated to a dead end. The spotlight, though, had always been on Singer. Could such an intense focus on the wrong suspect have caused even the most obvious clues to be missed entirely?

"The Brubaker house across from Arrowood, for instance," Josh continued. "It was empty at the time. The owners were on vacation, and the house was undergoing extensive renovation work while they were gone. Several different contractors had access to the house — painters, carpenters, plumber, electrician. I'm trying to find out if one of them was over there that day."

"Didn't they search all the nearby houses, though? I know they searched ours, more than once."

"Yeah, but they didn't get to every house right away. How much time passed," he asked, "before they started looking in your neighborhood? They were trying to find the gold car as quickly as possible. It was just the local police force, at first, before they called in the big guys for help. They didn't have any experience with kidnappings. They could have missed things. They *did* miss things, or we'd know what happened to your sisters by now."

"So we've gone from one suspect to the entire neighborhood. How do you rule people out seventeen years after the fact?"

"Most of them have alibis," he said. "I'm checking to see how strong they are, whether or not they were ever verified. Maybe someone lied for a husband or boyfriend back then, said he was home with her, and now her story's changed. Sometimes time and distance can bring things to the surface. Something that didn't seem significant then might stand out now. You never know."

"Thanks for keeping me updated," I said. "I appreciate it."

"Are you feeling better?" he asked.

"What do you mean?"

"From the other day. You seemed a bit shaken up after looking at the pictures. I just wondered if you were doing better now that you've had some time to take it in."

"I'm okay," I said. That was the answer people wanted, when they asked.

Shortly after breakfast, I stood on the front porch of Arrowood, working up the nerve to go next door and visit Lauren. The Ferrises' Gothic Revival was as familiar to me as my own—more so, maybe, as I'd spent so much time over there on my summer visits, especially that last summer, when I was fifteen. The Sister House wasn't the same that year. Aunt Alice had fallen and broken her hip and then developed pneumonia. By late July, Grammy was sleeping in Alice's hospital room, afraid to leave her alone overnight, and Dr. Ferris had offered to let me stay, temporarily, in one of their guest rooms. It was during that time that the mayflies began hatching on the river, and they swarmed into town by the millions to mate and die, their adult lives measured in hours. Dead mayflies lay in heaps at the bases of streetlights and storefronts, covered windshields and roads, and drifted into gutters like black snow. They were scraped from the sidewalk with shovels, into massive piles that smelled like rotting fish.

After a couple of days cooped up indoors to avoid the worst part of the swarm, Ben, Lauren, and I had ventured out to Dairy Queen one evening and then trudged back home in the fading daylight, sapped by the suffocating humidity and the stench of dead flies. The mayflies that hadn't yet died were dragging themselves through the languid air, bumping into us and clinging to our clothes and hair. Normally the streetlamps would be flickering on, but the city had shut them off to avoid attracting more of the insects, a move that hadn't seemed to help.

Dr. and Mrs. Ferris were visiting friends in Quincy that night and wouldn't be home until later, meaning that Ben, Lauren, and I could stay up late watching movies on the big screen in the family room without Mrs. Ferris glaring at us the entire time. Lauren kept insisting that she was old enough to watch *House of 1000 Corpses*, but we settled on a John Cusack flick instead. We clicked the window air conditioner to its highest setting, sprawled out on the stiff antique sofa, and covered ourselves with the cashmere throw Mrs. Ferris never wanted anyone to touch. About ten minutes into the movie, Lauren paused it.

"This is boring," she said, leaning her head on my shoulder. "Let's do something else."

"Like what?" Ben said.

Lauren sat up and picked at the fraying threads of a purple friendship bracelet that encircled her wrist. "We should go next door. To Arrowood."

Ben and I exchanged looks over her head. We had often talked about sneaking into my former home, and sometimes, in the dark, or in daylight when no one else was around, we would try a door or a window to see if it might open. I hadn't been brave enough then to smash a pane of glass.

"I'd like to," I said. "But we can't. It's locked up tight."

"Mom has a key," she said. "It's in her desk. I was digging through her stuff and found it. There's a label on the key ring that says 'Arrowood.'"

I felt a twinge, the beginning of a headache. "Are you sure?"

"It's probably old," Ben interjected. "Your parents had a key to our house, too, and we have one for the Niedermeyers' next door, in case something happens when they're out of town. It's a neighbor thing."

"Let's see it," I said to Lauren.

Her expression brightened and she got to her feet. We heard her trotting up the stairs to retrieve the key.

"Do you really think . . . ?" Ben said.

I twisted my head to the side until I felt a pop in my neck, ligament sliding over bone. "I don't know. Maybe the back door. The front one has a new lock."

Lauren returned with the key ring. A rectangular box was wedged under her arm, some kind of game or puzzle. I looked closer and saw that it was her Ouija board.

"Lauren." Ben's tone was stern, and she looked up at him guiltily, clutching the box tighter.

"I think we should try it," she said. "It didn't work over here, but maybe it will at Arrowood. I thought Arden would want to. You do, don't you?"

I nodded. "Sure. If we can get in." Lauren and I had used the Ouija board together many times, and the pointer never did anything more than jitter, refusing to spell out the answers we so desperately sought. Would her parents get divorced? Would I move back to Keokuk? Were my sisters still alive?

"All right." Ben took the key ring from Lauren and handed it to me. "Ready?"

I nodded, my fingertips tracing the bumps and notches of the key and hoping for a match. We slipped out the kitchen door and crossed the Ferrises' dark lawn, crunching mayflies underfoot. I wasn't terribly worried that we would get caught. It was just past ten o'clock, and I figured most people were likely indoors with their air conditioners blasting, cursing the plague of flies and the crippling humidity. When I tried the key, it slid into the lock without hesitation and the door opened into the laundry room.

It was completely quiet inside, all the night sounds silenced as soon as we closed the door. I inhaled the familiar scent of the old house, the enduring smell of polished wood and antiquity, and for one dizzying moment I was eight years old again, my body wanting instinctually to run up the back stairs to my sisters' room. I latched on to Ben's arm to anchor myself and looked around. The stairwell was dark, the laundry

room colorless in the moonlight that filtered through the voile curtains. My heart pulled in two panicked directions. *This is my house.*
This is not my house.

"What do you think?" Ben said.

"I need to see the rest." Lauren grabbed the back of my T-shirt, and
together the three of us crossed the room.

"Can't we turn on the lights?" Lauren asked.

"No," Ben said. "Somebody might notice."

He handed me the tiny penlight he'd brought along, and I shined it
into the hallway ahead of us. It was slightly brighter when we reached
the main hall, the stained-glass window on the second floor landing
allowing moonlight to bleed in. Drapes covered most of the windows
on the first floor, something I knew from years of trying to peek in from
the outside.

We moved stealthily from room to room. It was somehow more
disconcerting to discover that everything had remained exactly where
my family had left it, giving the impression that the house had frozen
in time the moment we'd stepped out the door. The one difference
was that each piece of furniture was covered with thick white sheets or
drop cloths to prevent fading and keep dust at bay, though there was
hardly any dust to be seen. The house was regularly cleaned and maintained, lending to the feel that Arrowood was not abandoned but
merely waiting for us to return.

I paused at the foot of the grand staircase, my hand resting on the
glossy banister. Sweat ran down inside my shirt, seeping into the waistband of my shorts. Ben and Lauren stood on either side of me, waiting
for me to take the first step, and when I did, they followed.

"We should try their room," Lauren murmured as we approached
the twins' door. I could feel the shape of the faceted glass knob in my
hand without touching it.

"No," I said. "Not yet."

Instead I opened the door to my childhood bedroom, savoring the familiar creak as it swung in. I grabbed the curtains and swept them back, the metal rings scraping along the rod. There was the river, down below, as it had always been.

Ben checked his watch. "Mom and Dad said they'd be home by midnight, so we've got maybe an hour on the safe side."

Lauren, who hadn't spoken a word since we entered the room, knelt on the bare wood floor and removed the Ouija board from its box. Ben sat across from her, and I sat facing the door. We scooted into a tight circle so that the board could balance on our knees. Lauren set down the planchette, a heart-shaped piece of plastic with a hole in the middle, and the three of us leaned forward to rest our fingertips on it.

"Hello," Lauren whispered to the board. We were close enough in the darkness that I could see the sweat beading on her forehead and upper lip. "We're going to ask some questions. Please answer if you can." My hands shook, and I concentrated on holding them still. The house was silent.

"Is anyone here?" she continued. We watched the board, waiting. The planchette remained motionless. Lauren glanced up at me. "Do you want to ask?"

I started to speak, but my voice came out gravelly and I had to clear my throat and try again. "I'm looking for Violet and Tabitha Arrowood. My sisters." I waited for a moment. My headache was growing more intense, like a drill slowly burrowing into my skull. "Can you tell me if they're alive or dead?"

I could feel Ben's and Lauren's knees pressed against mine, our legs slippery with sweat beneath the board. The planchette twitched, so slightly that I looked over at Ben to see if he had noticed, too, or if I'd only imagined it. Then I felt a tug beneath my fingers, and Lauren gasped. The plastic heart dragged itself across the alphabet from right to left and stopped. The hole in the heart framed the letter A.

"*Alive*," Lauren murmured. "They're alive."

Lauren and I had never gotten the board to work on our own, and I knew she wasn't pushing the pointer. This was the first time Ben had joined us, and I wondered if he was the reason it was working now, if there was a certain kind of energy that flowed between us. Ben and I had been closest to the scene of the kidnapping, the only ones to see the gold car.

The heart jerked again, moving to the right. It wasn't done. It slid past the L and instead halted over the R. It wasn't spelling *alive*. It kept moving, to the D and the E, before stopping at the N. *Arden*. It was spelling my name.

Lauren looked up at me, her eyes wide, the planchette pulling our fingers along as it began tracing increasingly energetic figure eights across the board.

"Arden," Ben said, his voice cutting through the syrupy air. "Do we let go?"

"You have to say goodbye," Lauren whispered.

I watched our hands swoop back and forth in the dark. I strained my senses for any sign of my sisters' presence—the scent of their hair, the rhythm of their breath. I waited for the smallest sensation, a vague hint of awareness in my heart. A hushed static filled my ears, the false sound of ocean waves when you listen to a shell.

"Goodbye," I said. The sharp creak of hinges filled the room as my bedroom door opened wider.

"On the board!" Lauren cried, shoving the planchette to GOODBYE and yanking her hands away. The piece stopped moving, and Ben and I let go, our fingers hovering above it. Tears spilled down Lauren's cheeks, and she clambered to her feet.

"The door's done that before," I said, unable to get enough air into my lungs. We all knew how old houses settled, the noises they made. "I don't think it was them."

"It spelled out your name." Lauren's voice trembled.

I wanted to believe that it had been the twins reaching out to me, though with each passing moment, doubt spiraled deeper. There were three other Arden Arrowoods who had died in the house. It was just as likely that one of them was announcing her presence as it was that a spirit had called me by name, and it was even more likely that no spirits had been involved at all. How could I be sure that our hands hadn't guided the pointer, not consciously, but out of our own fierce desire for it to move?

"I want to go home," Lauren said. Ben returned the board to its box, and Lauren grabbed his arm, dragging him to the door. He turned back and held his other hand out to me.

"Go ahead," I said. "I'll be right behind you."

I watched them disappear through the doorway, and then I was alone, the thin blade of fear that knifed into me not enough to drive me out of my room. I'd always thought if I snuck into Arrowood that I would take something back with me, something with good memories attached, like the string of bells that had hung on the mantel every Christmas. Now I couldn't summon the strength or the courage to climb up to the third floor and search through the boxes. I didn't want to be reminded of what was missing or what had changed, so I stepped over to the window, to look out on the river, the one constant thing. Mayflies had collected on the sill outside and on the terrace down below.

"Arden." Ben called to me softly from the door and I whipped around, jumpy despite his familiar voice. "I got Lauren home. I didn't want to leave you without a light."

He brought the penlight to me, and when I took it, his hand lingered on mine. "I'm sorry," he said. His breathing was labored from rushing up the stairs.

"It's okay." I wasn't sure what he was apologizing for—the light, or the lack of answers, or the long list of things that weren't as they should have been. None of it was his fault.

"You don't have to say that," he said. "Not to me."

I leaned against him, his arms circling my waist as though to keep me from falling to the floor. His T-shirt was wet, and his breath wheezed in my ear. I clamped my arms around his neck. As we stood pressed against each other in the stagnant heat, our bodies slick with sweat, I became acutely aware of the feel of his skin against mine. It was inno-cent—my wrist at the nape of his neck, fingertips grazing a shoulder blade—yet tinged with a flicker of anticipation I'd only felt in certain dreams. Never in life. Never before with Ben.

We should go back, he whispered. Neither of us moved.

I took a few deep breaths, which didn't help at all, and cut across the lawn, just as I had done a thousand times in my former life, to knock on the Ferrises' front door. After a minute or two of wondering if Mrs. Ferris had seen me through the window and decided not to answer, I heard movement in the house and the door pitched open. Lauren bar-reled out onto the porch and wrapped me up in a hug. She had been thirteen when I last saw her ten years ago. Twenty-three-year-old Lau-ren was a head taller than me, and all curves. Her hair was long and loose and tipped with magenta, and a thorny row of earrings pressed into my cheek as she hugged me.

She pulled back to look at me, smiling. "Damn!" she said. "You haven't changed. Come on in."

"It's so good to see you," I said, following her into the house.

"Ben says you might actually be sticking around?"

"I'm not sure yet," I said. "I don't really have any other plans."

"Plans are overrated," she said, pushing her hair behind her ear. "Wanna come upstairs and hang out, like old times?"

"Is your mom home?"

"No." She snorted. "She's in St. Louis on a shopping bender."

I glanced around the foyer and into the adjoining rooms. "It looks completely different," I said. "I know it's been a while, but I barely recognize it."

"Mom's redone every room in the house probably three times since you saw it last. She gets bored. Wallpaper's her latest thing. Dad loves to point out how much money we spent getting rid of the old wallpaper, just to get new wallpaper that looks old."

I followed Lauren upstairs to her slope-ceilinged bedroom, which had been papered in pink and white roses, with matching window treatments, upholstered headboard, and dust ruffle. I assumed the bedding matched, too, but the bed was unmade and covered with piles of laundry. Lauren kicked some books out of the way and we sat on the floor.

"Does this room give you a headache?" I asked, smiling.

"Isn't this so Mom?" she asked. "She turned it into a guest room the minute I left for college. Like we didn't have enough guest rooms already."

"What about Ben's old room?"

"Exact same wallpaper, in yellow. No joke. I think she was hoping it would keep us from moving back home."

"Ben said you're in dental school. Was he serious? Do you like it?"

"Do I like it? Not really. Do I think I'll flunk out? Possibly. It's too soon to tell." Lauren pushed up her sleeves, revealing a small bird tattooed on the inside of her wrist. "I only applied because I thought I wouldn't get accepted. Then Mom made Dad pledge a bunch of money to the dental school—probably my whole inheritance—and voilà, I'm in. Lucky me. It could be worse, though, I could be living here."

"I never would have guessed either one of you would end up working with your dad."

"Well, Ben started drinking Mom's Kool-Aid a while ago, around the time I stopped. She's got him squished right down inside the mold she carved out for him, and I think he likes it there. Or at least he doesn't complain anymore."

"He's happy?"

"Yeah, he is. He was going on about you when he called this morning." A slight blush warmed my face, and I hoped Lauren wouldn't notice. "Maybe now that you're back he'll break things off with Courtney. She's all right, but I'm pretty sure Mom had something to do with setting them up. I don't know how serious they are. I always thought you and Ben belonged together."

My throat tightened. Ben hadn't mentioned that he was dating anyone at dinner, but the subject hadn't come up. I hadn't talked about Dr. Endicott, either. "Ben and I weren't like that," I said. "We were just friends."

Lauren rolled her eyes. "Come on. It was embarrassingly obvious. If you guys were trying to keep anybody from finding out, you did a terrible job."

I shrugged. "That was a long time ago. Everything's different now."

"Whatever you say," she said. She picked at her fingernail polish, purple glitter flaking onto the floor. "You know, I'm sorry I stopped writing to you, Arden. I wish we would have kept in touch."

"It's okay," I said. We'd remained pen pals for quite a while after Ben and I stopped writing to each other, but I'd never been very good at maintaining long-distance friendships. When Lauren stopped responding to my letters, I stopped sending them.

"Something happened," she said. "I wanted to tell you about it, but I didn't. Then it didn't feel right, writing to you and talking about other things. I don't even know if it's worth mentioning now. You probably already know." She wedged her thumbnail between her teeth and bit down, a childish habit she had not outgrown.

"What was it?"

"It's about your dad. And my mom. She'd probably die if she knew I was talking about it." Lauren examined the jagged edge of her nail. "Did you ever think there was something going on between them?"

"I don't know," I said. "Maybe." I had never told anyone about seeing my dad kiss Mrs. Ferris at the Christmas party.

"There was a point where Mom was on the phone a lot, and she was going into her room and closing the door so I couldn't hear her. You know how she usually is on the phone, it's like she's yelling into a bullhorn. I wanted to know why she was being all secretive, so I picked up the phone downstairs, and she was talking to your dad. She heard the line click when I hung up, and figured out I'd been listening. She was all freaked out, asking what I'd heard, but I hadn't really heard anything.

"She said they were talking about your house. He was checking on it, maybe. But I didn't believe her. If it was just about the house, why would she bother to hide that from anybody? And why would she get so worked up about it? I told my dad, and he got all serious and admitted there'd been something between my mom and Eddie, but it was years and years ago and he and Mom went to marriage counseling, and everything was fine."

"Do you think they were still involved?" It seemed unlikely that they'd carry on an affair after we'd moved away. I wondered if my mother knew anything about it.

"I don't know," Lauren said. "I thought so at the time. I guess it doesn't matter now. I just wanted to tell you, so it wouldn't feel like I was keeping it secret from you anymore. Mom got back at me for telling Dad, by the way." Lauren smirked. "She sent me to one of those Outward Bound summer camps where they charge a fortune to torture you. She said she was doing it for my *health*, because I needed to lose weight or I'd end up with diabetes, but I knew it was because she was pissed at me for telling Dad she was talking to Eddie on the sly."

She grabbed my hand and squeezed it. "Anyway, I wanted you to know I didn't forget about you."

"I didn't forget about you, either," I said.

I tried to picture Lauren and her room as they had been before the pink and white wallpaper, before Lauren grew up. Sometimes, back then, I had pretended that she was my little sister.

"You really haven't changed, Arden," she said gently. "I know people always say that, but you're exactly the same."

I couldn't tell if that was supposed to be a compliment.

As much as I dreaded it, I needed to talk to my mother, and there was no telling when I would hear from her again if I waited for her to call me. On Monday, when I figured Gary would be at work, I picked up the phone and dialed.

"Hello?" she said. She always answered like that, a question in her voice, as if she didn't have caller ID and know that it was me.

"Hi, Mom," I said. As usual, the TV was blaring in the background, loud enough for me to hear every word. Rachael Ray was talking about making individual servings of meatloaf in muffin tins.

"So," she said. "Have you found yourself a job yet?"

"No, Mom." Rachael Ray listed ingredients, and I wondered if my mother was writing them down.

"Did you need something, Arden? I hate to rush you off the phone, but I have to leave for the women's ministry luncheon in a minute and I still need to do my hair."

"Yes. Okay, I—I wanted to ask you something. It's really awkward, so I'm just going to say it. Was there something going on between Dad and Julia Ferris?"

Rachael Ray made a joke about the tiny meatloaves, and the audience laughed.

"Yes," Mom replied finally. "Your father was unfaithful. Many times. That's a known fact, and I don't think we need to discuss it any further. I've given it all up to the Lord. God's judging Eddie now, and it's none of my concern."

That sounded like something Gary would say, and I didn't believe for a second that my mother harbored no bitterness toward my dad.

"When did it happen?"

"When do you think, Arden?" Her voice rose to a controlled shriek, and I knew for sure that Gary wasn't home, because she never raised her voice around him. "When we were living next door. But the same thing that put an end to everything else put an end to that."

She clicked her TV off, and I could hear her breathing. She wouldn't say it. *The thing that put an end to everything.*

"I really need to get going. You have a blessed day."

"I'm sorry, Mom," I said. She didn't answer. She'd already hung up the phone.

My mother had been depressed when we left Arrowood, and her condition hadn't improved over the course of our many moves. I understood it as mourning for the twins, because I'd felt it, too. It clung to me like my own shadow. Though looking back, I had memories of my mother's detachment *before*, and now that I was thinking about it more carefully, there had been evidence of her withdrawal even before my sisters were born. It had made sense to attribute my mother's exhaustion and distraction to being pregnant and taking care of newborn twins. But what if it had been caused by something else? Even then, she still made certain efforts, like curling her hair and playing bunco with the ladies in the neighborhood. That last summer, though, before the twins disappeared, I would sometimes find her sitting in her bedroom, holding the telephone and staring at the wall. Other times, she'd be standing at the sink, like she was about to do the dishes but couldn't muster up the energy to turn on the water. I'd say her name, and I'd have to say it ten times, my voice growing progressively louder, to get her attention.

For years my mother had been taking pills, and as a kid I hadn't thought it unusual. She called them her vitamins, and Granddad was the one who prescribed them to her. As far as I knew, all mommies took Xanax in the morning and painkillers in the afternoon and a little something to help them sleep at night. I was too young to realize that she was self-medicating, or to understand why. Now that I knew about my father's affair with Julia Ferris—ostensibly, my mother's friend—I wondered if that had been the thing that had begun to push her toward the edge, if the twins' disappearance had been not the start but the end of her undoing.

Josh had said our neighbors were all potential suspects, and that would include Mrs. Ferris. Ben claimed his mother wasn't in the house that afternoon, and he thought she might have been in the carriage house, which stood between our home and theirs. I assumed that she had been questioned along with everyone else, and as far as I knew she hadn't seen anything that was helpful to the case, though I had never come out and asked her. Was it possible that her affair with my father had somehow made her want to hurt the twins? She had told him at the Christmas party that she hadn't forgiven him, that he would have to make it up to her somehow, whatever "it" was. Had he done something so terrible that she would punish him through his children?

Maybe she had coaxed Violet and Tabitha into the carriage house while I was gathering dandelions. She couldn't have kept them hidden there for long, though; all the homes and outbuildings were eventually searched. Would she have been able to move them elsewhere before they could be found? It was hard to imagine that she would have intentionally harmed my sisters, though that didn't mean it wasn't possible.

I remembered the time Ben accidentally got gum stuck in my hair, when we were ten or eleven years old. Mrs. Ferris offered to help get it out, and I sat down at the kitchen table, expecting her to rub peanut butter into my hair like Grammy would do. Instead, she had pulled my hair taut and sliced out the gum with the kitchen shears, letting it fall into my lap. She had dropped the scissors onto the table with a clatter, and I had jumped up, startled, pieces of my hair scattering over the spotless floor. Our eyes met, and a glimmer of understanding crossed her face as my hands began to tremble, both of us realizing that I was afraid of her.

CHAPTER 10

Ben had arranged for me to talk to his mother about the holiday home tour, since Mrs. Ferris hadn't been home when I went to see Lauren. As much as I wanted to ask her about her relationship with my father, and the day the twins disappeared, I didn't know if I could summon the courage. I still pictured her as I'd known her in my childhood: severe eyebrows, pressed pants, headache-inducing perfume. Every time I had knocked on her door to see if Ben could come out to play, she had greeted me with a disdainful frown.

I picked through my work clothes looking for something decent to wear, and then I reminded myself that I was a grown-up, that I didn't have to dress to please Julia Ferris, and besides, even if I wore a freshly ironed blouse and khakis, she would probably still not like me. If I had to face an old enemy, I might as well do it in the comfort of my faded jeans.

I walked along the sidewalk instead of cutting across the Ferrises' lawn, atonement for my passive-aggressive wardrobe choice. Mrs. Ferris smiled primly when she answered the door.

"Come in, Arden, it's wonderful to see you," she said, extending her bony arm toward the front parlor.

As I walked past her, I was engulfed in her familiar, dizzying perfume, the synthetic sweetness of gardenia strong enough to turn my stomach. I sat on an antique love seat that had been reupholstered in flowery chintz, and she sat across from me in a matching chair, a spotless glass-topped coffee table between us. The window air conditioner whooshed on top speed, pumping the room full of frigid air.

Mrs. Ferris was older than my mother, closer in age to my father, though you wouldn't have guessed from looking at her. Mom would have been irritated to know that her former friend and rival had aged so well. She was thin as a stick of gum, and her skin was almost supernaturally luminous, as though it had recently been peeled and polished by an aggressive aesthetician. Her thick coffee-colored hair was cut into a precise bob. I held a notebook and pen in my lap, and my thumb clicked the pen open and closed, over and over, keeping time with the pendulum on the grandfather clock in the corner.

"May I get you some tea?" she asked.

"No, thank you," I said, trying not to be distracted by the curtains behind her. They were the same bold floral print as the upholstery, and they pooled extravagantly on the glossy floor in a way that I had only seen in magazines. I wondered if they ever got caught in the vacuum.

Mrs. Ferris's forced smile faded. "I want you to know how very sorry I am about your father," she said. "He'd be so glad to see you back in the house."

I nodded solemnly, though I couldn't imagine Dad caring what I did one way or the other. He hadn't been sentimental about Arrowood like I was. He mocked people who stayed still, living and dying in the houses and towns where they were born, a fate he had worked hard to avoid.

Mrs. Ferris plucked a Lee County historical society pamphlet from the coffee table and handed it to me, along with a flyer for a reception celebrating her contributions to the society and the Miller House Museum. "I suppose Ben already told you a bit about what's going on, though I'm not sure how well he explained it. Did he happen to tell you that Keokuk was recently named the worst town in the state of Iowa, and the second-most dangerous?"

I nodded.

"Can you believe that? I didn't. But the study was based on indisputable data—unemployment rate, median income, the number of vacant houses, crime. It was terrible news for the visitors bureau, and for all of us. I'm sure you agree that our town has a lot more to offer. This holiday tour is the first of our efforts to promote Keokuk as a destination for historical tourism. We're hoping, if it goes well, that we can make it an annual event and go on to add summer tours of certain homes and cultural attractions around town. The lock and dam, the Miller House, the steamboat museum. It could bring in some much needed revenue and improve our reputation."

"Sounds like a great idea," I said.

"You're probably aware that people are . . . interested . . . in Arrowood for various reasons, most notably, of course, for its connection to the Underground Railroad. The house has never been open to the public before, and I think it would make a nice draw if it were on our list." She smoothed back her hair, which didn't need smoothing, the knob of her wrist and the thin bones of her hand clearly articulated beneath her pale skin. "There wouldn't be much required of you, really, aside from writing a one-page profile of Arrowood for the guidebook, which I'm sure you'll have no trouble with. You'd need to put up Christmas lights and decorations—some vintage or antique ones would be nice if you have them handy. We're asking the homeowners to provide hot cider or cocoa, and maybe some sugar cookies. Then as people come in, you'd answer questions about the history of the house and let them look around."

"I'm not sure I can commit to that right now," I hedged. "I mean, I've been here less than a week. I haven't even finished unpacking."

"Oh, I know, but it's not until November. You'll have plenty of time to prepare, and I can help you if you'd like. I just need to know who's participating so I can get everything ready on my end." She smiled expectantly. "You'd be doing so much to help our town. And it would truly honor the memory of your grandparents. They were so proud of the house, and such avid supporters of the community."

I wondered how much good any fundraising efforts would really do, whether it was possible to slow down the rate of decay, let alone reverse it. Not that it mattered. She must have realized that mentioning Nana and Granddad would be enough to convince me. We both knew they would have wanted me to show off Arrowood.

"I guess it wouldn't hurt to open up the house for a few hours."

Mrs. Ferris sighed. "Thank you so much," she said. "Everyone will be thrilled to have you on board."

I clicked my pen open and closed, open and closed. How hard could it be to ask her the questions I really wanted answered? What was the worst that could happen? I remembered the sound of her kitchen shears slicing through my hair, the cold kiss of metal as they slid past my ear.

"I wanted to ask you something," I said.

"Of course."

"It's about the twins. The day they went missing."

Mrs. Ferris uncrossed and recrossed her legs, her navy-blue slacks rustling.

"Someone is trying to prove that Harold Singer is innocent, and thinks things may have been overlooked in the investigation. I wondered what you remember—any little details that might not have seemed important then. Ben said he thought you might have been out in the carriage house, so maybe you saw something from there that we couldn't see?"

Mrs. Ferris seemed to shrink into her chair, her mouth pinched shut. "No," she said, her lips curling around the word. "I didn't see anything."

"But that's where you were, in the carriage house, when they were taken? You didn't see the lawn crew, or anyone on the street?"

She shook her head. "I wasn't paying attention to anything that was going on outside the window."

"What were you doing?"

"Arden." She clasped her hands together, her eyes squinting and a deep vertical line appearing between her penciled brows. "I assumed you knew. I was with your father. It was kept quiet out of respect for your family, but it was known—your father and I were both questioned about our whereabouts and we told the truth."

"You were right there, both of you?" My face burned, hot blood rushing to the tips of my ears. "You were *right there* when it happened?" Would things have turned out differently if they hadn't been together that day? If my dad had been home with us instead?

"Yes, and I've lived with that guilt every day since. It was hard to even look at you, knowing what I'd done. Every time you came over to see Ben, it brought the whole thing back." She hinged forward in her seat. "You're old enough now that I can explain to you—your father and I didn't set out to hurt anyone. Eddie and I understood each other. We'd been involved off and on long before he met your mother. We weren't in love. It was just something that happened. He was a different man, though, after that day. We ended things."

"Lauren told me about you and my dad talking on the phone, years later."

She smiled wryly. "He asked to borrow some money from me. For an investment. That's all it was, later, when we were in touch. He needed the money, and I gave it to him."

"I'm guessing he didn't pay you back."

"No," she said. "And I never asked. Your father and I had a long history—we were friends, growing up. We were close, like you and my son."

Mrs. Ferris shut her eyes for a moment, and I wondered if she pictured my father through the same nostalgic lens I pictured Ben, if it had been hard for her to lose him even after so many years apart.

I closed my notebook, clipped the pen onto the front cover, and tucked the historical society pamphlet and flyer inside. I hadn't written down a thing. I stared at Mrs. Ferris's skeletal hands, the tips of her French-manicured nails an unnatural shade of white. Her wedding ring hung loose on her finger, the heavy stone tilting to the side.

"I thought you hated me," I said, my voice muffled by the bright upholstery, the blustering air conditioner, the gardenia perfume that I could taste in the back of my throat. "And I never knew why."

"I hated everyone for a while," she said. "Including myself."

Back at the house, my first piece of mail had arrived, a thick manila envelope from the lawyer. Now that I was the official owner of the house, I would periodically receive various documents related to the trust that supported it. The lawyer had promised that very little attention would be required on my part. I had the same problem with real mail that I had with email, tending to let it pile up unopened until it became too daunting to deal with. I forced myself to peel open the envelope and flip through the sheaf of papers, not wanting to look too closely at the details. There were property tax receipts, financial statements, and a list of expenses. My eyes caught on the last page, the balance of the trust, and my stomach hollowed out just as it had done when the lawyer first talked to me about it. It was far less than I had imagined. He had suggested that I let Heaney's contract expire at the end of the year as a cost-saving measure, since a caretaker wouldn't be necessary when the house was occupied. I could hire out any maintenance work as needed, to Heaney or someone else.

I stuffed the packet into a kitchen drawer, not wanting to think about what would happen if the trust ran out before I could find a decent job. I could survive on very little, especially now that I wasn't paying rent, but the house had needs of its own. My mother had warned me how greedy Arrowood could be, how impractical it was to live in a drafty relic with a million things waiting to go wrong; simply heating it through the winter would cost a small fortune. I, of course, hadn't listened to her. Already there were problems with leaks and moisture, the windows that refused to open. I thought of all the houses in town that were falling apart around the people who lived inside them and hoped that wouldn't happen to me.

I fixed my favorite childhood lunch, one I'd often prepared for myself and the twins when Mom was taking one of her long naps: slices of Oscar Mayer braunschweiger, which my father had kept stocked in the refrigerator at all times, and a bag of Sterzing's potato chips. I carried my lunch into the study and set it down on Granddad's desk, hoping to distract myself from thinking about the trust by working on the Arrowood profile for the holiday tour. I wanted to get it out of the way. I tied the heavy drapes back as far as they would go, to let in more light, and turned on my laptop.

It would be easy, I thought, to write about Arrowood. I knew most of the stories from memory—Nana would go on about family history in lengthy letters, before her arthritis made it too difficult to write, and every time she called on the phone—and now I also had access to all of her papers, including the documentation she'd used to get Arrowood on the National Register of Historic Places. She had kept it all in a box in Granddad's desk, and it was still there, nestled in the deep bottom drawer.

There were several articles detailing Arrowood's involvement in the Underground Railroad, all of which I had read before. The only new information I found among Nana's handwritten notes was the brief mention of a secret room in the basement that concealed the fleeing slaves who had sought temporary refuge at Arrowood. I'd never heard anyone talk about a hidden room, and I'd never found any hint of one while exploring the dirt-floored basement as a child. Most likely, it had been torn out at some point over the years as pipes and wiring were installed and updated beneath the house, the foundation repaired, the boiler replaced.

I sorted through pages of photocopied portraits of my relatives, many taken on Arrowood's front lawn. I had never understood my father's eagerness to sell the house. He was always too busy looking for the next big thing to see what he already had; he was the worst kind of gambler, never able to quit when he was ahead.

My dad came to visit me at college only once. He was passing through on his way to a sales convention, characteristically vague about what exactly he was selling. We ate gristly sirloins at a roadhouse on the outskirts of town, and he insisted that I drink a beer with him, scoffing when I reminded him that I was underage. He wore a cowboy hat and pointy-toed boots that looked like a disguise on him, though it was possible that that was who he'd become, someone who listened to country music and knew how to saddle a horse. I didn't ask, and he offered no explanation. I nursed my warm beer as he rambled on about a new boat he'd been eyeing, one I doubted he could afford. As far as I knew, he didn't live anywhere near the water.

He stopped talking and looked up at me, his bloodshot eyes turning wistful. *Remember the* Ruby Slipper? he asked, his voice gravelly from the skinny cigars he'd started smoking when he left my mother. *I loved that boat. Even your mom liked it, and didn't much make her happy.* His face had changed in the time since I'd last seen him, the skin loosened and sagging like a rubber mask. I wanted him to remove it, this ill-fitting façade of cigars and wrinkles and cowboy clothes, to reveal the father I remembered, the man who'd held me on his lap and let me steer the boat down the river.

Why did you marry her? I asked.

He cocked his head to the side and squinted, chewing a mouthful of steak. We rarely talked about my mother, and I didn't know whether he would answer. I wondered if they had once loved each other, or if he'd married her for her looks. She'd been wispy and delicate at twenty-three, with pale Scandinavian hair and skin that was so striking that people automatically assumed she was beautiful. Only upon close examination would someone realize that her features were actually quite plain.

She was working as a secretary at Sheller-Globe when she met my dad, and desperate to move out of the Sister House. According to Aunt Alice, my mother wasn't one to accept her station in life. She ran around with the well-to-do girls in high school and wanted all the same things they had: designer jeans, spring break trips to Fort Lauderdale, a car of her own. In the years after we left Arrowood, when my mother chased certain pills with a coffee mug full of Merlot, her tongue would limber up and she'd tell me about meeting my father for the first time, at a drive-in showing of *Sixteen Candles*. Eddie was tall and charismatic and drove a new Pontiac Firebird, and he had big plans for himself, which somehow overshadowed the fact that he was thirty-one years old, questionably self-employed, and still living with his parents at Arrowood. She saw him as her ticket to all the places she'd ever wanted to go. He had broken off a previous engagement to the Lee

County Corn Queen, which made my mother nervous and overly in-
dulgent, not wanting to do anything to scare him away.

She believed in me more than anyone else ever did, Dad replied, the
words muffled in his napkin as he wiped his mouth.

They had married for selfish reasons, each wanting what the other
could offer, though I supposed that was true of most people. It made
sense—more sense than falling in love—and it had been enough for
them, for a while. Maybe she held out hope that he would live up to
everything he represented to her, and maybe he relied on her belief in
him in order to believe in himself. I wondered if he'd waited to leave
her until he'd depleted the last of her faith in him, and she had nothing left to give.

It wasn't fair, though, to cast my mother as a victim. I had taken
care of myself for a long time, to spare her the burden, because I
thought that she was fragile and weak. However, after watching her
start her new life with Gary, it seemed that she had spent those years
selfishly hibernating, conserving her strength, waiting to emerge like a
frilly butterfly when another man with big plans came along.

I dug deeper into the box and pulled out a plastic sleeve containing
sketches of the house. Beneath the exterior renderings were diagrams
of the interior. House plans. The paper was brittle and discolored, but
there was no date, so I couldn't tell whether they were the original
plans. There was a second set done on a sort of tissue paper that crumbled at the edges when I touched it. Each layer detailed one floor of
the house, so that stacked on top of each other as the pages were, you
could see which rooms above lay on top of which rooms below. I
checked the basement level, careful not to tear the paper, but didn't
find anything to indicate a hidden partition. Of course, that wasn't
likely something one would document on a house plan, especially if
the room was intended to be part of the Underground Railroad.

I started typing up notes for the profile. Late in the afternoon, I was startled into awareness by the sound of running water, and couldn't tell if I'd been sleeping or merely daydreaming. My laptop screen had gone black.

I uncurled myself from the chair and stepped out into the front hall to listen, the floorboards cool against my bare feet. The sound seemed to be coming from above, like someone had left a faucet running upstairs, and my first thought was that the bathroom pipes Heaney had fixed were still having issues. I ran up to check the tub, but it was dry.

I stepped back out into the hall and paused at the third-floor stairwell. There was no real bathroom on the uppermost level, only a defunct, closet-size powder room with a marble sink and a toilet that looked like it belonged in a museum. Before Nana and Granddad moved out and Mom and Dad took over the master suite, my parents' bedroom had been up there. Mom told me she had hated sleeping in that room, with its fussy toile wallpaper, the same room where Arden Blythe Arrowood, age ten, had died of pneumonia nearly a hundred years before.

It didn't seem likely that I would have heard the powder room sink running from all the way downstairs, though it was possible that what I'd initially heard was the water running through the pipes in the wall. I wiped the remnants of a sagging cobweb away from the entry and leaned into the stairwell. I could definitely hear something.

The stairs were steep, the treads too small for normal-size feet, and I nearly fell when something tickled my arm, letting go of the railing in my hurry to brush off a tiny spider. The third floor was dim and claustrophobic compared to the rest of the house, with low ceilings and burgundy wallpaper and narrow windows set into the sides of the mansard roof. Dust was clotted everywhere, along the trim, on top of the doorknobs. It looked like someone had shaken out a down pillow. There were three closed doors on either side of the hall, and at the very end, the powder room door, which was ajar.

Once Mom and Dad had moved into Nana and Granddad's old

room, the entire third floor had been devoted to storage. Hardly any-thing that crossed Arrowood's threshold had ever been thrown away. There were rooms full of holiday decorations and tarnished silver serv-ing trays, baby carriages and bicycles, the remnants of various china sets, old-fashioned rug beaters, vintage General Electric fans with ex-posed blades that could sever your fingers. One room held all of Nana's coats and furs and winter clothes, things she hadn't needed in Florida but couldn't bear to give away, because that meant admitting that she would spend no more winters at Arrowood, that she would never again see the river freeze over. The room next to Nana's contained all the remaining possessions of my dad's two older brothers, my uncles who were killed in Vietnam. Nana was the only one who had ever gone in there.

The hinges shrieked when I pushed the powder room door all the way open to step inside. Dust shimmered in the weak light that filtered down from above, the ancient skylight held in place with narrow strips of trim and crumbling caulk, the glass clouded with years of grime. The marble sink was stained with rust where a thin stream of water flowed into the basin. I twisted the handle as hard as I could and it slowed to a steady drip.

It was a relief to find the source of the problem and to see that it was nothing serious. I would have to tell Heaney about the sink, and the skylight as well, which looked in danger of collapsing. It was under-standable that he might have neglected the tiny room; like the others on this floor, it was crammed with boxes. They were stacked on the tiled marble floor and on top of the toilet. They appeared to be the remains of Granddad's medical practice. There were financial records and patient files, and propped between the wall and the toilet, a large framed photograph of the building that had once housed his office, a building that had since been torn down.

I flicked through the tabs in a box of patient records, starting with the A's, and quickly came to my mother's name: *Arrowood, Sheila.* I wondered why Granddad had kept all this paperwork instead of shredding it, but I wasn't terribly surprised. He wasn't one for discarding things. I picked up the box, careful to support the spongy underside, and took it with me.

Back downstairs, I fixed myself a bowl of SpaghettiOs with oyster crackers for dinner and took the box into the study, where I opened my mother's file and spread the pages out on the desk. It was appalling, the number of medications Granddad had prescribed for her, but my mother seemed to have a complaint that fit each one. I had to look up the drugs I'd never heard of. First there was Prozac for depression and Xanax for anxiety. Trazodone to supplement the Prozac and help her sleep. Percocet for lingering C-section pain after the twins were born. She suffered from postpartum depression and a strained back. Zoloft. Valium. Klonopin for insomnia. Wellbutrin when the Zoloft wasn't working. It was clear that some of the drugs were not meant to be taken long-term, though that hadn't stopped her, and considering how much wine I remembered her drinking in her coffee mug back then, it seemed a small miracle that she had been able to function as well as she did.

I went upstairs not long after dinner and sat in bed with Grammy's scrapbook, the one she started when the twins were taken. She had given it to me my last summer at the Sister House. In addition to keeping a meticulous archive of newspaper clippings and information related to the twins' disappearance, she had written cards for them on their birthdays and holidays, checked in with the police station on a regular basis, and prayed for them daily without fail. She had never lost faith that the twins would be found alive.

According to the first newspaper clipping, from the *Daily Gate City*, Violet Ann and Tabitha Grace Arrowood, identical twins, age twenty-one months, were abducted by a man in a gold sedan from the front yard of 635 Grand Avenue at approximately four P.M. on September 3, 1994. Their sister, Arden Arrowood, age eight, was the sole witness, though a neighbor confirmed the sighting of a vehicle of similar description just prior to the incident. Police and volunteers searched for the vehicle and the children with no luck.

From the newspapers, I learned where my sisters had not been found: in the corn and soybean fields of Lee County; in the Des Moines River or the Mississippi; in a pumpkin patch near the river bottoms; in the city dump; in a ravine at the edge of town; in the pond at Rand Park; in the factories along Highway 61; in any of the barges or docks or trains or rail yards. They were not in the cemeteries, the woods, the hunting cabins or duck blinds, or any of the boats, stores, homes, garages, or cars that were searched, including our own. Then Singer was located, and after an exhaustive search of his property and a lengthy investigation, he too was eventually added to the list of dead ends.

There were a few other persons of interest over the years, each a case of unsubstantiated jailhouse bragging, and a false confession that made the news before being discredited. Grammy kept a record of all related possibilities, no matter how remote. In 1999, the desiccated body of a child was reportedly found stuffed in a trunk in the attic of a Fort Madison home. It was quickly determined to be a hoax. Human bones were discovered along the Des Moines River in 2001 after a spring flood, but testing concluded that they were Native American and had probably been there for decades. There were sightings of the twins reported across the United States and in a few foreign countries, but nothing came of any of them. The television show *Unsolved Mysteries* approached my parents about doing a segment on the kidnapping, but Mom and Dad didn't want to participate. It was too painful, they said. It would be overly sensationalized for ratings, and likely wouldn't amount to anything.

Out of all the reported sightings, one had seemed especially promising. An elderly woman in eastern Nebraska saw two little blond girls wandering barefoot through a cornfield in the spring of 1997. They were holding hands, wearing pink nightgowns that were too small for them and too thin for the weather. The girls looked to be about five years old, as the twins would have been at the time. Officers searched the area and discovered an abandoned farmhouse in the woods beyond the field. Inside the house, a family of five was found huddled together, hiding in an upstairs closet. There were three children: one dark-haired boy and the two little girls that the elderly woman had seen. The family had left a commune in Missouri, and they were wandering. The parents claimed that the girls were not identical twins, but rather "Irish twins" who were close in age and looked very much alike. However, they could not produce birth certificates for the children, who had supposedly been born on the commune and had never visited a doctor or hospital or been enrolled in school. The girls resembled Violet and Tabitha, or rather, age-progressed images of the girls as they might look at five years old, and DNA tests were performed to see if they were the missing Arrowood twins. They were not.

I'd found a lengthy thread on Midwest Mysteries where people speculated about my sisters' demise. Not everyone was convinced that Singer had taken them. Some people thought maybe they were alive and well, snatched by someone desperate to have children. Others suggested that they were being held captive and might one day escape, like kidnapping survivors Jaycee Dugard and Elizabeth Smart. Quite a few theories centered around their potential value on the black market: Where might fair-haired, fair-skinned identical twins fetch the highest price? Most people, though, assumed that Violet and Tabitha had been killed, their bodies dumped in the Mississippi soon after they were taken. It was the theory that made the most sense.

Would I have been able to discern a moment when my sisters ceased to exist? Was it possible that they were murdered minutes after touching my hand, and I didn't feel a thing, didn't sense that loss of connection? Dead or alive, they were gone, had been gone far longer than they had been with me.

I closed the scrapbook and placed it in the rolltop desk. Outside my window, in the darkness, pinpoints of light marked the dam and the power plant downriver. The crab apple tree in the backyard wavered in the wind. I left my room and moved slowly, noiselessly down the hall, though there was no need to be quiet; I was alone in the house. I opened the door to the twins' room and stepped inside, the humidity condensing on my skin. Moisture trickled down the windowpanes, dripping over the sills and splattering onto the floor. I lay down next to the cribs, shutting my eyes and taking myself back to the fever dream I'd had the day the twins disappeared, the one where they were home safe and everything was fine. I let the false sense of relief seep through me, thawing, temporarily, the frozen space inside. I felt something trail lightly across my face, delicate as a thread, and as I lifted my hand to brush it away, a soft exhalation of breath warmed my ear, a wordless whisper. My heart seized up and my eyes snapped open, searching the darkness. There was nothing there.

CHAPTER 11

The phone was ringing, and I thought maybe it was Josh, that I had overslept and missed our meeting. He had mentioned that he'd be in town to restock his books at the Miller House Museum gift shop, and asked if he could stop by to talk. I had suggested that we meet at the lock and dam instead, not quite sure about the idea of bringing him into the house. In my groggy state, I swiped around in the sheets trying to find my phone and inadvertently knocked it off the bed. It clattered onto the wood floor, and I realized the ringing wasn't coming from my cell, it was coming from the house phone. It had been ringing every few days, the number always unknown, sometimes no message, other times a man's voice—*Arden, are you there?*—with a brief interlude of staticky silence before the beep. Since the caller wasn't saying anything creepy or threatening, I mostly ignored the calls, figuring whoever it was would eventually give up.

I rolled onto my stomach and dangled my arms between the bed and the wall to fish out my phone, flinching when my fingers unexpectedly encountered something soft and fuzzy, though I quickly realized it was only a dust bunny, one of many. I got down on the floor to get a better reach, and as I slid my phone through the carpet of dust under the bed, an envelope slid out with it.

I recognized the handwriting right away. My own. It was one of the many letters I'd sent to the twins at Arrowood, this one postmarked 1996. The envelope flap was open, though I couldn't tell whether someone had carefully opened it or if the glue holding it together had simply dissolved over time. I pulled out the sheet of blue-lined notebook paper and unfolded it, dust gritting my fingers.

Dear Violet and Tabitha, I have read A Little Princess *three times now. It is my favorite book.*

I would have been ten at the time, living in a drafty Illinois farmhouse among the wheat fields, imagining myself as Sara Crewe, the privileged schoolgirl forced into terrible circumstances when her doting father dies. My father was still alive then, of course, and though he hadn't ever doted on me, our former life at Arrowood had been idyllic in comparison. The letter went on to explain that Dad was now gone most of the time, trying to work himself to the top of a promising pyramid scheme after taking a Dale Carnegie course called How to Win Friends and Influence People. Our kitchen cabinets were packed with useless, unsold products—shake mixes and dietary supplements and homeopathic remedies and freeze-dried meals. The point, Dad explained, wasn't to sell the products, but to recruit people under you to sell them. Even if they failed, you'd still make money, because they had to buy their way into the pyramid. The pipes in the rented farmhouse had frozen and burst that winter, and we had moved again.

I squeezed half under the bed and used the light on my phone to search for more envelopes, but didn't find any. If this letter had made it to Arrowood, maybe the others were somewhere in the house as well, though I wasn't sure why this one had ended up in my room, under my bed. I stuck the letter in my rolltop desk and hurried to get ready to meet Josh.

He was waiting for me on the concrete overlook. "We got lucky," he said. "There's a barge coming." Watching barges pass through the locks was a popular local pastime, especially for kids. Grammy and I had done it all the time. Three young boys pressed their faces to the chain-link fence, their mom sitting on a bench behind them. The oldest wanted to know how long the boat was, how wide, how many containers, and she told him it wasn't close enough yet to tell.

"How was the Miller House?" I asked.

"Good," he said. "They were all sold out of my book on the Mark family massacre. Are you familiar with that case?"

"Never heard of it."

"A farmer, Leslie Mark, his wife, Jorjean, and their two kids, who were only one and five years old, were shot to death up near Cedar Falls in 1975. Leslie's older brother, Jerry, was convicted on some pretty convincing circumstantial evidence, and he's in prison in Fort Madison. The story made a lot of sense, the way the prosecutors pieced it together. Jerry was angry that his little brother had inherited the family farm. He lied to police about some key things that incriminated him. But there were no witnesses, and the methods for analyzing the physical evidence could all be disputed today. A while back, DNA testing proved that cigarettes found at the scene weren't his. That wasn't enough to overturn his conviction, though. Without definitive proof, we're left with a story. If the story makes sense, we believe it."

Like my story. Singer. All the pieces had fit.

The boys along the fence pumped their arms, hoping for the captain to blow the horn, but the towboat was still too far back to see them. *Look up there,* the mom said, pointing to the underside of the elevated bridge that carried traffic across the river to Illinois. *See the birds? Do you know what kind they are?* She wasn't talking to me, but I couldn't help looking. A colony of mud nests clung to the bridge like giant barnacles. Cliff swallows.

"Anyway," Josh continued, "I've been going over the timeline from the day the twins disappeared, and I wanted to run a few things by you."

"Sure."

"You thought it was around four when Singer's car drove away. That matches up pretty closely with your mother's call to the police. But now we know he was there around one. That's a three-hour difference. For argument's sake, let's assume Singer didn't come back again at four, that you only saw his car at one, when he took the pictures. Do you remember what happened between the time you saw Singer and the actual time of the disappearance?"

"I don't know. I can't remember a gap. I remember it the way I remember it, them being gone after he drove away."

"Do you remember at what point your dad came home, what time it might have been?"

"I'm not sure. I was sick, and I hadn't slept much the night before. I think I might have fallen asleep for a while, or maybe that was later on, at the Sister House—part of the day is blurred together and always has been."

The barge, now penned in, began to lower, gradually, as the water drained out of the lock to match the level downstream. The boys rattled the fence, trying to get the attention of a crewman at the front of the towboat. *Three containers across*, the boys' mother said. *Five long. How many does that make?* The boys ignored her.

"I've been looking into your dad a bit, you know, just checking out every angle. I realize you might have been too young to pay attention to this sort of thing, but do you remember him having trouble with anyone? I know he was involved in some questionable business dealings. Maybe there were conflicts related to fraudulent investments or gambling? Someone he owed money to?"

"I wasn't really aware of him having any enemies back then. He was good at talking people into things, convincing them to invest in whatever worthless idea he was pitching, and eventually they'd realize he was the only one coming out ahead. I never saw anybody mad at him, though. It wasn't until later on, after we moved, that he started having problems. He was gambling too much. Couldn't rely on his family name anymore to get him out of trouble."

"That's what I thought," Josh said. "I haven't found evidence that anyone in town hated him enough to want to hurt his kids. The consensus seemed to be that the good tempered the bad. Even when he pissed people off, they still sort of liked him. One of the receptionists from your grandfather's practice called him a 'charming asshole,' and she was smiling when she said it."

I paused, watching the mother on the bench watch her boys. "What about Julia Ferris? I assume you know they were together that day?"

"They were each other's alibis."

"And more."

The captain finally blew the horn, a low mournful wail. The two older boys rattled the fence and cheered and the younger one started bawling.

"An affair isn't a crime. Or a motive, as far as I can tell," Josh said. "Not in this case."

"You've already thought this through."

"Yeah," he said, chewing his lip. "There has to be a reason, a believable one. Why would Julia want to take the girls? The affair itself isn't enough. There'd have to be something more going on, and I haven't found anything." A daddy longlegs crawled up onto the bench between us, and Josh picked the spider up by one leg and dropped it on the ground. "Oh, something else—you remember how I was looking into the Brubaker house across the street? Trying to find out who had access to the place while it was being worked on?"

"Yeah?"

"Turns out Dick Heaney was on the list. He was doing some plaster work."

"Heaney? Does it mean anything that he was on the list? Was he over there that day?"

"He had an alibi," Josh said. "He said he was visiting his father at the nursing home."

"Okay. So that rules him out, right?"

"Probably."

"Probably?"

"I can't verify it because his father's no longer living, and the nursing home doesn't keep visitors logs from that far back. But I'm almost certain someone would have checked the log back then. It was noted that he'd done some work for your grandparents way back when he was a teenager, but he hadn't had any contact with the family in years by the time of the twins' disappearance. Nothing to make him a person of interest."

"So I shouldn't be worried?"

"I don't think there's any reason to be."

The lower lock gates opened, releasing the barge, and it lumbered downstream, slowly gaining momentum. The three boys held on to the fence, pressing their faces against the chain link, and I let my eyes unfocus, waiting for that dizzy, disconcerting feeling that I was the one moving, while the barge and the river and the rest of the world stood still.

———

Even though Josh didn't think there was any reason to be suspicious of Heaney, I decided not to call him about the leaking faucet on the third floor. It wasn't bad enough that it would make a difference on the water bill.

Without work or classes or a schedule, the days were muddling together, distinguished mainly by the meals I ate: Hostess powdered doughnuts for breakfast; Slim Jims for lunch; Sonic—which was growing on me more than I cared to admit—for a late, deep-fried dinner. I ate out on the terrace, or on the sofa in the drawing room, or while hovering over the sink, uncomfortable sitting alone at the cherrywood table in the dining room, staring at eleven empty seats.

Most mornings I didn't bother changing out of my nightgown. I'd grown used to the stale air in the house, the amphibious stickiness of my skin. Hours would disappear while I wandered through the rooms, wiping dust out of grooves in the walnut molding and clearing away the delicate spiderwebs that seemed to regenerate in the window frames each night. I listened to the house, training my ears to identify all its secret sounds. Floorboards settling, chimneys sighing, branches scraping the glass of an upstairs window like a long-nailed witch trying to get in. Occasionally, somewhere in the walls, a faint metronome tick like water dripping. Sometimes I listened so hard to nothing that the silence itself grew into a deafening static.

I kept thinking Ben would call me, and then I finally realized that I had his number but he didn't have mine. I texted to see if he wanted to hang out or grab dinner. *I'm busy this week*, he replied, *but let's plan for next Saturday. It's your favorite of all the agricultural-themed festivals!* He followed up with a string of emoji: jack-o'-lanterns, ghosts, bats. It was a joke between us. Surrounded by farmland as we were, every festival revolved around a harvest: grapes, watermelon, sweet corn, apples. Any excuse to set up a beer tent and rickety carnival rides.

The pumpkin festival, though, was arguably the best. *It's a date*, I typed. Moments after clicking Send, I had texter's remorse. Should I have phrased it differently? I wasn't sure that it was a date in the technical sense—not that I didn't want it to be.

Before Ben mentioned the festival, I hadn't even noticed October's arrival. The Arrowood profile was due the first of November, and I decided that I would give myself a deadline, to finish it in one week. I had read in a self-help book that if you completed a simple task and crossed it off your to-do list, it would give you the confidence to attempt more difficult tasks. Maybe, if I could finish the profile, I'd be motivated to work on something much harder: making a life for myself here. I'd expected that everything would somehow fall into place now that I was home, but so far living at Arrowood wasn't much different from those last dreadful months in Colorado, spending too much time on my own.

I knew it shouldn't take long to write a brief history, but I was having the opposite problem that I'd had with my thesis. There was too much to say; I couldn't distill it down to one page. I wanted to explain on paper what it had once meant to be an Arrowood in Keokuk, before the name had become synonymous with tragedy and an empty house. I could almost hear Dr. Endicott chastising me for making it too personal.

By the time Heaney rang the doorbell the following Saturday, I had written dozens of pages about the Arrowoods and forced myself to complete several drafts of the one-page version, none of which captured what I was trying to say. I hadn't left the house or seen another human being all week, and maybe for that reason, I didn't mind seeing Heaney on the porch, bearing a wooden crate.

"Morning," he said, smiling too broadly, his pale lips stretching over his teeth. "I brought you something." He set the box down and knelt to pick through the netted bags piled inside. "Flower bulbs. Got some tulips, hyacinths, daffodils, crocuses, snowdrops." He stood up and brushed off his hands. "I was thinking how this place doesn't have much in the way of flowers anymore. I thought we could start getting it back to how it used to be."

We did have flowers before, ones that had been there my entire life and probably other lifetimes as well. Annabelle hydrangeas with softball-size clusters of white blooms bordering the porch; lilac bushes and pink peonies and bearded irises around the sides of the house; orange daylilies clustered at the iron fence out back, along with tall yellow cannas that had died after Nana and Granddad moved and no one bothered to dig them up for the winter. The lack of flowers wasn't something I would have expected Heaney to notice or remedy.

"If it's all right with you, I'll go ahead and start planting," he said. "It's a perfect day for it. And I thought maybe if you're not busy, you might like to help."

I hoped that Heaney was better with flowers than I was. I had never planted anything that survived. In grade school, when we grew marigolds in old milk cartons for science class, mine were the first to die.

Heaney fetched me a pair of gardening gloves from his truck and told me where I could find two small trowels stored in the laundry room. I dug holes in the empty flower bed by the porch and dropped the bulbs in, pointy side up like he showed me, without paying attention to what went where. I noticed that Heaney was planting his in orderly rows, grouping the hyacinths and crocuses in the front so they wouldn't be hidden among the taller flowers. He hummed under his breath while he worked, a tuneless, white-noise sound, like a refrigerator running.

When we had finished planting the bulbs, we shook out our gloves and Heaney pushed up his sleeves. As he did so, I noticed that he wore a wristwatch very similar to the one my father used to wear, a stainless steel Rolex that Nana and Granddad had given him for his high school graduation.

"My dad used to have a watch like that."

Heaney looked at me, his forehead wrinkling up. After a moment, he unclasped the watch and handed it to me. Like my dad's watch, it was a Rolex.

"Turn it over," he said.

I flipped the watch over in my palm and saw my father's initials engraved on the back: ELA. Edward Louis Arrowood. "How did you get this?"

"Your dad showed up here a while back. He wanted to come in the house, and I'm sorry to say, but I wouldn't let him. He knew he wasn't supposed to be here, and I didn't know what might happen if he got inside. He made some threats, but once he saw it wouldn't do any good, he broke down. Said he needed money and begged me to buy his watch. I felt bad for him."

I brushed my thumb over my father's initials. I wondered what it had been like for him, to show up and not be allowed inside—if he had blamed Heaney, or Granddad, or if he blamed himself for leaving Arrowood in the first place.

"Keep it," Heaney said. "It should be yours."

"I can't," I said, handing it back. "You paid for it. I'm sure it was expensive."

Heaney shook his head, trying to refuse it, but I pressed it into his hand. "I didn't give him anywhere near what it's worth," Heaney said. "Probably about the same as he'd get at the pawnshop."

"Did he say what he needed the money for?"

"No." Heaney sat down on the porch steps and I joined him. "I didn't ask."

"You knew him, though, right? From high school? Wasn't it hard not to let him into his own house?"

Heaney groaned, looking up into the branches of the mimosa tree. The frilly pink blossoms that adorned it in the summer were gone, re-placed by clusters of ugly brown seedpods.

"Was it hard? It was and it wasn't."

"What do you mean?"

He laughed ruefully. "I don't know that you need to hear about it. I don't want to speak poorly of your father."

"I know how he was," I said. "It's not like you're going to ruin him for me."

"How about this. I'll tell you, if you let me give you the watch. Please."

He held it out, and I let him slip it onto my wrist. It slid halfway up my forearm, the metal warm from being cupped in his hand. I knew I would take it off the moment he left.

"I used to work for your grandparents a long time ago," he said. "Starting back when I was in high school. Did you know that?"

I shook my head, though Josh had mentioned it.

"I did all sorts of errands, odd jobs. Your granddad was a good man. He and my dad were in Rotary Club together, old friends. My dad was severely disabled in an accident while he was working down at the lock and dam, and Dr. Arrowood took me under his wing after that, giving me a job, encouraging me to stay in school when I wanted to drop out. He told me I was a hard worker, that I had potential. He even helped me get started in community college, though I never did finish. I spent quite a bit of time over here, and your granddad thought it might be good if Eddie and I got to be friends. I made bad grades but liked to work, and Eddie was lazy but smart. Maybe together, we might even each other out. It didn't happen, though.

"I always got the feeling that your dad didn't like me hanging around, didn't like your granddad paying so much attention to me. Then one day Dr. Arrowood told me I wouldn't be working for him anymore. Eddie's car had been crashed the night before, and he'd told his dad I was the one who did it. I had copies of all their keys, because I would take the cars in to the shop whenever they needed oil changes or new tires or what have you. I could tell your granddad didn't really believe I had done it, but he felt he had to side with his son. That was that. To his credit, he never told anybody about it, never asked me to pay to fix the car. I think he felt bad about the whole thing.

"Then ten years back, when the first caretaker retired, I was working maintenance at the nursing home where my dad lived, and I got a call about the job here at Arrowood. That was right before your grand-dad passed. I like to think he had something to do with me getting the job, making things right."

"I'm glad it worked out," I said. "Sorry about what happened with my dad, though."

He shrugged. "He never appreciated what he had, how much his parents did for him. He didn't appreciate your mother, either, in my opinion. She deserved better than him."

"How well did you know my mom?"

"She never talked about me?"

I bit down on the inside of my cheek, not wanting to answer. Heaney stared at his shoes, the skin on his broad forehead turning pink in the awkward silence.

"We dated awhile, starting back when she was in high school."

I did my best to maintain a neutral expression. I couldn't picture my mother with Heaney. When I had mentioned his name on the phone, she'd acted like she didn't even remember him. I wondered if he was telling the truth.

"We stayed friends. I tried to warn her about Eddie when she started seeing him. He had a reputation for messing around, and everybody knew it. Your mother made up her own mind, though, and she usually got what she wanted. She'd get that stubborn look on her face, same one you had the day you moved in here, when you wouldn't let me carry your things."

So that was the resemblance he'd seen between me and my mother. Nothing more than a stubborn expression.

Heaney shook his head and whistled through his teeth. "Enough about that, huh? I have an idea." He got up from the steps and tucked his gloves under his arm. "I'm gonna play hooky the rest of this beautiful day and take my boat out to Little Belle Isle. Why don't you come fishing with me?"

"I can't today," I said, though that wasn't completely true. Ben wouldn't be picking me up for the pumpkin festival until dark.

"Come on, you sure? It'd do you good to get out of the house. You ever been out on the islands?"

I shook my head. I'd seen Little Belle and Grand Belle when we'd sped past them in the *Ruby Slipper*. They had always looked odd to me, forested outposts in the middle of the river, little cabins up on stilts to avoid the spring floods.

"I've got a place out there, perfect for a bonfire and fish fry this time of year."

I tried to picture the two of us sitting around the fire together and couldn't quite make the pieces fit. Were we supposed to be friends? Employer and employee? Was he trying to forge a relationship of some sort between us, or did he simply pity me, that I was alone? And why did he say that it would do me good to get out of the house? Did he know, somehow, that I hadn't left in days?

"Maybe next time," I said, not meaning it.

"All right." Heaney squinted down at me. "Next time, then. I'll hold you to it."

As soon as I closed the door behind me, I realized I'd left the trowels out on the porch. I popped back out to retrieve them, just in time to see Mrs. Ferris hurrying away from the carriage house. She cast a fleeting glance in my direction and then turned back toward her house as though she hadn't seen me.

CHAPTER 12

Ben arrived to pick me up as darkness fell. He had promised to help out a friend with the jack-o'-lantern auction fundraiser, though that wasn't until later in the night. He was going to serve as the auctioneer. I wondered if the friend was Courtney, the girl Lauren had mentioned, whom Ben still hadn't told me about. We parked on Main and walked down to the riverfront. The street was lined with hundreds of flickering jack-o'-lanterns, and the moon loomed over the water, the color of bone.

I hadn't been to the pumpkin festival since I was ten, when Grammy drove to Illinois to bring me back for a long weekend visit. I had worn the Halloween costume she'd made for me that year: Dorothy from *The Wizard of Oz*, with long underwear underneath to keep me warm. My ruby slippers were old rain boots she had painted red and dusted with glitter. Grammy let me march in the costume parade with Ben and Lauren, though she'd followed right behind, not comfortable letting me out of her sight. I had wanted to ride the Himalayan, a mini-coaster with sparkly snowcapped mountains painted on the side, but I wasn't tall enough. Instead, I was stuck riding the merry-go-round and the kiddie train with Lauren and the other little kids, though I secretly enjoyed it. Later, Grammy allowed me to go into the House of Mirrors with Ben, after making him promise he would not let go of my hand.

"I've missed this," I said to Ben as we walked down the crowded midway. He smiled and linked his arm with mine as we approached the ticket booth. Ghosts roamed through the crowd on stilts, their white sheets rippling in the breeze. Halloween was always my favorite holiday, but I hadn't done anything to celebrate it in years. I couldn't remember the last time I had put on a costume or carved a jack-o'-lantern.

"Do you think any kids will come to my door to trick-or-treat?" I asked. "Or do they avoid Arrowood like we used to skip the Stone House down the street?" In the 1920s, the owner of the Stone House had shot his wife as she fled down the staircase, and then hanged himself in the attic. His wife bled to death at the foot of the stairs, and despite repeated attempts to remove the bloodstain, including sanding down and refinishing the floorboards and then finally replacing them altogether, the stain always reappeared. Oddly, as kids, that was not what scared us the most. To reach the door of the Stone House, you had to walk beneath an arch of pointed stones that resembled a mouth full of fangs. I'd never been brave enough.

"Kids aren't scared of the Stone House anymore," Ben said, handing a twenty to the lady in the ticket booth in exchange for a strip of tickets. "The new owners give out full-size candy bars. I bet the same trick would work for you."

The air smelled of fry grease and cotton candy and funnel cakes dusted with powdered sugar. I glanced around at the rides, hoping to see the Himalayan, knowing, of course, that there were probably no more Himalayans in existence, and that even if I found one, it wouldn't be as glittery and enticing as my memory claimed. We passed a carousel, colorful blinking lights distracting our eyes from rickety gears and cheap fiberglass animals, and I was glad not to see the run-down carnival in daylight. Darkness was kind, cloaking disappointing truths in mystery.

"We are totally riding the Scrambler," Ben said, pulling me into the line.

"Don't you hear that noise it's making? It's probably going to fall apart any minute now."

"Come on," he said. "You need to loosen up. Be a little bit more adventurous."

"Fine," I said. "But you'll be sorry if I puke on you."

I screamed for the entire two minutes the Scrambler spun us around. Centrifugal force pressed us together, and I buried my face against Ben's leather jacket until it was over.

"Did we really used to enjoy that?" I asked as he helped me down.

"Yeah, we did. We used to get wristbands at the county fair so we could ride all day, remember?"

"I think I'm too old to have my brain sloshing around in my skull like that anymore."

"Well, we've got a bunch of tickets to use up, so let's rest your brain for a minute and then get back to it."

"Can we sit for a sec?"

"Sure."

We walked over to a bench facing the river and sat down, the cool night air soothing my nausea. Behind us, there was carnival music and laughter and the screech of machinery, but the river, as always, was silent, keeping all its secrets to itself.

I could feel Ben watching me, and I turned to look up at him. "Better?" he asked.

I wanted to tell him that I was not better, though it helped, having him here. He had loved me, once, and I remembered how he had looked at me back then, the heat that had kindled in my chest like a fever. A long-dormant tide swept over me, and I imagined my old self flickering to life in the shell of my body, warming my bones, flushing my skin from the inside out. Neither of us looked away.

"I think we have time for one more thing before the auction," he said. I watched his lips as he spoke, and I held still, waiting, willing him to angle closer, press his mouth against mine. He didn't. "You're not too old and feeble for the House of Mirrors, are you?"

"I think I can handle it."

We made our way back into the crowd. The House of Mirrors looked the same as I remembered it, though it wasn't likely the same one after all these years. Come morning, the whole thing would be folded up neatly onto a flatbed truck, but in the dark, with Halloween approaching, it evoked a tinge of nostalgic childhood fear. Ben handed over our tickets, and we slipped through the black canvas curtains.

Inside, the passageways were lit with dull, failing bulbs, the floor gummed with spilled soda and who knew what else. Music was piped in, a tense, tinny melody like the kind that played as you twisted the handle of a jack-in-the-box. Ben moved on ahead of me, barely pausing to look in the mirrors, but I took my time. I watched my reflection morph into a dozen slippery versions of myself, retreating and reshaping as I navigated the maze, until I found a mirror that made me disappear. I stepped back into the shadows, and then forward, reappearing, disappearing. Each time I drew close to the mirror, my reflection narrowed until it swallowed itself. Ben's voice echoed from the exit, calling my name, and I hurried to catch up to him.

A crowd had gathered around the auction site, and I squeezed in for a look while Ben went to find his friend. The historical society had done a series of jack-o'-lanterns featuring prominent Keokuk homes, all carved by local artists. I recognized the Grand Anne, a Queen Anne–style Victorian that was now a bed-and-breakfast, and the Katie John House, former home of author Mary Calhoun. Then the man in front of me moved aside, and I saw Arrowood, its arched windows lit from within. The detail was stunning. Whoever carved it must have traced a real picture of the house as a guide. The wind blew and the candle inside the jack-o'-lantern guttered and flared, shadows moving inside the little house like ghosts.

I backed away into the milling crowd. Ben stood off to the side, listening attentively as a young woman with long wheat-colored hair spoke to him, waving her hands around for emphasis and then laughing as she squeezed his arm. Envy soured my stomach as I watched them together. This had to be Courtney. I had hoped Ben's silence meant the relationship wasn't serious, that it wasn't worth telling me about.

I headed for the food stands in the parking lot by the riverboat museum and looked around until I found one selling caramel apples. They'd been my favorite Halloween treat when I was a kid, though I was pretty sure they hadn't cost five dollars back then. I admired the apple's smooth, glossy coating. This was how caramel apples were meant to be served: impaled whole on a Popsicle stick, not cut into finger-friendly slices and served with caramel on the side. I tried to maneuver my mouth around to take a bite, and ended up with caramel on my nose and in my hair. As it should be, I told myself. No wonder my mother had hated it when I ate these things.

I was uncomfortably sticky after finishing the apple, and I wiped my hands and face with wet paper towels at one of the portable sinks. I spotted a man who looked like Heaney walking in my direction, the same slouching gait and receding hair, and I hurried off before he could catch up to me. I didn't feel like talking to him after our strange conversation earlier in the day. On my way back to the auction, I came across a tent labeled MADAME YVONNE, FORTUNE-TELLER. The tent itself was typical dirty canvas, but the entrance was draped with tie-dyed scarves. The flap was open, revealing an empty chair and the reek of incense.

"Are you coming in or not? I can see your feet," a voice called from inside. The accent was heavy and obviously fake, a feminine version of Count Chocula.

I ducked under the scarves and into the tent. The fortune-teller looked younger than I expected—younger than me—which didn't give me much confidence in her abilities, though to be fair, I didn't have much confidence in any fortune-teller's abilities. Madame Yvonne was the sort of girl I'd always envied, one with an abundance of hair. It sprawled down her back and over her shoulders, dark and glossy, and formed a widow's peak low on her forehead. Gold chandelier earrings glittered down her neck. Everything about her was striking and overdone: thick eyebrows, black eyeliner, purple lipstick, henna tattoos covering every inch of her hands.

"You want me to read your fortune?" she asked. Her eyelids drooped low like she was sleepy or high. Maybe both. She shuffled tarot cards on the wobbly table in front of her. They made shushing sounds as her hands worked them back and forth.

"Sure," I said. "Why not?"

She nodded toward a metal cashbox with a slit in the top. It was chained to the table. "Ten dollars."

I slid the money into the box, and she abruptly stopped shuffling.

"I'm Madame Yvonne. What's your name?" she asked.

"Does it matter?" I'd visited psychics before, and had seen plenty of fake ones on TV. I knew better than to give away any personal information.

Madame Yvonne shrugged and smacked her gum. "Not to me."

She handed me the deck of cards. They were new enough to be slippery, the edges still sharp. The red and brown design on the back reminded me of an Oriental rug rolled up in the storage room at Arrowood. "You shuffle, then cut the deck."

I had never mastered the art of shuffling, and Madame Yvonne sighed impatiently as I spread the cards out, mixed them up, and then tried to fit them all back together. When I finished, I handed the deck back to her.

"No," she said, refusing to take them. "You do it. Think about whatever it is that you came to see me for. Deal three cards, lay them out in a row."

I did as she said, thinking about the twins. I heard voices behind me. "Form a line!" Madame Yvonne barked to whoever was outside. "Wait your turn."

She studied the cards, and then looked into my eyes. "These cards are your past, present, and future. The Six of Cups card, here, represents your feelings and emotions." An illustration of two yellow-haired children in a garden. They were smiling. My stomach twisted like it was being wrung out. "Happy memories. Clinging to the past. The Cups suit is associated with the element of water." *I was born at the confluence of two rivers*, I thought. *My heart orients itself to the Mississippi. Everything in my house is inexplicably damp.*

Madame Yvonne watched me for some response, her dark eyelashes flapping like an ostrich's, and I sat perfectly still.

"The second card," she continued, tapping it with a black-painted fingernail, "is the Wheel of Fortune. It can help or hinder you on your journey." The card depicted a golden eight-spoked wheel surrounded by a sphinx, a snake, an Anubis, and four winged creatures of the zodiac. The zodiac figures appeared to be reading books. "The sphinx represents life's mysteries," she said. "The Wheel of Fortune is unpredictable. It's a turning point. Everything rests on the way the Wheel turns, and your reaction to it. You can't choose your fate, but you can choose how to respond." She nodded emphatically, as though this was both very important and very true, her chandelier earrings swishing back and forth.

"Your third card, here, the Ace of Wands, that represents vision and intuition." She pushed it closer for me to get a good look at the cartoonish hand reaching out of a cloud, holding a stick. Madame Yvonne watched me through her lashes, waiting to see if I would ask for more information. I wasn't sure she knew what she was doing. Maybe she had learned to read tarot from Wikipedia, same as me.

"How do I know what it means?"

She frowned. "The Ace of Wands represents potential. Opportunity. It is not about intellect but inner vision. What it says to me is, you'll have to rely on your gut to see clearly."

In college, I had saved up to visit two reputable psychics, one of whom was also a medium. The first psychic declared unequivocally that the twins were no longer living, and hadn't been for some time. The medium could not make contact with them, and thus concluded that they must still be alive. I didn't cry either time. I listened to what they had to say and left with an empty wallet.

The incense was beginning to irritate my throat, and I coughed to clear it. Madame Yvonne swept her hand over the cards with a flourish, like a magician revealing a trick. "I hope you found the answer to your question."

"No," I said, my eyes lingering on the Six of Cups, the smiling blond children. "But I wasn't really expecting to."

Madame Yvonne raised an eyebrow. "You want more, it's gonna cost more."

"Thanks," I said, starting to get up.

She reached out and jabbed the Six of Cups with her fingernail. "This card," she said. "This one spoke to you."

I hesitated, then fished another ten out of my pocket. "This is all I have."

She held out her hand to take it, and instead of putting it in the cashbox, she stuffed it down into her bra. She looked a bit more alert now, pleased that her hustle had worked.

"You're clearly a water sign," she said, leaning forward and sliding the Cups card toward me. "The element of water is your guiding force. It's no mistake you are here, between two rivers. You were drawn to this place. You're looking for something that wants to be found. Let the water speak to you, guide you."

Something that wants to be found. I felt a chill down the back of my neck. I thought of my sisters' small bodies sinking into the river. If they were there, I'd never find them.

"Your Ace of Wands card tells me that you need to follow your intuition. You need to trust yourself. Listen to your gut. When you don't know what to believe, remember that the truth comes from within." She began to gather up the cards, expertly slicing them together and tapping them into a neat stack. "I don't know whether you'll get the answers you want," she said, flipping her long black hair over her shoulder. "But you're going to find what you're looking for."

The auction was under way when I returned. Ben was hamming it up, trying and failing to yodel like a real auctioneer. The wheat-haired girl was standing off to the side, laughing along with the crowd of bidders, and as she turned her head in my direction, the moonlight illuminated her face and I realized that I knew her. Lauren had said Ben's girlfriend's name was Courtney, and the girl watching Ben was a grown-up version of Courtney Wells. I remembered her from the pool, part of a clique of girls who were shaving their legs and wearing mascara the summer after sixth grade, while Ben and I were still waiting for our bodies to change. I remembered smiling at her in the pool locker room and Courtney averting her eyes, rendering me invisible.

"Hi, Arden." Josh was standing in front of me. He wore his standard windbreaker and cap, and he cradled a pumpkin in his arms. Even with the candle extinguished, I could tell it was the Arrowood jack-o'-lantern.

"This is for you. Got into a bit of a bidding war, and then it turned out the other guy was Dick Heaney, so I guess you would have gotten it either way." He smiled sheepishly. "He seemed kind of pissed off that I beat him. Anyway, I was going to leave it on your porch, but now here you are."

"Oh," I said. "Thanks. I might be walking home, though, and I'm not sure I want to carry it all the way back." I wasn't sure I wanted it at all.

"No problem," he said. "I can drive you. I was ready to go anyway. I mean, if you are. Or we could hang out here for a while if you want."

I looked over at Ben. Courtney was watching him attentively, an easy smile on her face, her long hair fluttering in the breeze. *We're so happy,* I imagined her telling her friends. There were still a dozen jack-o'-lanterns on the table.

"I'm ready," I said.

I texted Ben to let him know not to wait around for me. When Josh and I got back to Arrowood, he carried the pumpkin up the front steps and set it on the porch.

"Thanks," I said. "For the jack-o'-lantern. And the ride."

"You're welcome." He stuck his hands into his jacket pockets. I got out my house key and reached for the door.

"Hey," he said. "I was hoping we could talk for a minute. Could I maybe . . . come in?"

I hadn't had any guests at the house since I'd moved back, aside from Heaney. Josh would be the first.

"Sure." I unlocked the door and we walked in. I paused in the entry, not certain that I wanted to let him in any farther than that, but it felt awkward standing there, so I led him to the drawing room at the back of the house and turned on the lights. He sat in one of Granddad's old leather armchairs, and I sat on the sofa.

"This is quite a house," Josh said, glancing around the room. I hoped he hadn't wanted to come inside just to get a peek at the interior for the sake of his book.

"What did you want to talk about?" I asked.

He looked at me and swallowed hard, cracking the knuckles of one hand and then the other. I was used to his straightforward manner, not holding anything back to spare my feelings, and now I worried that he seemed to be hesitating, gauging my ability to take in what he was about to say. "I tracked down one of Singer's old neighbors, at a nursing home over the river in Hamilton. Jean Shirley. She lived across the street from him. I asked her if she ever knew Singer to have a dog, and she said yes, he had an enormous Rottweiler back then. She remembered because the dog would run loose, and it would come across the street and scare *her* dog." He paused and adjusted his glasses. "I asked if she'd ever seen him with a little white dog, and she said no, but that her dog, the one Singer's dog was always harassing, was a white-haired Maltese."

My teeth ground together while I waited for him to continue. I already knew what he was going to say.

"Her dog went missing just before Labor Day. She couldn't remember the year, but she said it was right around the time of the Arrowood kidnapping."

My chest felt tight, like a balloon was expanding inside it, making it hard to breathe. "You think he stole her dog, and he had it with him that day."

"Yes," he said. "I do. It all fits. It makes sense."

I didn't want it to be true, but he was right. It didn't seem like a coincidence. I ran the movie in my head, the door slamming, the flash of white, the car driving off.

"There's something else." Josh shifted in his chair. "I have some interest from a small press, for my book. They were thinking it could draw a bit of media attention if they schedule the release to coincide with the twentieth anniversary of the kidnapping, and that would give me plenty of time to finish it. It's all riding on the theory that Singer wasn't involved like everyone thought he was." I sat there, not saying anything, waiting for him to continue. "That really opens the whole case back up again, makes it fresh," he said. "In a way, it's more of a mystery than ever, but with the chance to look at it from new angles that might lead to it being solved. That's how I pitched it, anyway."

He stopped and looked up at me, apologetic and expectant. His face was flushed, and it was obvious that he was excited by the new developments, and probably hoped that I would be excited, too. "I wanted to make sure you're okay with it," he said. "With the book, with telling people you were wrong about what you saw, that you no longer believe Singer took them."

I didn't care if he told the world I was wrong about Singer. What was devastating was the realization that I had been the one to throw the investigation off track from the beginning. Now that it seemed Singer hadn't taken the twins, I had to accept that there was something missing from my recollection of that day. In my head was a movie that had played over and over for nearly twenty years. What other parts had I gotten wrong? The truth had been revised by memory, my imperfect recollection the only version that remained.

"It's your book," I said. "Do what you want."

"I really think something good will come out of this, even if I'm not the one to solve it," he said. "Maybe somebody knows something, and they'll come forward. I want the answers as much as you do."

"I doubt that."

"I'm sorry, Arden, I didn't mean—you know what I mean. I want to know what happened. Not for the same reasons, exactly, but I want it for you, too."

"I know," I said. "Do whatever you need to do. It's fine with me."

I walked him to the door and told him good night. He reached out, his hand on my arm, his fingers curving around to the underside, where my scars hid beneath my sweater. I froze. We stood there, tenuously connected, the barely perceptible weight of his touch somehow swaying me off balance.

"I'll keep you in the loop," he said. "Talk to you soon."

I pushed the door shut behind him and locked it. Josh was being nice, asking for my permission, which he didn't need, before moving forward with the book and exposing my mistake. He was doing everything he could to solve the mystery of my sisters' disappearance, regardless of whether he was doing it for himself or for me.

I went to the kitchen and dug through the junk drawer until I found a book of matches I'd brought from Colorado. They were from a hotel bar called Paradise, where Dr. Endicott and I had sipped cloying, brightly colored cocktails while attending a conference in Denver. The drinks had made my stomach hurt, and the pain got worse as I rode the elevator up to my room and waited ten minutes, as instructed, before sneaking down the hall and tapping lightly on my adviser's door.

I held the matchbook in my teeth as I unlocked the front door and removed the singed lid from the jack-o'-lantern to light the candle. The wind blew out the first few matches as soon as I lit them. I huddled over the pumpkin with my back to the wind, cupping my hand around each newly struck flame, and still the candle would not light. On the last match, the wick flared and then went out. I threw the empty matchbook across the porch, tears of frustration blurring my eyes, and then the candle flickered on, all by itself. The flame held, and shadow ghosts wavered in the windows of the miniature Arrowood.

CHAPTER 13

"Please, please, please," Lauren whined. "You have to come. Mom said she invited you."

"She didn't invite me: She gave me a flyer when I was at your house. I don't even know if she gave it to me on purpose." I'd been surprised to get a call from Lauren, to hear that she was back in town so soon.

"That counts," she said. "I'm only going because I don't have a choice—they're honoring my mother, and God only knows what she would do to me if I didn't show up and act like we're the world's happiest family. But you love that museum, I know you do, so why don't you just come along and keep me company? Ben says he hardly sees you, that you barely leave the house."

"How would anyone but me know how often I leave my house?"

She cleared her throat theatrically. "Mom spies on you, I think. It's really hard to pretend you're not home when everyone can see your car parked outside. Now go change into something nice. Or don't. Mom's the only one who'll care."

The Miller House was all lit up when we arrived. The museum was the former home of U.S. Supreme Court Justice Samuel Miller, now owned and operated by the Lee County historical society. All three stories of the painted brick Italianate, built in 1859, contained bits of Keokuk history, including an alcove filled with antique dental equipment to which Ferris Family Dental had contributed.

Dr. and Mrs. Ferris and Ben were standing just beyond the rotunda entrance, near the portraits of Chief Keokuk and Justice Miller. I shook their hands, and Ben, who looked surprised to see me there, gave me a quick hug. Mrs. Ferris aimed a tight-lipped smile at Lauren, motioning for her to join the family receiving line next to her brother. "Don't leave without me," Lauren hissed, before taking her place in line.

I wandered around the upper floors—the children's playroom, the office, the walk-in closet, which was unusual for its time, with a pulley system for hanging items high on the wall. The closet shelves were filled with hatboxes from the days when five different millinery shops had operated on Main Street. I found two of Josh's books in the first-floor gift shop: *The Mark Family Massacre* and *Unsolved Iowa: A Collection of Cold Crimes.* One day his Arrowood book would sit here along with the others. I wondered what the title would be, which picture might be used for the cover.

I saved the basement for last, my favorite part. This was where the kitchen had been, and the laundry, and while it was the working portion of the house, it was every bit as spacious and beautifully detailed as the living quarters. The world's largest denim overalls were on display in the laundry room, next to a framed article from the *Daily Gate City* about how the workers from the local Irwin-Phillips Company had sewn them for the "World's Fattest Man." Along with the article was a photo of four of the factory women standing inside the overalls, two in each leg.

I hesitated before entering the small corner room, which housed a collection of portraits of well-known Keokuk homes. A cluster of people were blocking my view of the Arrowood exhibit, so I squeezed into the corner to look at the photos of the Hubinger Mansion, the finest, most expensive home ever built on Grand Avenue. Hubinger had made his fortune in elastic starch, and had spared no expense on the house—a three-story castle with twenty rooms—and grounds, which boasted a man-made lake with an island. The walls of his home had been covered not with wallpaper but with velvet and silk. All that remained of the house were pictures; it was hard to imagine a time of such opulence in Keokuk that a lavish mansion was torn down for another mansion to be erected in its place.

The crowd around the Arrowood display broke up, and as they moved past me to exit the room, I came face-to-face with Courtney.

"Hi!" she said brightly. "You're Arden, right?"

"Yes."

"I'm Courtney. Wells. Ben's girlfriend?"

"I know," I said. "I remember you. From the pool, back in junior high."

"Of course," she said. "Ben can't shut up about how happy he is to have you back! You know they renovated the pool? It looks completely different now. Way better than it was back then."

"That's great," I said, thinking I would have liked it better if it hadn't changed. "I'll have to go see it."

"Yeah, you should." She smiled awkwardly, nodding, her long hair swishing around her shoulders. "Well. I'd better get back upstairs. I just wanted to say hi." She dug around in her little clutch purse. "And here's my card. If you ever need a real estate agent, I work at Sutlive Real Estate. That's how Ben and I—I helped him buy his house. I guess you're probably not looking for a place at the moment, but if you ever want to sell Arrowood."

Courtney left, and I stood alone in front of the framed portraits and articles, staring at a plaque listing all the Arrowoods who had fought and died in wars, including my two uncles. I let Courtney's card slip out of my hand and fall to the floor, and then, because I knew I was being childish, I quickly knelt and picked it back up.

"Was it Franklin or Theodore?" Lauren sidled up to me. "I get them confused with the Chipmunks."

"What?"

"Which Roosevelt stayed at my house? Someone just asked. Mom will die if I said the wrong one."

"Theodore," I said, guiding her across the room to the picture of him standing in front of the Ferrises' newly built carriage house. "And there is no Franklin in the Chipmunks. Maybe that will help you re-member next time."

Lauren reached out and pressed her fingertip to Roosevelt's face. "Doubt it."

"So what's your mom doing with the carriage house these days?" I asked. At one point she had talked about using it as an office for an interior design business she never started. And now, of course, I knew it had been used to rendezvous with my father.

"I don't think she's using it for anything," Lauren said. "I couldn't tell you the last time she was out there."

"Last week," I said, suddenly remembering. "I saw her coming out. She looked right at me and then turned and rushed back to the house without saying anything."

Lauren scrunched up her face. "That's kind of weird."

"I went to talk to her the other day," I said, lowering my voice.

"There's this guy, he's writing a book about the kidnapping, and he's convinced it wasn't Singer—"

"Ben told me about it," Lauren interrupted. "The guy from that website, right?"

"Yes. He had me thinking, what did I miss, who else might have seen something? I asked your mom what she saw that day, and she admitted that she was out in the carriage house with my dad. It just made me wonder if she knew something, if she had anything to do with it."

"Jesus." Lauren looked around to make sure no one was listening. "I know she can be a bitch, but do you really think she could do something like that?"

"No. I don't know. Josh doesn't think so."

Lauren fidgeted with her earrings, twisting the studs one by one like she was tuning an instrument. "Do you think we should go check it out? Just to be sure there's nothing up there that she's trying to hide? We should go right now, while she's busy."

I shrugged. "If she had anything incriminating, she would have gotten rid of it by now."

"It might make you feel better, just to look and see that there's nothing there. And I, for one, am dying to see what kind of hideous wallpaper she's got up there."

It was almost enough to make me laugh. "I thought you were supposed to be here all night."

She sighed. "I've done my duty. I smiled and shook hands and listened to everyone drone on and on about how wonderful my mother is. I think she'd probably be thrilled if I leave before I screw something up."

The lower level of the carriage house was unfinished and unlocked, and the key to the upstairs room was hanging just inside the door, by the stairs. Either Mrs. Ferris wasn't worried about what anyone would find up there, or she didn't think anyone would bother to look. Lauren went in first and I crowded behind her in the dark, both of us fumbling to find the switch. She flipped on the light and let out a disappointed sigh. There was, indeed, hideous wallpaper, a migraine-inducing ikat print. Clothing racks lined the walls, shopping bags on the floor. The room looked like an overflow closet, a place to hide things she didn't want Dr. Ferris to know she'd bought.

Lauren kicked a giant Nordstrom bag and it tipped over, shoes spilling out. "These are old," she said, shoving the bag aside and surveying the room. "Maybe this is all the stuff she's saving to take to Goodwill. I wonder if she'd notice if I took a few things and sold them on eBay."

I wasn't looking at the shoes or the clothes. I was eyeing the red metal step stool, which looked exactly like the one my grammy had in her kitchen at the Sister House. I waded around bags of Mrs. Ferris's discarded clothing to get to it. Sitting on top of the stool was Grammy's sewing basket, and inside the basket, her tomato pincushion, her seam ripper, her good fabric shears, and a little cellophane package of duck-shaped buttons, still bright yellow, four remaining from a package of ten.

"What's all that?" Lauren asked, a pair of patent leather pumps tucked under her arm.

"It's from the Sister House." There was more, piled in cardboard boxes: Aunt Alice's jar of marbles, the squirrel nutcracker, the buffalo-check blanket that had lain across the back of the sofa.

"Why is it up here with all this stuff she's getting rid of?"

"I don't know," I said, my chest tightening. "I guess we'll have to ask your mother."

Mrs. Ferris remained calm, though I could tell from her murderous expression that she wanted to choke me. Lauren stood behind me, and

Ben and Courtney hovered in the corner of the floral chintz sitting room, doing their best to blend into the puddled curtains. Ben looked troubled, and Courtney's mouth gaped open, as though she could not believe anyone would talk to Mrs. Ferris like I was talking to her now. Dr. Ferris had made a hasty exit under the premise of getting everyone something to drink, and I doubted he would return from the kitchen. He avoided conflict whenever possible.

"I wasn't keeping your grandmother's things from you," Mrs. Ferris said, an edge to her voice. She wasn't pleased that I was ruining the end of what had been, for her, a lovely evening. "I was saving them to give to you. The other day, when you saw me, I'd been up there getting everything together. I just hadn't figured out yet how to do it without upsetting you."

"What does that mean?"

She rubbed her temples. "What did your mother tell you she did with everything from the Sister House after your grandmother died?"

Sweat collected on my scalp, inched down the back of my neck. "She said she sold the house at auction. We needed the money. Grammy's things went into storage. We were renting a tiny duplex and didn't have room for it all."

"The house did sell at auction," Mrs. Ferris said carefully. "The contents were sold at an estate sale, every one of your grandmother's earthly possessions laid out with a price tag on it. I bought what I could to save for you, things I thought might mean something. There are some old family pictures in frames. A few photo albums. A Bible. How was I supposed to tell you that your mother did that? I couldn't understand it myself."

Her face puckered up with pity. Mrs. Ferris couldn't understand, but I did. My mother hadn't wanted to drag any more history around with her. She had wanted to unharness herself from every part of her past, to be new and clean, to live a life completely devoid of the dust and grief and memories she had left behind. In some ways, I couldn't blame her.

Lauren walked out with me, and Ben followed. "Can I talk to you a minute?" Ben asked. I nodded, and Lauren turned back toward the house, leaving us alone.

"I'm so sorry," he said. "I didn't know anything about that."

"I know."

"Are you all right?"

"Why didn't you tell me about Courtney?" I said. "She introduced herself tonight, as your girlfriend. You could have said something."

"I know. I'm sorry."

"She used to walk right past us like we didn't exist."

"Arden, that was a long time ago. We've all changed. We're not the same people we were in junior high."

I shook my head. Ben was the one who had changed, boxing up his former self and putting on a grown-up costume to play the role his parents had written for him. I wasn't so sure about myself. I didn't feel like I had changed in a long, long time.

"You were my best friend," Ben said, his voice softening. "The first girl I loved, the first girl to break my heart. When I saw you in the office, all those feelings came rushing back. But we're not fifteen anymore. We were just kids then—everything feels so big and important when it's happening for the first time. You fall in love and it's all-consuming, like you've been set on fire."

I remembered. I could still close my eyes and feel the heat of his skin. When I lay beneath Dr. Endicott in the sweating dark, I had wanted him to be Ben.

"I didn't hear from you for ten years, Arden. We're in different places now. We can't pick back up where we left off."

He sounded uncertain as he said it, though maybe I imagined it. His face was flushed, I could see it even in the moonlight. I wanted to reach out to him. I wanted to say all the things I was ten years too late to say.

"Ben?" Courtney approached in the darkness. "Sorry to interrupt, but I need to be getting home. It was good to meet you, Arden."

They turned to go and Ben glanced back at me, an unspoken apology on his face. I slipped away across the lawn. It was all I could do not to break into a run.

CHAPTER 14

Mrs. Ferris brought Grammy's things over the next evening, harboring no ill will after our confrontation, or so she claimed.

"Here are the photo albums," she said, stacking them on top of Grammy's step stool. She clicked her nails over the spines and slid a marbled blue album out of the pile, handing it to me. Its cheap cardboard cover was peeling apart. "This one's your mother's. I can't believe she didn't even want her own pictures."

I flipped through the pages. High school pictures. Mom and her friends in their cheerleading uniforms, their feathered hair stiff with hairspray; her senior portrait, wearing a boatneck sweater and pearls, her fist tucked demurely under her chin. I stopped at a prom photo, where she stood beneath cardboard palm trees in a poufy taffeta dress, a huge cluster of pink carnations and baby's breath strapped to her wrist. A boy in a white tux held her by the waist. He had coppery hair and an athletic build, and he was smiling so hard his lips had lost their color. He looked familiar, though his hairline was lower, his face more balanced without so much of his skull exposed. Heaney had been telling the truth after all.

Mrs. Ferris peered over my shoulder. "So lucky. Natural blonde. Lots of girls would have killed to have her hair."

Mom's hair was white as an albino rabbit in the picture, as always, but her normally pale skin was a bronzy orange, like she had smeared on self-tanner for the occasion. The photographer had caught her mid-laugh, her mouth open, teeth showing, eyes half closed. I didn't know what she had seen in Heaney, before my dad came along and blinded her to other men, but she looked happy. Maybe she had liked his over-attentiveness, the way he always wanted to take care of things. Maybe he had big plans back then. Or maybe he didn't, and that became a problem.

"How long did my mom date Dick Heaney?"

"Hmm." She folded her skeletal arms across her chest and leaned down to get a closer look at the picture. "I'm not sure. I didn't really know her before she met Eddie. I do remember her saying Heaney had a hard time moving on when it was over, though. And your dad didn't care much for him, I know that, but I've never had any problems with him all the years he's been working here."

"Why didn't my dad like him?"

"It was a bit ridiculous, actually. He was jealous, I think. Your grandparents were charitable people. Your grandfather did a lot of mentoring through the Rotary Club, and he helped Heaney out quite a bit. Felt sorry for him, with no mother, and his dad on disability. He wanted to give him opportunities he wouldn't have had otherwise. Eddie felt like Heaney was trying to worm his way into the family. He came home from college on summer break to find Heaney was practically living with them, and Eddie didn't want him there."

I turned a page in the photo album, the image of my mother's orange skin and white hair from the prom picture still flashing behind my eyelids when I blinked. There were more shots of Mom with Heaney. Mrs. Ferris looked them over, tapping a fingernail on my mother's face.

"You know," she said, "I wonder if she was the reason all the cleaning ladies he hired for Arrowood were always pale, with that same platinum hair as hers. Well, not quite the same. Most of them were bleached, and not professionally. I could tell that from across the yard."

That seemed a bit creepy, that he hired women who resembled my mother, though I knew some men were attracted only to a certain type of woman. Maybe he simply liked blondes.

"I've been meaning to ask," Mrs. Ferris said with forced brightness, "how's the profile coming along? It's all right if you're not able to get a full page of text. We can always pad it with pictures."

"I'm getting close." That was an exaggeration. Mrs. Ferris needed one page, and so far I had written over a hundred, covering everything from timber baron William Sr.'s arrival in Keokuk in the 1800s to my father's death on a blackjack table at the Mark Twain Casino. I was nowhere near close to condensing it down to one perfect page, though not for lack of trying. The more I wrote, the more deeply mired I became. My ancestors seemed noble and purposeful, building fortunes and working for the abolitionist movement and volunteering to fight in wars, while I spent my days rattling around in the empty rooms they'd left behind, eating Pop-Tarts and wiping dust from the molding. The Arrowood family as it had been in its heyday—when it was large enough to fill the entire house—felt like a party I was a hundred years late for. I was one of them, stuck in the wrong time, looking back at what I had missed. It was something I had always loved about history, an advantage it held over the present. My family was there, everyone I had lost: my sisters and uncles and grandparents, my distant cousins, the three other Ardens. If you went back far enough in time, everyone was still alive.

"The sooner the better," Mrs. Ferris said. "I'll be waiting for it."

I had dialed my mother before Mrs. Ferris made her way down the porch steps.

"Hello?" she said. I recognized the voice of Lisa Robertson on TV, my mother's favorite QVC host for the past sixteen years. She was extolling the virtues of Diamonique rings.

"It's me."

"What is it? My show's on right now." Her voice was sludgy, as though she'd been drinking. Gary must have gone to a conference or a men's fellowship retreat. She never got full-on drunk when he was around.

"Why did you act like you didn't know Dick Heaney?"

"What are you talking about?" I heard a clink and imagined her tipping a wine bottle into her coffee mug.

"I saw a picture of the two of you at prom."

There was a muffled crash, like she had knocked something over. Maybe the wine bottle going into the trash. I knew she would pile newspapers on top so Gary wouldn't see it.

"So what?" she slurred.

"You didn't find it worth mentioning that you dated the caretaker?"

"Why would it matter? Was I supposed to tell you about every man I ever dated?"

"It's just a little awkward. He looked really disappointed when I told him you were married. He thought you might move back here."

She snorted. "I'd sooner chew off my own arm."

"How long did you date him?"

"Do we really need to have this conversation?" she snapped. "You want to know the intimate details of a relationship I had before you were even born? Fine, I liked him because he was old enough to buy beer for me and my friends. He'd do just about anything I asked him to. He beat up a guy who was rude to me at the bowling alley and nearly sent him to the hospital." She sounded a bit too pleased about that. "It was fun for a while, but he got too clingy. He was always talking about getting married. And no way in hell was that gonna happen."

She had to be blind drunk to stay on the phone with me for so long, to tell me those things. I wondered what had her drinking so heavily. I hadn't heard her this bad since she'd married Gary.

"Was that enough?" she asked. "Do I need to get more explicit?" *Explicit* lisped out with too many syllables. Her shrill laughter cut into my ear, and when it finally trailed off, she said she had to get back to her show, because Lisa Robertson had finished selling all the Diamonique and was moving on to fine jewelry. I tried to imagine Heaney, with his thick forearms and stretched-out smile, beating up a man for insulting Mom. It was disturbing, though I almost felt sorry for him, that he had been so taken with my mother. He hadn't stood a chance.

I turned on my laptop and peeked at my credit card statement online. I had been using my Discover card for expenses so that I could conserve my cash, and the balance was creeping steadily higher. I had applied for the jobs at the Super 8, the gas station, and the phone-answering service, and hadn't heard back from any of them. I knew that if I wanted to find a job teaching history, which was what I'd been working toward for so long, I would have to complete my thesis and get my degree. That should have been my top priority, right after dashing off the one-page Arrowood profile, which shouldn't have taken more than an hour. Avoidance, however, was one of my greatest strengths (my superpower, Ben used to say), so instead of getting started on either of those things, I decided to do some laundry. I'd noticed specks of mildew on the towels.

Around nine o'clock, I changed into my nightgown and went to move the laundry from the washer to the dryer. I stepped in something cold and wet, and jumped back. Water was spreading out from the washing machine and across the floor. I tried to ignore the leaden weight in my stomach, telling myself that the washer had overflowed because I'd overfilled it, cramming all my towels in on top of my clothes, not because of some disastrous issue with the plumbing. If there was a bigger problem, I could worry about it later. I needed to sop up the water from the painted floor before it could do any damage.

I grabbed a mop and bucket out of the storage closet, but the mop was old and stiff and didn't seem to do more than spread the water around. I glanced over at the pile of sheets mounded in the corner, the ones that had been covering the furniture, and I couldn't think of a better idea. I spread them out on the floor and swished them around with my feet.

I worked from the outer edges of the room, pushing the water toward the center and then wringing out the sodden sheets in the laundry sink. I thought I was making progress until I noticed a still-growing puddle surrounding the washer. I pinched my eyes shut, trying to think. There had to be a shutoff valve somewhere, probably in the basement.

I kicked the wet sheets aside and unlatched the basement door. The basement showed Arrowood's age more than any other part of the house. The walls were stone and mortar, the floor hard-packed dirt. My mother had always hated it, and she refused to go down there for any reason, even on the few occasions tornado sirens had blared outside and the TV weatherman advised us to seek shelter. She had wanted a clean, finished basement with carpeting, like the one she had now, where she hosted a monthly Bible study with Gary. I hadn't minded it so much. I had liked to explore down there as a kid, turning on all the lights, digging through musty steamer trunks, dragging out the antique croquet set that no one but me had used in years, filching bottles of Coke that Granddad kept stacked in cases under the stairs.

I could feel the temperature drop as I descended below the house, goosebumps ridging my bare arms. The basement smelled a bit like the river, dampness and rotting wood and silt left behind by a flood. I held my breath for the three quick strides from the bottom step to the dangling chain that turned on the light. A wide pool of standing water spread off into the darkness, reminding me of a cave my dad had taken me to when we lived briefly in the Ozarks. We entered by canoe, the dark passageway narrowing and the ceiling dropping while the guide told a story about a group of tourists who had drowned. I didn't want to call Heaney, but I didn't want the house to flood, either.

Heaney came over right away, brushing off my apologies and calmly assessing the situation. I tried not to think of him in a white tuxedo with his arms around my mother. "It wasn't your fault," he said. "Drainpipe's clogged, and the hose is about rotted out. I'll have to get a replacement hose tomorrow, and finish clearing out that drain, so no using the washer in the meantime. You're welcome to do laundry at my place if you need to."

"Thanks. I think I can wait."

"How about you come on down with me and I'll show you where the main shutoff is. Good to know in case something like this happens again."

I followed him down the stairs. The sump pump was making gurgling sounds somewhere in the shadows, like someone struggling to breathe. Heaney showed me where he'd turned off the water supply, and pointed out the labels on the fuse box, in case I ever needed to shut off the electricity.

"You must know everything about this house after working here for so long," I said.

"I know it as well as any of the Arrowoods."

"Maybe you could help me with something. My grandmother wrote about a hidden room down here that was used as part of the Underground Railroad. Do you know anything about that?"

He looked surprised by the question and cocked his head to the side, thinking it over. "Well, there is one thing. Back here."

He stepped out of the pool of light cast by the bare bulb and disappeared into the furnace room. I followed him, my bare feet inching along the wet dirt floor, my stomach twisting uneasily as I crossed into the darkness. I knew there was another pull chain hanging somewhere nearby, another bulb waiting to fill the room with light, but I couldn't remember exactly where it was. I tried to recall the layout of the maze of rooms that burrowed under the house, windowless nooks with low ceilings dripping wires and pipes and clusters of gauzy spider eggs.

There was a metallic scraping sound, and I flinched as the light flicked on. Heaney stood next to the furnace, an ancient behemoth with pipes coming off it like the arms of an octopus.

"I had to repair the boiler a while back," he said. "I accidentally tore up part of this wall taking out a pipe. There's storage space on the other side, and it seems like it goes the whole way back, but when I was measuring things to get it fixed up, I realized it doesn't. There's dead space in there. It's not big enough that you could call it a room, really."

"Did you go inside it?" I asked.

"Nah. Chipped out a little hole in the mortar and shined a light in. Couldn't find any sort of door, or any way to access it."

"And? What did you see?"

"Nothing," he said, chuckling. "Empty. It could've been used for cold storage at one time, or maybe there used to be an old pipe or chimney there, and it got sealed up, who knows?"

I wrapped my arms around myself to stave off the chill. "Maybe there used to be a way in." I was thinking of the house plans I'd found. I could check and see what lay above this section of the basement.

Heaney shrugged. "Could have been, a hundred years ago." He

pulled the chain and the room went black. "All right, why don't we go flip the water back on, now that we know nothing's leaking."

We crossed back over to the shutoff, in the narrow alcove near the stairs, and I reached up for the handle. I froze when I noticed Heaney staring at my arm, the long pink scars snaking over my skin. He chewed his lip and shifted his gaze up to my face, to look me in the eye. I could feel his breath in the tight space, his flannel shirt brushing my shoulder.

"It's nothing," I said. "I was in an accident."

"Some accident."

"It was," I said. "But I'm fine now."

He backed out of the alcove and I squeezed past him, taking the stairs up two at a time. After Heaney left, I piled the wet sheets in the laundry sink and got out the house plans. I gingerly lifted the top two layers of the tissue-paper blueprints and pressed down on the layer for the first floor, to see what lay beneath. By my approximation, the hidden basement room was directly below the mammoth antique armoire that sat along the wall in the laundry. I didn't see anything out of the ordinary on the floor around the armoire, and when I attempted to push it aside to see if there was anything under it, I couldn't get it to budge.

When my phone rang Thursday morning and Josh's name popped up on the screen, I hesitated a moment before answering. I wondered if he had news about the case, and whether it was news I'd want to hear.

"Hi." He sounded surprised when I answered, like he would have preferred to leave a message. "I know this is coming out of left field, but I wondered if you might want to go to a Halloween party with me Saturday night. I mean, if you don't already have plans. It's a costume party my friend's throwing, and I figured it might be a chance for you to meet some people. If you want. I won't be offended if you say no."

"A costume party?" My instinct was to turn him down, though I had just been thinking about how much I missed celebrating Halloween. I hadn't been to a party of any kind in a long time. I knew it might be awkward to hang out with Josh and his friends as the third wheel, but I wanted to go. "Are you dressing up?"

"Yeah," he said. "You don't have to, though, if you're not into that."

"It sounds fun," I said. "Sure."

I had an idea for a costume, and I headed out that afternoon to find what I needed. As I drove through town, I noticed that the leaves had begun to turn, the reds and oranges muted and already muddying to brown. It took some time to locate the Goodwill store. It had moved to a crumbling stucco building behind the carwash, though on the inside, nothing had changed. The walls were still lined with old console televisions that no one would ever buy, the shelves cluttered with stained Tupperware, cracked picture frames with pictures still in them, and worn-out shoes molded to the shape of their former owners' feet. In the summers, I had often begged Grammy to take me to Goodwill so I could dig through the bin of cassette tapes and CDs, and she would complain that the place was too depressing for old people. She would browse around and find jewelry and cross-stitch samplers and collections of ceramic pigs that had belonged to recently departed friends, dismayed that their families had thrown out everything the dead had held dear—exactly what my mother had done.

I flipped through racks of dresses until I found a pale satin gown with spaghetti straps, perfect for a 1970s prom. The fabric was stained and discolored with age, but that wouldn't matter. More digging unearthed a pair of white dress shoes, possibly from someone's wedding, and a princess crown studded with plastic rhinestones.

"Got a big day coming up?" the elderly cashier asked, carefully folding the dress before stuffing it into a crinkled grocery sack.

"Just a party," I said.

"Well, you found a great outfit. You'll be the prettiest girl there."

She smiled as she handed back my change, her hand shaking with some sort of palsy, her eyes magnified behind greasy glasses. I didn't tell her that the dress was for a costume party, that I would be covering it with blood.

By Saturday night, I was jittery, uncertain about my decision to go. I put on my costume, complete with a long blond wig I'd bought at Walmart, and stood in the tub to drench myself with a bottle of fake blood. I poured it over my head, across my chest and bare arms, obscuring my scars. Syrupy red globs rolled down my dress and splatted onto the white porcelain, where they crept in slow motion toward the drain. When I climbed out of the tub and turned on the water to rinse it out, the shriek of pipes was as sharp as an icepick in my eardrum.

When I showed up at Josh's apartment, he knew exactly who I was.

"Bloody prom queen," he said. "You're Carrie, right? I like it."

Josh had colored his salt-and-pepper hair dark brown, and it was disorienting. I couldn't stop staring at him. He was dressed in an orange prison jumpsuit instead of his usual cap and windbreaker, which I also thought of as a costume. "I get that you're a convict," I said. "Are you supposed to be anyone in particular?"

"Are you serious?" he said. "You can't tell? I'll give you a hint. I'm a famous serial killer." He pointed at his inmate number, 069063.

"Sorry," I said. "That doesn't really help. Are you . . . Jeffrey Dahmer?"

He shook his head. "Dahmer had lighter hair. Maybe I was over-shooting by going for someone so handsome and charismatic." He took off his glasses. "Ted Bundy?"

"Oh, yeah, I totally see it now," I said. "The glasses were throwing me off."

"Liar." His mouth curved into a teasing smile and heat rose unexpectedly to my cheeks. I'd never seen this playful side of him. He was always so serious when discussing my sisters' case, and that was what we usually talked about.

"That's okay," Josh said. "Just don't get used to the hair—it's tempo-rary." He held up a grocery sack. "You like gin and tonic? We could stop at Hy-Vee and get something else if you want."

"Gin's fine," I said. I hated gin, but that didn't matter. I wouldn't be drinking it for the taste.

Josh's friend lived in a brick bungalow on a dead-end street, close enough to the Mississippi that the basement probably flooded every time the river rose. I could see the Ready Mix concrete plant in the distance, sloping piles of gravel glowing in the moonlight. Josh cut the engine and we both looked out at the dark house. There were no other cars around. "Are we early?" I asked.

"No," he said. "They're not the most punctual people."

"Where do you know these guys from?" I asked. "Are they friends from school or something?"

"I met them at GameStop," he said. "Travis works there. We all play *Warcraft* together."

"*Warcraft?*"

"It's an online game." He drummed his fingers on the steering wheel. "Maybe they're still at the liquor store. Do you mind waiting around?"

"Not at all," I said. "But maybe we should have a drink while we wait. What do you say, Ted Bundy?"

"Great idea, but I don't have any cups."

I pulled the Tanqueray out of the bag. "I'm game if you are."

"What—drink out of the bottle?" He eyed me like he wasn't quite sure if I was serious, if this was something I would do. It was part of the fun of dressing up, I thought, pretending to be someone else. Forget-ting the rules we usually lived by.

"Like you've never done it?"

He laughed. "Probably not since I was sixteen."

"We'll pretend we're in high school, then."

Josh groaned and grabbed the bottle of tonic water. "Fine. Chaser."

"Okay, let's do this." I unscrewed the cap and took a swig of gin. It was warm and bitter and seared my throat. We switched bottles and I chugged the tonic. I watched the line of his jaw as he drank, two quick swallows.

"You may not believe this," Josh said, "but this is my first time drinking in my van with a prom queen."

"Pretend prom queen," I corrected. "I was never voted into high school royalty, not even as part of some sinister plot."

"Really?" he said. "I wasn't, either. I did submit a lot of embarrassing poems to the school literary journal, though. Luckily they were all rejected."

I took another turn with the gin and handed the bottle back to him. "Maybe we would have been friends."

"Maybe so."

"You really wrote poetry?" I asked. The wig was making my head itch, and I tried to readjust it, pulling loose all the bits of blond hair that the fake blood had glued to my skin.

"Yeah. Doesn't every dorky teenage boy?"

I shrugged. "I had you pegged for school newspaper."

"You may have greatly overestimated me." He waved the gin in front of me. "Another?"

I nodded. "Poetry's not dorky." I had been obsessed, in high school, with confessional poets, envious of their ability to lay themselves bare on the page. I wanted to write my own poetry, but I'd hold the pen and stare at the paper and nothing would happen.

Two cars pulled into the driveway. People spilled out and filed into the house, and lights came on inside. Another car drove past and parked in front of us.

"I guess we can go in now," I said.

"Or, we could just hang out in here and recite poetry."

"Only if you go first."

He screwed the lids back on the bottles, pretending to consider it and then shaking his head. "I guess we'd better go in, then."

Inside the house, someone had switched on a black light, giving everyone blue skin and glowing teeth. I was relieved to see that nearly everyone was in costume. Josh introduced me to his friends, though Travis was the only name that stuck. He was dressed as Alex from *A Clockwork Orange*, with a black hat and spidery fake eyelashes dangling below one eye. All of Josh's friends looked too young to be drinking, though maybe that was only because the two of us were clearly the oldest people there.

I stood in a corner of the living room next to a dead ficus tree while Josh talked about computer viruses with a guy sporting red contact lenses and devil horns. I tried to pay attention to the conversation, but I couldn't follow it, and then someone turned the music up so loud that I could barely hear them anyhow. I leaned against a brown and gold velour sofa with wooden armrests shaped like wagon wheels. The upholstery was dotted all over with melted black burn marks, as though someone had been chain-smoking and stubbing cigarettes out on the couch for years. Pinned above the couch was a poster I recognized from my freshman dorm, depicting a Malibu beach house at sunset and a garage filled with sports cars. JUSTIFICATION FOR HIGHER EDUCATION. The poster should have specified that it didn't apply to anyone with a humanities degree.

The house slowly filled with bodies, and I began to sweat inside my satin dress. I excused myself and made my way through a cluster of girls in eighties costumes (either that, or the eighties had come back in style without my knowledge, which was entirely possible) to reach the tiny kitchen, where the light was normal and the windows were open to the breeze. Travis was there, pumping the keg and smoking a clove cigarette. His pupils were enormous.

"Beer?" He held out a cup for me, and I took it.

"Thanks." I leaned against the counter. It vibrated with the bass from the throbbing stereo.

"Hey," Travis said. "Are you having a good time?"

I swallowed a mouthful of beer and wiped foam from my lips. "Yeah."

He filled a cup for himself. "I've never seen Josh with a date before," he said. "You must be something special."

"It's not a date," I said. "We're friends, I guess." I wasn't sure quite what to call Josh. We weren't friends, exactly.

"Ah, sorry. How did you two meet? Are you a gamer?"

"No," I said. "We met through his website." It was the closest I could come to the truth.

Travis picked at his fake eyelashes, which seemed to be coming unglued. "Wait a minute, did he say your name was Arden? Are you that Arrowood chick?"

I shook my head.

"I never heard of any Ardens around here except for that one."

"Really?" I murmured. "I know three others." *In the cemetery*. I dumped the rest of my beer into the sink and plucked a bottle of sour apple schnapps off the counter.

"What did you say?" Travis cupped his hand behind his ear, but I didn't repeat myself. I pushed my way back into the living room, where Josh now stood alone, picking shriveled leaves off the ficus, his teeth glowing in the black light.

"Schnapps!" he said. He had to lean in close to my ear to make himself heard. "This is getting classy."

I filled the cup halfway and handed it to him, keeping the bottle for myself. The schnapps was thick and went down like cough syrup. I was buzzed, but I wanted to be drunk. Josh took one sip from the cup before abandoning it on an end table.

"Dance with me!" I yelled. I grabbed Josh's arm without waiting for an answer and dragged him into the crowd, tripping on the shag carpeting and nearly pulling him to the floor on top of me. He lifted me to my feet easily, stronger and steadier than I expected him to be. I leaned against his chest and he placed his hands uncertainly at my waist, his arms tensed to grab me again if I should fall. I closed my eyes and swayed, letting the music and the liquor blur my thoughts. I didn't want to think about anything.

At the end of the song, the stereo switched off and one of the eighties girls came in with a jumbo pack of toilet paper. "Time for the mummy contest!" she hollered. "Find a partner, grab a roll of paper!"

I squeezed my way over to the toilet paper and brought a roll back for me and Josh.

"We're doing this?" he asked.

"You know you want to."

"Okay!" the girl yelled. "When I say 'Go,' wrap your partner up like a mummy. You have to use the whole roll. Whichever team finishes first wins a Jäger Bomb!"

"Is that really a prize?" Josh hissed in my ear.

"You wrap me," I said.

When the girl said "Go," Josh started at my ankles, loosely winding his way upward, careful not to touch me too intimately. The paper slid down as he went, coiling at my feet.

"You suck at this," I said, grabbing the roll. I wrapped him as tightly as I could, reaching my arms around his back as I got to his chest. We were face-to-face, his breath sweet with schnapps, a strange energy buzzing between us. The eighties girl hollered for everybody to stop, and behind us we heard the high-pitched screams of the girls who won the Jäger Bomb, but we didn't bother to turn around and look. Josh and I stood there staring at each other as the music started back up.

"Do you want to go?" I asked. My hand circled his wrist and I could feel his pulse shuddering through my fingertips.

"I don't think either of us should drive right now."

"Let's walk," I said, tearing the paper off of him and letting it fall to the floor. "It's not that far."

"Won't you be cold?"

"I want to. Come on."

I pulled him back through the house to the door, not saying good-bye to anyone, and we stepped out into the night, shedding the last of the toilet paper as we went. The wind whipped my dress and wig, and I turned to face it head-on as Josh retrieved my bag from the van. The numbing chill felt good against my skin after the heat of the house, and I inhaled the crisp scent of frost and dead leaves. I chucked the schnapps bottle toward a garbage can and missed, nearly twisting my ankle in the process.

"You sure you're okay?" Josh asked.

"Why did you invite me to come tonight?"

"What do you mean?"

"Why did you ask me to come here with you?"

He didn't answer. He didn't have to. Everything he was holding back burned clearly in the way that he looked at me.

I grabbed his arm and ran. We made it to the end of the next block before my lungs seized up and I had to slow down. Josh brushed hair away from my face, and I took his hand, lacing my fingers through his, pressing our palms together, wanting to feel his skin against mine. He exhaled slowly, heat radiating from his body, his breath turning to smoke in the cold air. By the time we reached his apartment, I was shivering and my feet had blistered in my secondhand heels. I pried off the shoes and staggered to the bathroom to pee as soon as we got inside.

I heard Josh put on music, something brooding and instrumental, and when I looked up from washing my hands, my reflection startled me. So much blood, caked in the tangled blond wig, staining my face, snaking down my neck, saturating the bodice of my dress. I looked like someone the worst had already happened to. Someone with nothing to lose.

Josh was standing barefoot in the living room. I walked toward him, and he watched me intently, with no trace of his previous uncertainty as I leaned in to kiss him. He kissed me back, softly at first, the heat of his touch spreading over my skin, and then I was unzipping his jumpsuit and tugging at the sleeves to get it off, sliding my hands under the T-shirt he wore beneath it. Josh took me by the wrist and led me into his dark bedroom, where he undid the back of my dress and let it slide to the floor. I imagined us as our costumed selves: the broken prom queen, the charismatic killer. I pulled him down onto the unmade bed and wrapped myself around him, pressing my face against his throat to feel the warm thud of his pulse.

CHAPTER 15

When I woke up next to Josh hours later, daylight slicing in through the shades, I felt like I'd been struck in the head with an ax. I eased myself out of bed and crept to the bathroom naked. My wig had come off as I slept, leaving my hair a matted mess, and the fake blood on my skin had begun to flake and peel. I turned on the shower, and while I waited for the water to heat up, I dug around in the medicine cabinet and found some Advil for my headache. I scrubbed myself in the shower, trying to remove the pink stains left behind by the blood, and washed my hair with Josh's dandruff shampoo.

When I finished, I wrapped myself in a towel and returned to the bedroom, digging quietly through Josh's dresser to find a long-sleeved shirt and a pair of pajama pants. I knew it would probably be easier to leave before he woke up, to avoid any awkward discussion of the previous night, but I wanted to lie down for a few more minutes, just long enough for the Advil to kick in.

Josh lay curled on his side, snoring lightly, the covers bunched up around his waist. I tugged the bedding loose to pull it over me, and something caught my eye. His T-shirt had ridden up to expose a line of black script on his lower back. A tattoo.

I carefully slid his shirt up to get a better look. It wasn't one line of script, as I had initially thought, but many, twisting together and branching upward like vines. I couldn't pull his shirt up any farther for fear of waking him, so I couldn't see the whole thing. The lettering was intricate, the words ornamented with leaves and thorns, and as I tried to make them out, I saw that they were not words, exactly, but names. *Paul Andrew Kyle 1996.* His brother, the one who had run away. *John David Gosch 1982. Eugene Wade Martin 1984. Marc James Warren Allen 1986.* The Des Moines paperboy abductions. *Heather Leigh Campbell 1989.* The girl from Burlington who was never found. All unsolved cases, children who had gone missing without a trace. Then, along his spine: *Violet Ann Arrowood 1994. Tabitha Grace Arrowood 1994.* My sisters' names etched into his flesh. I let go of his shirt, and he stirred in his sleep, burrowing deeper into his pillow.

I scooted backward out of the bed and gathered up my things, closing the bedroom door softly behind me so as not to wake him. In the living room, his orange jumpsuit lay on the floor where it had fallen the night before. I leaned against the desk for balance as I strapped on my Goodwill shoes, my hand resting on a pile of folders. The one labeled ARROWOOD sat on top. I wanted out of the apartment, but I couldn't help myself. I flipped the folder open and shuffled the papers aside to get to the pictures, the ones he'd shown me to prove Singer's innocence.

I felt a weight in my chest, as though my heart had been filled with wet sand. There were the twins, exactly as I remembered them on that very last day, brought into focus in the one photo where I was a blur. I picked through the smiling close-ups of me with my sweaty bangs and missing tooth, the shots of my eight-year-old body, my end-of-summer tan, my thin arms hanging loose and relaxed.

Below those were other pictures that Josh hadn't shown to me. School pictures of me over the years, from elementary on. I wasn't sure where he had gotten them. Part of his research, I supposed, getting close to his subjects—scouring the Internet, looking for people I knew, finding out what he could about me and my family, details for his book. At the bottom of the stack was a yearbook photo from my freshman year of high school in a windswept corner of Nebraska, where my dad was swindling farmers by selling them unnecessary insurance. I wore a lavender button-down blouse with a warped collar, and there were hollows under my eyes, as though I hadn't been sleeping well. I remembered how the wind had kept me up night after night, rattling a broken windmill in the yard of our rented farmhouse. My hair was tucked behind my ears and I was frowning, as I always did when my picture was taken *after*, so that if anything happened to me, people would see my face on a poster or on the news and know that I had seen it coming, that I was not one of those smiling kids who thought the world would not hurt them. I imagined Josh examining these photos of me long before we met, thinking that he knew me, how I felt, what I wanted; that he understood me from studying two-dimensional portraits of my pain.

Josh had no claim to my sisters or my grief. He had no right to wear their names on his skin, to obsess over someone else's loss, to group it in with his own as though we all suffered equally. We had loss in common, a thread that had drawn us together, but my story didn't belong to him. I grabbed my bag and walked out of the apartment, taking the pictures with me.

The temperature had dropped overnight, the last day of October bringing frigid winds. Frost etched my windshield, and I scraped it off with the edge of an empty cassette case that had been sitting on the floorboard since the tape player had broken years ago, that last mixtape permanently wedged inside. I felt light-headed, like I might throw up. I hadn't been hungover in quite a while, and it was worse than I remembered. I cracked the window to let in the cold air and drove down the river road, which was littered with newly fallen leaves. I wondered what Ben was doing, if he lay next to Courtney in his half-finished house, which he still hadn't invited me to see. He had warned me that there was something off about Josh, and I hadn't listened.

The sky and the river were two shades of gray, winter colors. As I cut around the bend nearing the town of Montrose, a flock of starlings scattered from the trees and swept into the air, turning and wheeling in fluid formation and then swooping over the car like crashing surf, their maneuvers beautifully synchronized. In a manner inexplicable to humans, the birds were connected, in tune to an improvised master plan. Each bird knew from moment to moment what would come next, without having to think, without having to be taught. I envied them, their ability to connect to those around them, to move through life with unstudied ease, never looking back. As I pulled away from the starlings, my hands tight on the wheel, the flock spun and each bird spun with it.

As soon as I got home, I stripped off the clothes I'd borrowed from Josh and tossed them into the laundry sink, along with my bloody costume. I wondered if he'd be surprised when he woke to find me gone; if he'd expected me to stay, make conversation, eat breakfast. I'd assumed the night before that we were acting in silent agreement, pretending to be people we weren't, indulging a mutual need. I couldn't deny there had been a connection between us, though it was different from what I'd felt for Dr. Endicott—the carsick feeling that was better than being alone—or my nostalgic longing for a version of Ben that no longer existed. It was something all its own. I couldn't quite name it.

I put on some sweats and turned up the heat, imagining the utility bill escalating with each degree. I'd have to go to the store later to buy candy for the trick-or-treaters, though all I wanted to do was lie on the couch until my stomach stopped its ominous churning. It didn't help that the last day of the month was winding down. I knew it was irrational, but I was dreading November first. As a kid, the days after Halloween were always a letdown, but it was more than that for me. I had never liked the beginnings of things—mornings or Mondays or the start of a new month or year. The hours before midnight were never as empty and lonesome as the ones that came right after. Single-digit days were too bare and new. I was aware that it was all in my head, that each day was simply a continuation of a long line of days marching into winter and back out again, their numbers meaningless and repeating. January first was no different from the day that came before. Still, I could feel it. Tomorrow November would arrive, and soon, a new year. I had been at Arrowood for more than a month, and it hadn't turned me back into the person I used to be.

I woke up on the couch early in the evening, as the sun was starting to fade. I had a voicemail and a text from Josh. The text was brief: *Make it home okay?* I didn't listen to the voicemail. My head felt much better, and my stomach growled, though I still wasn't hungry. I made my way to the study at the front of the house and peeked out the window. Already, little fairies and goblins and ghosts were making their way down the street. No time to run to the store for candy. I wasn't sure that I could face them anyway, all those happy children spilling onto the porch, their bright chorus of trick-or-treats and thank-yous. Instead, I headed up the stairs past the third floor to the tower.

I hadn't been out on the widow's walk since I'd moved back, and had never been allowed up there as a kid unless someone went with me. It took some muscle to scrape the door open from the tiny tower room, and then I stepped out onto the roof. The wind lashed my hair across my face, and I closed my eyes, listening to the rustle of dead leaves, the muted voices of children far below, the ghostly call of a train as it cut between the river and the bluffs.

I remembered trick-or-treating as a witch the year after the twins were born, going up and down Grand Avenue to all our neighbors' houses while Grammy stayed with Violet and Tabitha. I was secretly giddy to have a night alone with my mother. She held my hand as we walked the moonlit sidewalks together, leaves crunching underfoot, my little plastic cauldron slowly filling with Hershey bars and Tootsie Rolls. She told me stories about soaping windows and toilet-papering yards with her friends on Halloween, talking to me like she used to, when I would sit at her dressing table, when I was her only child. Mom used up a whole roll of film taking pictures of me that night, the first time I'd been photographed alone since the twins were born, and I had a furtive thought: *What if it could be like this all the time?*

I opened my eyes and leaned against the wrought-iron railing, where Arrowoods had long ago watched for barges bearing timber, my pulse quickening. If the railing gave way, a fall from that height would easily kill me. The sky was rapidly darkening, the air sharp and clear, and as I looked out over town, I could see porch lights blinking on and the warm glow of jack-o'-lantern flames. It seemed a miraculous thing: The town was dying, yet the people who remained kept on living, like there was no other way around it.

When it was completely dark, I went back downstairs to the kitchen to fetch some matches. It would be a shame, I decided, to let Halloween pass by without at least lighting the jack-o'-lantern. I crept carefully out the front door, not wanting to turn on the porch light and attract trick-or-treaters with a false promise of candy. The jack-o'-lantern wasn't at the top of the steps where it had sat the night before, and I wondered if someone had stolen it. A group of kids shuffled by on the sidewalk, trailed by a lone parent. None of them glanced in my direction. I moved to the edge of the porch, and there at the bottom of the steps were the pulpy remains of the pumpkin. I had never understood the fun in destroying other people's things. I told myself it wasn't personal, that whatever teenage jerks had done this had likely smashed every pumpkin on the block.

I tucked the matchbook into my pocket, and as I turned to go back in the house, something caught my eye. Beneath the branches of the mimosa tree, two shadows moved up the moonlit walkway, footsteps silent on the brick. I watched in disbelief as two platinum-haired girls emerged from the darkness, standing side by side. They wore matching baby-doll dresses, their hair tucked behind their ears and held in place with barrettes. In the dim light, I couldn't make out their faces, only the hollows of their cheeks and eyes.

"Trick-or-treat!" they said in unison, their voices high-pitched and screechy, like a record played too fast.

I couldn't move. It took me a minute to push words up from my throat. "I—I'm sorry. I don't have any candy."

"Arden?"

"Who are you?"

The girls looked at each other and giggled. "Can't you tell? We're Violet and Tabitha. The Arrowood twins."

"We saw a light on upstairs, in our room," one of the girls said, pointing up and to the right, toward my sisters' room.

The other girl nodded, and they slid closer. They were older than I had first thought. Taller. They looked wrong in their little-girl dresses and hair clips. I took a wobbly step backward, and another, a tingling sensation rushing up my spine to the base of my skull and prickling over my scalp.

"What's the matter?" one of the girls said as they glided up the steps and onto the porch. "Did you think we were dead?"

I reached the door, panic fumbling my fingers so that I could barely turn the knob. The girls were laughing, terrible shrieks ribboning out of their mouths. Once I managed to get inside, I sank to the floor and sat on my shaking hands. I leaned back against the door and then flinched as a loud thud, and then another, struck the other side. It sounded like they were trying to kick down the massive door. I waited for them to give up and go away, and after a minute of pounding, it went quiet. I got to my feet and listened. A thin, scrabbling sound pricked my ears, like fingernails scratching at the window. I sucked in a few rapid breaths, telling myself how ridiculous it was that a couple of teenagers had me cowering in my own house. I yanked the door open, ready to chase them away. There was no one on the porch. My heart thudded as I scanned the yard. Dead leaves scuttled along the walkway, the empty sidewalk, whispering. My skin itched like someone was watching me, but I couldn't see anyone in the dark. I shut the door and stood there in the center hall staring at it, willing my heart to slow down.

Bam-bam-bam-bam. A rapid-fire knock. "Go away!" I screamed, the words tearing my throat. The knob rattled and turned, and before I could think to run, the door pushed open and there was Heaney, dressed in Carhartts and a stocking cap, wielding a hefty flashlight the size of a thermos. My breath wheezed in and out, my hands trembling.

"What happened?" he said. "I just saw a couple kids running for the backyard."

"What are you doing here?"

"I was on my way over to keep watch. I guess I didn't get here in time."

"Keep watch?"

He shut the door behind him, and I inched back toward the stairs.

"I didn't want to worry you," he said. "There's been trouble here before on Halloween when the house was empty. Kids trying to break in, vandalize the place. Usually not until later at night. I was planning to keep an eye out, just in case, though I figured people might be less likely to try anything now that the house isn't vacant anymore. I guess I wasn't thinking about the crazies who might want to come around for that very reason—because they know you're here."

I pulled my hands into the sleeves of my sweatshirt so that he wouldn't see them shaking.

"Something really scared you, didn't it?" he said gently. My teeth rattled in my jaw.

"Sorry I burst in here," he continued. "I saw those kids take off, and I saw the pumpkin, and then when I knocked . . ."

"It's okay," I said. "I just want to make sure they're gone."

When Heaney finished looking around the yard, he checked all the doors and windows from the outside to make sure they were either locked or had been jammed shut for so many years that they were in no danger of opening.

"It might be a good idea for me to stay here tonight," he said. "That way I'll be right here in case anything else happens. Folks'll see my truck outside and know you're not here alone."

I thought of Heaney and my mother, how he had beaten up a stranger for her. He could handle the situation if someone broke in. I brought down a pillow and blanket and made up the drawing room couch, while Heaney went around the house checking behind closet doors and shower curtains the way my dad had once done a very long time ago when I had awoken from a nightmare that the three other Ardens had come for me.

———

Heaney was still there when I got up. He had made coffee for me and was puttering around the first floor, looking for things that needed fixing. It was different, having someone there, though I didn't mind it. It was comforting to hear the small sounds of him moving through the house when I came downstairs.

I took my coffee out onto the porch and huddled on the steps in my baggy sweater. Frost tipped the grass in the places the sun hadn't yet reached, and I noticed that the smashed pumpkin was gone. Heaney must have scraped it up and disposed of it. I had almost finished my coffee when Josh's van pulled into the driveway and parked behind Heaney's truck.

"Hi," he said, approaching the porch cautiously, as though he thought any sudden movements might spook me and send me darting into the house. He was back to the familiar windbreaker and hat, though the bit of hair sticking out was still brown instead of gray. "Nice truck."

"Heaney's," I said.

He handed me a cherry ChapStick. "You left this in my van. It must have fallen out of your bag."

"You drove all the way here to bring me that?"

"No," he said softly. "I wanted to make sure everything's okay. I had a great time with you the other night, and I'm not just talking about what happened at the end."

I kept my eyes on my coffee mug, a white elephant gift from the history department's holiday party. The text was chipping off. WHO NEEDS HISTORY? IT'S NOT LIKE IT REPEATS ITSELF!

"I felt like we were starting to get to know each other," Josh said. "Then you were gone in the morning, and when you didn't call back, I wondered if I did something, or . . . I saw that you took the pictures from the folder. Not just Singer's, but all those pictures I had of you. . . . I hope it didn't make you uncomfortable, that I had them. I thought maybe that was why you didn't call back."

"We shouldn't have—done what we did," I said, my voice low. I didn't want Heaney to hear us and come outside.

"I'm sorry," he said. "I wasn't really thinking at the time. I mean, neither of us was. I'm not expecting anything. If that's all you're worried about, we can just forget about what happened and start over as friends."

"It wasn't just the pictures you were hiding," I said, looking up at him. "I saw your back, while you were sleeping. Your tattoo. Were you planning on telling me about it?"

His shoulders dropped and he swallowed hard. "I didn't think there was a reason to bring it up," he said. "Does it bother you?"

"My sisters' names on your skin?"

Josh's lips pressed into a tight, bloodless line, and he sat down next to me on the steps. "I got the tattoo when I was eighteen. I might not make the same choice today, but I don't regret it. It wasn't a spur-of-the-moment thing—it means something to me. Each one of those names was a lost person that I didn't want forgotten. My brother ran away, and yeah, maybe that made me a little obsessed. I can't help but want to make sense of things, find answers. Some people might think it's strange, but I'm a normal guy. It's just that this is the thing that drives me. And I want to understand what drives you, too."

"How come you never told me what really happened when your brother disappeared?" I asked. "That you were there?"

Josh was silent for a minute, his jaw twitching. Finally he shrugged. "I figured you'd find out if you wanted to."

"Ben told me."

"What did he tell you? Did he tell you that Paul only took me camping with him because he knew that was the only way our parents would let him go? That he had planned the whole thing just so he could run off, that he left me alone in the woods overnight, with no supplies, no way to get home—not caring what would happen to me, what people would think? He told me he wanted to spend some time with me before our parents sent him away. I believed him. Even after he was gone, I kept thinking he'd come back to see me. Sometimes I'd rather think he's dead than think he's out there living his life, not even missing me."

"You could have told me all of that," I said. "You already know everything about me. It's not fair to hide so much of yourself."

He glanced over at me, studying my face. "So you knew. And you weren't worried I'd killed my brother and left him in the woods like everybody was saying back then?"

"No," I said. "I wasn't. I was thinking how scared you must have been, waking up alone, trying to drive back, the accident."

"Then you know me better than you think you do. We have something terrible in common, Arden. Whether you like it or not, or want to believe it or not, we get each other. We do. I think there could be more, if you want there to be."

My heartbeat was audible, thrumming in my skull.

Josh reached out and lifted my hand from my lap, turned it palm up, and slowly, gently, used his thumb to push my sleeve above my wrist to reveal my scars. "You didn't hide these," he said. "But you didn't talk about them, either."

I snatched my hand back. I opened my mouth to speak, but I didn't know what to tell him. "I didn't try to kill myself," I said finally, "if that's what you're thinking. I did something incredibly stupid. I broke into someone's house and cut myself going through the window." He looked a bit uncertain, and I couldn't tell if he believed me. "And I think we should forget about what happened last night. Nothing has to change. We can still stay in touch about the book. You can call me if anything new comes up."

He nodded slowly, biting his lip. "If that's what you want."

"Yeah."

"So we're okay?"

"We're okay."

As I turned to go back in the house, a shadow slipped away from the door. Heaney, watching, keeping an eye on me.

CHAPTER 16

I'd switched off the ringer on the house phone, tired of receiving unknown calls, and when I finally checked the messages to get rid of the furiously blinking red light, all of them except for one were dead air, the caller waiting to see if I would pick up and then hanging up when I didn't. The only actual message was from the lawyer, reminding me that I needed to sign and return a form from the packet he'd sent.

It took me a minute to remember which drawer I'd shoved the papers into, and once I found it, I had to read through everything to figure out what exactly I was signing. I sat at Granddad's desk, and the more I read, the more confused I became. There was a summary of charges from earlier in the year, before I had come to Arrowood, including things like utilities and property taxes. Most of the items, however, were listed in vague categories such as exterior maintenance and repair, so I couldn't tell exactly what the trust had been billed for. It seemed that I had not only overestimated the Arrowood fortune, but also underestimated the cost of keeping the place in good repair. I wrote a note to the lawyer, asking for further documentation, including copies of the invoices if possible.

I set aside the trust documents and attempted to straighten up the desk, putting the old photos in the drawer and stacking all my notes and books in piles. As I returned my mother's medical file to the box I'd brought down from the third-floor powder room, I noticed a familiar name on the very last tab. I plucked out Julia Ferris's folder, and while I knew what an intrusion of privacy it was to look at someone else's medical records, I barely hesitated before opening it.

Mrs. Ferris was anemic. Her cholesterol levels were normal. She had needed an inhaler for a lingering case of bronchitis. It was all perfectly mundane, and I felt ridiculous for reading it, until I reached one entry that stood out. In the summer of 1992, Mrs. Ferris had undergone a D & C. I knew what the procedure was, and that it could be performed for various reasons. I flipped the page and saw that she had had a positive pregnancy test just prior to the procedure, four years after Lauren was born. That meant that Mrs. Ferris had either lost or terminated the pregnancy. Based on the dates, this would have happened during the same time that my mother was pregnant with the twins.

It wasn't fair, I knew, to assume anything about Mrs. Ferris's situation. One way or another, she had suffered the loss of a child. Still, I couldn't help but wonder if my father had been involved — if Mrs. Ferris had thought the child was his. Was this what she had not forgiven my father for, the thing she told him he would have to make up to her? Had he pressured her to end the pregnancy, or abandoned her after a miscarriage? I could understand her anger, losing a child while my mother went on to have twins. Could that have been enough to push her to hurt my sisters? It wasn't something I could ask Mrs. Ferris, and even if I did, I wouldn't expect her to tell me the truth. I wondered if Josh knew about this, if it was the sort of thing he might consider a believable motive.

Later that night, while soaking in the tub, I examined the pink lines on my arm, trying to decide if they were fading. They were mostly hidden on the underside, and when visible, they weren't severe enough to draw stares, except maybe the thicker one at the base of my wrist. The scars might become less noticeable over time, though they would always be with me. I'd be an old woman with my skin hanging down like curtain swags, and the scars would still be there, concealed in the folds.

Josh had been wrong, in a way, comparing the secret marks on our bodies. He had chosen his tattoo. Scars, too, were reminders of the past, though we rarely got to choose them, and most likely preferred to forget whatever it was they commemorated: an accident, a surgery, a mistake. It wasn't the marks on my arm that bothered me, it was what they reminded me of, the reason I had left school without finishing.

When my mother came to Colorado to get me, to take me back to Minnesota with her after my accident, she wouldn't listen to my explanations. She was convinced that I had tried to kill myself over a relationship with Dr. Endicott. That was one of the most shameful parts; despite what had happened, I could never think of him as Charles or Chuck. Even when we were intimate, I had thought of him as Dr. Endicott.

My original adviser, Dr. Browning, had suffered a stroke after my first year in the program and had to take an indefinite leave, at which point I was switched over to Dr. Endicott. I'd taken one of his courses and admired his work. He was the professor who would gladly join students for happy hour, or hold class outside on the quad when the weather was nice. He was in his forties, with dark, heavy brows and wavy hair and a constant five-o'clock shadow. He had a stubborn paunch, which drove him to try every new fitness fad, and while he wasn't especially handsome, he was confident and charming, and that made him attractive. The undergrads that crowded around during office hours had crushes on him.

I felt lucky to have Dr. Endicott as my new adviser, though he was not initially a fan of my thesis topic. Nostalgia didn't interest him. I thought it was unusual that, as a history professor who spent most of his waking hours absorbed in the past, he found little emotional attachment to it.

He liked to have our meetings somewhere other than his office, at the pizza place or coffee shop or pub at the edge of campus. I liked talking to him, though most of the time I was listening, and sometimes our meetings would stretch on much later than necessary, which I didn't particularly mind. One day he asked if we could meet at his house, since he would be at home grading papers, and we sat in his backyard roasting marshmallows in the fire pit and talking about things that were not at all related to my thesis. After that, we always met at his house, and we met when we didn't need to.

As our discussions grew more personal (I knew, for example, that Dr. Endicott had fallen out of love with his wife and was going through a divorce), he asked me about the kidnapping and what my life had been like after, and I did my best to explain the things that I had a hard time putting into words. I hadn't talked to anyone about it in a very long time. It was rare that anyone asked. He took my hand as I spoke, his fingers sliding between mine, a jolt of unexpected intimacy that gave me a weightless feeling, like I had stepped into a rapidly descending elevator.

You can't change the past, he said. *You can't go back.* He kissed me then, and undressed me on his sofa, and we made love with a framed picture of him and his soon-to-be ex-wife and their children staring down at us from the mantel.

We were together, secretly, for the rest of the fall semester. I hadn't been with a man before, not like that, though I wouldn't have admitted as much to Dr. Endicott, who never asked if he was the first. I hid my initial discomfort and inexperience because I craved the warmth he provided, the weight of his presence, the way the air in a room felt different when he was there and I was not alone. When he held me against his chest, I felt a glimmer of possibility, like a train was approaching from a long way off, and while I couldn't yet see or hear it, I could feel the vibration in the tracks. It made me wonder about my mother, if that's how it had been for her, with my father and with Gary, and maybe even with Heaney—if she had felt less empty, if she'd thought it might somehow be possible to be full.

Dr. Endicott didn't want me to leave any sign of myself at his house, or to show him any affection in public. It wouldn't be wise, he said, because even though we were doing nothing wrong, he was still my adviser. If anyone in the department found out, it would make things awkward for both of us.

My father died in February, and while I didn't want to believe that it had any impact on me, it was then, when I returned from his funeral, that my focus began to further deteriorate. I had struggled with my thesis all along, penning brilliant phrases in my head only to have them dissolve when I began to type. I loved history, but some days I wondered if I was fooling myself, if I had stayed in school for so many years to avoid facing whatever came next, pursuing a master's only because there was still money in my college fund. I credited Dr. Endicott with what progress I'd made—I had forced myself to put words on the page because I wanted to please him—but after the funeral, whenever I opened the file, I felt sick to my stomach and closed it without writing anything.

I spent spring break in my tiny basement apartment, staring at my laptop screen, while Dr. Endicott went skiing in Breckenridge with his two grown children. I didn't miss him, exactly, but I missed not being alone. The other graduate assistants, the ones who were usually up for happy hour or coffee or a movie at the dollar theater, had all gone to visit family or headed up into the mountains or driven a punishing number of hours to get to a beach. Instead of utilizing my free time to work on my thesis, I got out a notebook and pen, and I wrote a poem. I'd never written one before, though I had tried. I'd never been able to get the right words to come. This time, I just started writing, spilling my thoughts messily onto the page. I closed with an unattributed quote stolen from Flannery O'Connor's *Wise Blood*, which had never felt so true to me as it did on the long drive back west after Dad's funeral, my heart clenched in protest as I traveled in the wrong direction: *"Where you come from is gone, where you thought you were going to was never there . . ."*

I had promised Dr. Endicott that I would go to his house over break to water his houseplants. He had given me a key for that specific purpose, and I was to leave the key in the house when I was done. I had the poem with me, folded in my pocket, and while I was there, watering the philodendron in his home office downstairs, I slipped it into the middle drawer of his desk on an impulse, tucked beneath an address book and a thin stack of takeout menus. I hadn't written the poem for Dr. Endicott, but for me. It was not for or about him. He hadn't wanted me to show my feelings in public, hadn't wanted me leaving any trace of myself behind. Now I had left a piece of my hidden self, exposed, and I was electric with the knowledge that it might possibly be discovered.

Dr. Endicott was fidgety when he returned from break and didn't have much time for me. One night, as I was getting dressed to go back to my apartment after spending the evening with him, he confessed that he had been feeling guilty about our relationship and was no longer sure that it was a good idea. He wanted to break it off. We would go back to being adviser and advisee, and nothing more.

I didn't feel anything at first, white noise, empty air. Soon after, when there was talk in the department that he was trying to reconcile with his wife, I remembered my poem, that piece of myself I had left behind. It had been stupid of me to leave it with him, and I wanted — needed — to get it back, without him ever knowing it had been there.

I drove to his subdivision when I knew he was teaching a night class, parked down the block, and walked to his house, sneaking into the backyard and onto the patio where we had once roasted marshmallows.

The sliding glass door was locked, so I scooted one of the patio chairs over, climbed up on it, and tried the office window. I kept jiggling the window long after I realized that it wasn't going to open. I was growing frustrated and angry with myself, that I couldn't do this one simple thing. I was so close to getting my poem back, but instead Dr. Endicott would find it and feel sorry for me, embarrassed. I imagined him reading it to his wife or putting it in my student file, things he wouldn't likely do, but could, because I had laid myself bare on the page, and he had it in his possession to do with it as he pleased.

I took off my jacket and balled it around my fist, like I'd seen people do on television. The glass was flimsy in its frame, so I knew it would shatter, though not how easily. I punched with all my strength and my arm went straight through, so far that I fell forward. I stood there a moment, slightly panicked by what I'd just done, and then my adrenaline spiked and I knocked out the remaining shards and pulled myself through the window.

I was shaking as I opened the center drawer in Dr. Endicott's desk and slid the poem from beneath his address book. Red drops spattered onto his pencils and Post-it notes, and as I looked for its source, blood dripped down my fingers, blooming darkly along the edge of the paper I clutched, threatening to blot out the words. Blood spotted my jeans and shoes and left a trail across the floor. I realized that I must have slit my arm on the broken window glass, and I was bleeding more than I had ever seen myself bleed before. I fainted then, more from the sight of all the blood than the loss of it.

A dog-walking neighbor had heard the window break and shined a flashlight in to see me lying on the floor in a puddle of blood. He called the police, and then Dr. Endicott, who thankfully didn't want to press charges against me for breaking into his house. However, he did insist on calling my mother. The poem was still crumpled in my hand when I was found, and the officers had read it and shown it to him. He was certain that I'd tried to kill myself because he'd broken up with me.

I was admitted to the hospital for the night and given a psych evaluation, but I was released when my mother came for me the next day. She drove me back to Minnesota, sighing heavily every time she turned to look at me. When she finally spoke, I thought she would recite some Bible verses, tie everything back to God in the way that Gary had taught her. I was wrong. She shook her head. *I thought if you learned anything from me, it was not to ruin yourself over a man.*

I had told her twenty times that I hadn't tried to kill myself, that I had cut my arm breaking in, and that I wasn't breaking in to vandalize or steal, I only did it to retrieve something that was mine. Yes, the cuts ran along my veins, the smart way to do it, none of that wrist-slashing, cry-for-attention bullshit. But really, if I'd wanted to die, would I have bothered making shallow cuts up to my armpit? Would I have wanted to be humiliated, found dead on my adviser's floor clutching a terrible poem?

This is temporary, she'd said when we pulled up to her and Gary's ranch house. *It doesn't do any good to sit around and mope.* Ironic advice from a woman who'd spent ten years swallowing pills in her bedroom.

Mom and Gary laid their hands on me and prayed that I would be saved from sin and born again through the Lord Jesus Christ. My

Catholic baptism apparently hadn't done any good, and there was talk of submerging me in the pool at Gary's church. I pictured myself sitting in a dunk tank, Gary throwing Bibles at the bull's-eye to get me to fall into the water. When Gary was home, my mother cooked and vacuumed and worked out on her elliptical machine while reading scripture, and when he was gone, she bought things from the Home Shopping Network and drank white wine in a coffee mug and ate chocolate chips out of the bag while she curled her hair.

I felt like an alien in their house. Mom would make unfamiliar meals, things she'd learned, perhaps, from watching so much Rachael Ray; and she and Gary would both crumble Nacho Cheese Doritos on top of their Mexican casserole, like it was the natural thing to do, and I would sit there and watch them eat, thinking theirs was not a family I belonged to. Each night at dinner, Gary lectured me on the importance of faith and belief, quoting his favorite televangelists and offering up Bible verses. *"To every thing there is a season, and a time to every purpose under the heaven." You've got yourself stuck in a long, dark season, Arden, and it's time to let in the light.* As though it were as simple as opening up the blinds.

When a week had passed with no signs of me wanting to harm myself, Mom and Gary were glad to put me on a plane back to Colorado. I didn't have much left to do to complete my degree besides turn in my thesis, but I hadn't told anyone—especially not Dr. Endicott—that my thesis wasn't finished. After what had happened, I didn't see how I could go back to school. A few of my friends from the history department called and emailed to check on me, to ask where I was and what was going on. I didn't know if I should lie, or if Dr. Endicott would tell everyone what I'd done anyway.

I wasn't thinking, at the time, that he would want to keep everything quiet to avoid revealing to his colleagues and his estranged wife the details of our somewhat inappropriate relationship. I just knew that I couldn't face him, so I returned to my basement apartment and stayed there, sleeping at random times and staring at the blank screen on my computer, ignoring messages from the other graduate assistants, until the lawyer called with the news about Arrowood—letting me know that Granddad had always planned for the house to go to me, but not until my father died.

Coming home hadn't been the new start that I thought it would be. The house didn't feel the same as it had *before*, and neither did I. I had been altered by grief, remade as a version of myself that I would not have chosen to be but couldn't help being. The girl I was meant to be had been stolen along with the twins, spirited away to some dark place where I would never find her.

CHAPTER 17

"I brought you something," Josh said. The sweating Styrofoam cup was almost too big to hold in one hand. It was a forty-four-ounce root beer from A&W. I took a sip, and though the ice had mostly melted during the drive from Fort Madison, it still tasted divine. "I need to talk to you for a minute about the open house," he said. I let him in.

"There's been some discussion on the website about people coming to see Arrowood on the holiday tour," Josh said. "None of the people seem threatening, that I can tell, but I thought you should know. I was thinking maybe I could be here, to help keep an eye on things. If you don't mind."

"Sure," I said. "That's fine." I sipped my root beer, the taste taking me back to Grammy's Chevy Nova with the textured cloth seats that left patterns on the backs of my legs. She had stolen one of the miniature A&W mugs from the drive-in tray, tucked it under the seat for me. She hated the idea of stealing, but I had begged her.

"I found something you might want to see," I said. "It's about Mrs. Ferris." I got her file from the office and brought it to him, watched as he read it. "Could that be a motive?" I asked. "If she thought the baby was my father's? Maybe she was jealous, that she lost her child and my mother had twins. She said she and my dad weren't in love, but I think she might have been lying." I was thinking of how I'd loved Ben but had never managed to tell him. "Or maybe she wanted my dad to leave my mom, and he wouldn't do it because of us, and she decided to do something about it."

"I've talked to her several times at the Miller House," Josh said. "She's a bit overbearing, but she doesn't strike me as that kind of crazy."

"How can you be sure? Can't people snap sometimes under the right circumstances, people who seem normal otherwise?"

"Anything's possible. But this is someone who cares very much about appearances, about her reputation. Her affair with your father was kept very discreet. I don't think she would have committed a big splashy crime that would draw attention. It just doesn't fit. And there's still that three-hour window," Josh said. "If they disappeared at one and the police weren't called until four . . . why did it take your mom three hours to make the call?"

"That's only if they were really gone right after I saw Singer's car. I was wrong about everything else, I could be wrong about that, too. If there was a gap, though . . . My mom was on a lot of medication back then. She was always tired, and kind of zoned out. I was tired that day, too, and sick. Maybe we fell asleep. Maybe we were all napping and someone came into the house."

"Maybe," he said, though he didn't sound convinced. He was looking not at me but through me, and I imagined him with a Rubik's Cube, twisting it in a hundred different directions trying to get all the colors to line up.

I had another visitor later in the day, one who rang the doorbell so many times on my way to the door that I was ready to chip through the wall and disconnect the wires, as my mother had done years before. My stomach dropped when I peeked out through the sidelight and caught a flash of familiar platinum hair. I couldn't think of a good reason why Mom would show up at Arrowood unannounced—or at all. It quickly registered that my mother would never wear a stretchy pink hoodie and short denim skirt from the juniors department, like the blonde on the porch was wearing, and then the woman leaned forward to jab the doorbell again and I got a good look at her face. She was younger than my mother, though not by much. In her forties, probably, with thin lips and an overbite and too much eyeliner. Her skin was pale to match her hair, and I remembered Mrs. Ferris saying that Heaney had hired cleaning women who resembled my mother. I opened the door.

"Oh, hi," she said, forcing a polite smile. I was clearly not the person she had been expecting.

"Hi," I said. "Can I help you with something?" She didn't answer right away, and I looked out to the driveway, at the little Hyundai parked there, but didn't see any sort of sign on it. "Are you from the cleaning service?"

"What? No." She snorted, shaking her head. "Sorry I'm just standing here like a goof. I'm Deirdre. I was looking for Eddie."

"Ah . . . are you a friend of his?" I wasn't sure why anyone would be looking for my dad here, since he hadn't lived at Arrowood in years.

"Yeah," she said, shrugging. "Friends. Is he not home?"

I didn't know what to say, so I simply answered the question, thinking that might be enough to make her go away. "No, he's not home."

"Maybe you can give him a message for me?" She shifted back and forth in her scuffed stiletto boots. "I tried to message him, but he didn't message back."

I figured it was only fair to let her know that Eddie would not message her back, ever. "Um. I hate to tell you this, but he passed away."

"He did? When?" She looked more surprised than upset.

"February."

She frowned. "But I just saw him at the bar over in Hamilton a month ago. He told me he was gonna be busy for a while, that his daughter was moving home. That's you, right?"

Nausea pooled in my stomach. She couldn't have seen my father a month ago.

"How do you know Eddie?"

She made a face, scrunching up her nose. "I'm not sure he'd want me talking to his daughter about that."

"What does my dad look like?"

"Big forehead. Sort of reddish-brown hair. Why are you asking?"

"Because that's not Eddie, and this isn't his house."

She stood up straighter, indignant. "It is so. I've been over here before. He had me put on his letter jacket, and his name was embroidered right on the front, *Eddie*. That was his thing, you know, like he wanted to relive his glory days. Some of the older guys are like that."

"Well, he's not here," I said. "And you shouldn't come back."

I shut the door on Deirdre, feeling like I might vomit. The blond women Mrs. Ferris had seen at Arrowood were not housecleaners after all. Heaney had been indulging in a fantasy with women who looked like my mother. And he had told Deirdre that he had a daughter. It was disturbing, if not exactly criminal. His contract would expire at the end of the year, and I wouldn't renew it. I could avoid him until then, and let the lawyer take care of the details. I wouldn't be letting him back in the house, no matter what needed fixing.

My deadline to turn in the Arrowood profile was the first of November, which I missed by a week. I wasn't happy with the end result, which sounded too dry on paper, though I knew it didn't matter, that no one would read the profile with the same care I had put into writing it. In my haste to send it off, I sent the wrong file first, the long one, and Mrs. Ferris had emailed back almost instantaneously to ask if I'd somehow misunderstood about the length.

She came by Arrowood about a week before the open house to discuss a long list of action items I needed to attend to before and during the event, and she was shocked to see that I hadn't yet made any preparations.

"I don't see any holiday décor," she said, smiling aggressively, her face shiny and pink like she had recently undergone a chemical peel.

"Yeah, it's all up on the third floor," I said, though I hadn't checked to make sure. "I just need to bring it down." I felt jumpy and uncomfortable having her in the house, after my discussion with Josh.

"Mm-hmm, and what about lights for the porch? Are you going to be able to hang them by yourself? Because the outdoor lighting is crucial. You know what, I'll send Ben over to help you. He knows exactly how I want it done."

"Sure," I said. "If he wants to help, that's fine." I hadn't seen Ben since the night Lauren and I had snuck into the carriage house, though we had texted back and forth a few times about nothing in particular. *How's everything going? Not bad, how about you?*

Mrs. Ferris made a note to herself and moved down the list. "We're going to have a girl from the high school here with her cello, so you need to have an area in the foyer where she can set up, and you'll need to figure out where to put the cookies and drinks. I have a folding table if you need it. Oh, and I was thinking you might want to make an informative poster for the hidden room in the basement, the one you mentioned in the profile. People are very excited to see an actual stop on the Underground Railroad. Everyone's going to want to see that room."

"I'm not sure anyone will be able to look inside. It's sealed off from the rest of the basement. I'd have to pry up a floorboard or something."

"Oh, just have Ben do it when he's over here hanging the lights. I'm sure he won't mind. He's become quite the handyman, working on that house of his."

"I don't know," I said. "I was thinking maybe we could limit the tour to the first floor. I'm not sure I'm comfortable with people roaming through the whole house."

She snapped the cap back on her pen and looked up at me. "I know this must be hard for you," she said, "opening your home up to strangers. Ben was worried that people would come here out of, what did he call it, 'morbid curiosity' about your sisters. There will always be people who seek out that sort of thing, but you don't have to let it be about that." She came closer and I reflexively shrank away from her. "I think it's perfectly reasonable to block off the stairs so that no one goes up to the twins' room. But don't forget why we're doing this. If you highlight some of the fascinating details of this house, and your family, it will help keep the focus where we want it to be: on the rich history of Keokuk. We're using that past to build a future."

I was fairly certain I'd seen that exact line in the historical society brochure, the idea that our history could somehow save us. "Do you really think it'll work?"

She shot me a stern look. "Not everything is a lost cause," she said. "You don't know until you try to prove it otherwise."

Ben showed up after dinner two days later, carrying a toolbox and a six-pack of beer.

"Hey," I said. "I'm sorry your mom made you come over here to help me with all this stuff."

"Are you kidding?" he said, taking off his coat and hanging it on the newel. "You should see what she had me doing at the Shermans' up the street. Mr. and Mrs. Sherman are about five feet tall with twelve-foot ceilings, and too frail to get up on a ladder. I think I changed every lightbulb in the house. This'll be a breeze in comparison."

I had worried that things might be awkward between us after our last conversation, when he said we couldn't pick up where we'd left off, but I felt better now that he was here. He'd always had a way of putting me at ease.

"Did your mother mention that she wants you to tear up the floor in the laundry room?" I asked.

Ben twisted the cap off a beer and handed me the bottle. "She's a gifted delegator."

"Yeah, she is."

"So," he said, taking a swig of beer. "All we need to do is lug some boxes down three flights of stairs, break into a secret room, and hang about five zillion Christmas lights."

"Only three things," I said. "Easy peasy."

The boxes of Christmas decorations were stacked at the back of the second storage room we checked, next to Nana's red velvet love seat, the one my mother had hated so much that she made my father drag it up the narrow stairs the minute Nana and Granddad moved out. The night Ben, Lauren, and I broke into Arrowood, I had wanted to come up to the third floor and steal a string of Christmas bells. After the incident with the Ouija board, I'd forgotten about the bells entirely until days later, when the last of the mayflies had died. Ben and I had sat together in the dark, on the stone floor of the carriage house, hoping Lauren wouldn't come looking for us. Outside, the streets were still black with dead flies, the air heavy with the overwhelming stench of decay. I had told Ben about the bells, how I'd wanted to retrieve one small piece of my past. He suggested that we sneak into Arrowood again, but I wasn't ready to go back into the house. We sat facing each other, our knees nearly touching, both of us aware of the new current running between us.

I'll go, Ben had said. *I'll get them for you.* And I had felt it again, the fluttery sensation that had first appeared when we'd held each other in my old bedroom at Arrowood. I had leaned forward, there in the carriage house, and touched my lips to his. Our first kiss.

I wondered if Ben still thought about that night in the carriage house, or all the other nights that summer when we had snuck away from his sister to be alone. I hadn't known that it would be my last summer at the Sister House, that Aunt Alice would go into the nursing home, both she and Grammy within a year of dying. I hadn't known that I would stay with my mother the next summer, working at McDonald's to earn money to buy a used car.

Ben stacked the two larger boxes in his arms and I took the smaller one. We carried them down the back stairs, and when we got to the laundry room, I wiped the boxes with an old towel and attempted to brush the dust off Ben's shirt.

"One down," he said. "I think we deserve to finish our drinks before moving on to step two."

I opened up one of the boxes while Ben went to retrieve our beers from the front hall. Beneath the top layer of tissue paper lay the garland of bells that my mother had always hung on the mantel in the living room. Ben had never come back to the house to get them. Mom had once told me that she knew when Santa had filled our stockings because she'd hear the bells tinkling as he brushed against them on his way back up the chimney.

"So," Ben said, returning to the laundry room with his toolbox and the beers, "are we ready to destroy your floor to appease my mother?"

"We can try. I looked over the house plans again after talking to your mom, and I did some measuring up here and down in the basement, and I think our best bet to get into the hidden room would be along the wall right here, under the armoire."

"All right. Let's move it out of the way, then, and see what we have."

I got on one side of the massive antique cabinet and Ben got on the other. With both of us pushing and pulling, we were able to slide it a few feet along the wall. We squatted down to examine the floor.

"Look," Ben said. "It's been painted over, but you can just barely see a square outline here. With the way the boards are lined up, you probably wouldn't notice it unless you were looking for it. What do you think? Are you really okay with tearing up the floor?"

I nodded. Ben dug around in his toolbox and got out a hammer and chisel. Slowly and carefully, he tapped all the way around the outline and then dug the chisel in deeper to pry up the boards. After a few tries, the edge of a section of flooring popped up, making a sound like a gasp of breath, and Ben removed it in one piece. I got chills peering down into the hole, thinking about the people who had sheltered here as they fled north, seeking freedom.

The opening was less than two feet square, barely large enough for a grown person to squeeze through. There was a narrow iron ladder attached to the stone wall below. The light from the laundry room got swallowed up before it reached the bottom, though I guessed the space couldn't be more than ten feet deep.

"Anything down there?" Ben asked.

"Doesn't look like it," I said. "Hard to tell in the dark, though. You want to go down and check it out?"

He laughed. "Ladies first."

"Fine with me."

"I was kidding," he said. "That ladder could fall apart and then you'd be stuck down there with a broken leg."

"It would be worth it," I said. "This is a piece of history. How can you not be excited right now?"

"It's great," he said. "But I can enjoy all the historical significance from up here."

"Well, I can't. It's not that far down. Let's see if the ladder will hold me."

Ben sighed and held out his hand. "All right, but take it slow, and if it feels like it might give way, I'll haul you back up."

I held on to Ben as I placed one foot on the ladder and carefully tested my weight. A dank, musty chill emanated from the hole, the smell like roots poking blindly through the earth, toadstools with moist accordion caps. I took a step down, and then another, letting go of Ben's hand when I could grab the top rung. The cold crept up my legs, as though I stood in rising water.

"Be careful," Ben said as I descended beyond his reach.

Once I passed through the opening, I got a better sense of the room's size. It was narrow enough that I could reach out from the ladder and touch the rough stone wall on either side, but I could feel the empty space stretching out behind me, and when I looked over my shoulder into the darkness, I couldn't see the back wall.

I stopped near the bottom of the ladder, the air so damp and close that moisture collected on my skin and beaded on the rungs. I tried to imagine what it must have been like to hide down here in this dark, silent vault of earth and stone, sealed in and praying not to be found. How scared they must have been. I was hesitant to step down from the ladder onto the hard-packed dirt floor.

"What do you see?" Ben called down.

"Nothing so far," I said. I took my phone out of my pocket and clicked on the light. Black lichen covered the wall in front of me, flaking off like old scabs. I held on to the ladder with one hand and turned to shine the light across the room with the other. I could make out the far wall, maybe ten feet back. Lichen crusting the stone. Chunks of crumbled mortar on the ground. I swept the light to my left and yelped, dropping the phone. The light had caught on something in the far corner. It had looked like someone was standing there. I froze, my heart juddering.

"Arden?" The phone had landed with the light facing down, and as Ben leaned over the hole to see what was wrong, he blocked out much of the light from above, plunging the room into darkness. My lungs constricted in a sudden flash of claustrophobia, and I couldn't breathe. Dizziness washed over me and I dropped to the floor, scooting away from the corner where I'd seen the figure. The ground was ice-cold, and I had the disconcerting feeling that I was sinking down into it, the opening up above stretching farther and farther away.

Ben disappeared from the hole for a moment and returned with a light of his own, shining it down on me. "What happened? Did you fall?"

I couldn't answer right away. I was wheezing. I snatched up my phone and whipped the light back and forth. Something glinted in the corner, but it wasn't a figure, like I'd thought. Along the seam where the walls met, water seeped through the stone, the light reflecting off it. That was all. Still, I couldn't shake the jittery feeling that I hadn't been alone in the room.

"You're freaking me out. Say something, or I'm coming down to get you."

"I'm coming up." I hurried up the ladder, my heart hammering with the irrational fear that something would reach out and grab my feet, pulling me back down. When I was almost to the top, Ben reached down and helped me out of the hole, kneeling next to me on the floor.

"You're shaking." He held my face in his hands, his eyes lit with concern.

"I thought I saw something, and I panicked. I was just scaring myself. There's nothing down there."

"Breathe," he said, taking my hands. We knelt on the floor, breathing together until I calmed down, our chests rising and falling in the same rhythm. He was watching me closely, his skin flush with heat despite the chill in the room, his fingers curled around my wrists. I wondered what he saw when he looked at me; if he thought of the old me, the one hardly anyone knew. If he remembered how he had felt at sixteen. I couldn't forget. I leaned forward and kissed him, fiercely, ten years' worth of pent-up longing coursing through me, and he answered without hesitation. I pressed myself against him, inhaling his warm, woodsy scent, and as I slid my hand up to the nape of his neck, I felt him go still. It happened quickly, as though his mind had caught up to what his body was doing and put a stop to it. He retreated, gently, his fingers lingering on my cheek for a moment. I could tell, as soon as it was over, that it wouldn't happen again.

"I'm sorry," I said. I was sorry, but I didn't regret it. I could stop wondering, now, if there was a chance that Ben and I could be together. It was better to know.

"Don't be," he said. "It wasn't just you." We sat together on the floor, enough space between us for someone else to sit there. "It was selfish of me not to talk to you about Courtney right away. I'm sorry for that. But I don't want to mislead you. I'm serious about her, more than I've been about anyone in a long time. I think you'll like her, too, if you give her a chance."

I couldn't deny that Courtney had been perfectly nice when she had spoken to me at the Miller House. Maybe it would be possible to be friends. I wanted to be happy for Ben, and I knew that any lingering attraction I felt for him was part of my disease, nostalgia creating a visceral response to my memories. It was my own fault that things had turned out the way they had. After that last summer, he had written to tell me that he was in love with me. He had made a little comic book, drawing scenes of the two of us over the years: wading through piles of mayflies, doing cannonballs into the pool, sitting cross-legged on the stone floor of the carriage house. *I love you*, the illustrated Ben had said in the last panel. *I always have. I always will.* The bubble drawn next to my mouth was blank, waiting for me to fill it in. I never wrote back.

In the years that followed, I wrote him dozens of letters, letters I tore up and didn't send. I asked if he remembered the night we broke into Arrowood, if he had pushed the pointer on the Ouija board to spell out my name. I told him how I felt when he kissed me for the first time. I told him how much I missed the river, and asked if he still thought of me when the mayflies came. I hadn't kept in touch with Ben, or Lauren, or anyone else. I had let my old friends slip away, and the new ones I made I always kept at a careful distance.

It was too late to tell Ben that I had loved him, too. I had wanted to tell him, back then, but I couldn't. I was waiting for the twins. I had spent my life waiting for them to come back, to catch up to me, not wanting to leave them too far behind. It was my fault that they had been outside alone, my fault that they were taken. Ben's comic book arrived on the anniversary of their disappearance, and I took it as a sign. It didn't feel right to move forward, to be happy and fall in love, to fill in the empty spaces, and so I had stood still and saved their place while the rest of the world moved on.

The night before the open house, I hooked up Dad's old stereo and put on Bing Crosby's *White Christmas*. It was early for Bing, not quite Thanksgiving, though my father would have approved. Arrowood looked much as I remembered it from my parents' long-ago holiday parties, except that I had not hung any mistletoe or bought a twelve-foot spruce. There were garlands on the staircase, bells on the mantels, and mercury glass ornaments on the lopsided artificial tree that a woman from the historical society had loaned me. Nana's antique nativity set was displayed on the table in the hall. Earlier in the day, Mrs. Ferris had carted over six gallons of apple cider, cups, napkins, and several boxes of sugar cookies. *In case you run out,* she said, clearly aware that I'd forgotten about refreshments altogether. She also brought a gift, tucked in a bag of crinkly tissue paper: candles that smelled like pine trees and cinnamon apple pie. Fake holiday scents to disguise an empty house.

I lit the apple pie candle in the foyer, and it smelled enough like hot cider that I could close my eyes and listen to Bing Crosby croon about going home for Christmas and picture my father standing in the doorway, wearing his tweed sport jacket. *Hi, sweetie. Did you see the mistletoe?*

He had been kissing Mrs. Ferris, not for the first time or the last, and my mother had begun to draw into herself. My life had not been perfect before the party, though that was the first time I felt it tilt hard off-center. The loss of the twins may have been our undoing, but we were in trouble long before.

I stepped out into the cold to admire the lights Ben had hung on the house. They wound around the posts and railings and outlined the roof of the porch. On the left side, one strand had come loose and dangled down, too high for me to reach. Mrs. Ferris had noticed, and called me to see if I could have Heaney come fix it. That wasn't going to happen.

I had received another package from the lawyer earlier in the day, erasing all doubt as to what had been going on. There had been no mistakes. I had a stack of signed invoices from Heaney to prove it. He had been charging the trust for things he hadn't done, like a labor-intensive project to replaster all the walls—walls still covered with their original antique wallpaper. I'd left a message with the lawyer to call me back first thing Monday morning.

I stared at the lights, transfixed, my eyes watering in the frigid air. The house was beautiful, and it was all I had left. A collection of stone and wood and glass.

I was still standing on the front walk in my socks and flannel night-gown when headlights spilled into the drive. My face and ears had gone numb, and the bitter wind cut through my gown as though I wore nothing at all.

"Arden?" Heaney called, approaching me in the dark. "You'll freeze out here! What are you doing?"

"Looking at the lights," I said dully.

"I was driving by and noticed that some of them came down. Figured I'd put them back up for you so it'll look good for tomorrow. Why didn't you tell me about the open house? I could have hung the lights for you, helped get things ready. I didn't know until I saw it advertised in the paper." He unzipped his coat and shrugged it off. I stepped back as he tried to wrap it around my shoulders.

"Let's get you inside," he said. "I mean it," he added when I didn't move, taking me by the elbow and guiding me up the steps.

I didn't want to confront Heaney about the trust until I'd talked to the lawyer, but I couldn't continue to have him in my home acting like he belonged here, as though he had somehow replaced my father. I pulled away and turned to face him.

"I got a detailed list of invoices that were paid by the trust," I said. "I know what you were doing."

Heaney froze, and then realization flickered across his face and his eyes widened. "Arden—it's not what you think," he said, his head swiveling side to side.

"You were stealing," I said, backing up to the door and wrapping my hand around the knob. "It's obvious. There was a bill for a new washer and dryer. Did you buy them and return them, and keep the receipt? You went to a lot of effort. Don't try to tell me it was an accident."

Heaney looked stunned. His jaw tightened and he swallowed hard. "I'm so sorry," he said finally. "But you don't understand."

"A woman named Deirdre came looking for you, too. She thought you were Eddie, and that I was your daughter. Did I misunderstand something about that?"

"Arden—"

"Please leave," I said. "Please."

I didn't wait to see if he did. I yanked the door open and darted inside, locking it behind me and sinking down to the floor. *White Christmas* had finished playing and the house was silent.

CHAPTER 18

My bedroom floor was ankle-deep with discarded outfits. I'd waited until the last minute to get dressed, as usual, and nothing looked or felt right. My go-to green dress was too summery, and I couldn't wear anything that needed ironing, because I still hadn't located the iron. I settled on a conservative wool skirt that hit below the knee, a turtleneck sweater, and faux leather boots that looked nice but pinched my feet. The skirt was tighter than I remembered, the waistband cutting sharply across my stomach, the result of two months of nostalgic eating. I was sweating before I made it down the stairs.

Cookies and cider sat out on a folding table in the center hall, and fires burned in all the fireplaces on the first floor, just as they had at my parents' last Christmas party. A red ribbon stretched across the grand staircase, dangling a DO NOT ENTER sign, and another ribbon draped across the middle of the laundry room in an attempt to prevent guests from climbing the back stairs or falling into the newly opened hole, while still allowing them to get close enough to peer inside.

I was exhausted from trying to get everything ready in time. The house looked cheerful and festive, and it only made me feel more alone. Ben was busy helping his mother next door, and while Josh had insisted on coming, to keep an eye out for any suspicious activity, he hadn't yet arrived.

I walked through the house a final time as the clock ticked toward six, my heart ricocheting in my chest. A line had formed outside the front door. The cellist Mrs. Ferris had arranged from the high school ran her bow back and forth over the strings, but I couldn't hear the music. All I heard was the rush of my pulse and the din of the crowd as I opened the door.

I retreated as people flowed in, stopping only when I could go no farther, backed up against the fireplace in the drawing room. Strangers approached to shake my hand and ask questions about the house. They spoke of the twins among themselves, in whispers, as though they didn't want to offend me by saying their names out loud. One older gentleman in a plaid golf cap gave me a probing look as he shook my hand. It made me uneasy, the way he stared at me, as though he knew me somehow. His voice sounded vaguely familiar, though I couldn't place it, and then he was crowded out of the way as Lauren pushed through to crush me in a hug.

"Surprise!" she said. "Mom bribed me into coming back for the weekend to help out. I had to sneak off for a minute to come see you. Jesus, did she dress you, too? We look like Stepford children." Lauren wore a long plain skirt similar to mine with a matching cardigan set, her hair swept into an elegant French twist, though I could still see streaks of magenta and a new bit of blue and the procession of studs riveting her ears.

"You look nice," I said. "How's the crowd over at your place?"

"Not quite this bad. Ben wanted to come say hi, too, but Mom has him, Courtney, and Dad pouring cocoa and telling everyone in earshot about how one of the Roosevelts spent the night at our house."

"It was Theodore."

Lauren rolled her eyes. "How do you always remember that? I'd better get back before Mom notices I'm gone. Oh, hey, did you know that Midwest Mysteries guy is here? He's right out there in the hall, cornered by some groupies. Looked like he was trying to make his way in here. I can see why you agreed to help him with the book. You didn't tell me he was kind of hot. Something about the gray hair, right?" She winked and pinched my arm, then squeezed back through the crowd.

The man in the golf cap was still standing there, waiting, a wadded-up handkerchief tucked in his palm. His hands were blotched with liver spots. "I'd very much like to continue our conversation," he said. I tried to remember if he'd told me anything more than his name, which I'd already forgotten, and the fact that he'd driven up from Quincy. "Could we talk privately, please?"

I glanced around. People were walking in and out of the room, no one paying particular attention to us. "If you have questions about the house," I said, "there's a detailed write-up in the guidebook." I was growing increasingly hot and uncomfortable in my thick sweater and too-tight skirt, and my skin had begun to itch. I wanted to sneak outside to cool off, and hide on the terrace until everyone had left.

The man edged closer, pushing rimless glasses up on his nose. "I'm not here about the house. I need to talk to you. You never answer your phone."

"What?"

"I've been calling," he said. "I don't know how many times. You never pick up."

All those calls, dead air on the machine. The messages where he'd spoken my name. We were surrounded by people, yet I felt strangely detached, a surge of nauseous unease making me light-headed. Josh had said he wanted to be here to keep an eye on things, in case any Midwest Mysteries fans got out of hand, but I wondered if his real reason had been something darker. If he'd thought that the kidnapper might take this opportunity to revisit the scene of the crime, to meet the girl he left behind. This man had not come here to see the house. He had come to see me.

"Why were you calling me?"

He clenched the handkerchief in his hand. "Let's step outside for a minute, out back, where we can be alone."

"No." It came out louder than I intended, cutting through the chatter in the room and drawing curious stares. I caught sight of a familiar cap, and there was Josh, striding toward us.

"Something wrong?" he asked, casually wedging himself between the man and me.

"No," the man said, clearly agitated. "Please excuse us."

"He says he's the one who's been calling me and hanging up," I said.

"What?" Josh twisted around to face me. "Why didn't you say anything about that before?"

"I wouldn't have hung up," the man said, "if she'd answered the phone."

"Right," Josh said. "Listen, Miss Arrowood is busy right now hosting this open house, so it's not the best time to bother her. I'm Josh Kyle, from Midwest Mysteries." He reached out and the man reluctantly shook his hand. "Let's get you something to drink and then you can talk to her in a bit." He put his hand on the man's shoulder and guided him out of the room, turning to shoot me a quick reassuring glance before they disappeared into the hall.

By the time Josh came back, the cookies had all been eaten, the fires had died down, and the high school girl was preparing to pack up her cello. I felt like I had been up for days, a tension headache gnawing at the inside of my skull.

"I had my cousin down at the station check him out," Josh said. "He's who he says he is."

"And who's that?"

"A retired minister from Quincy. He was your dad's sponsor. Some twelve-step program for gambling."

"What did he want?"

"To talk to you," he said. "He didn't want to stick around, though, after we left the station. I'm afraid we rattled him a bit, but I thought it was better to get the police involved and make sure he wasn't a threat. He gave me a message for you." He adjusted his cap, his fingers brushing over the spot where the thread embroidering the Midwest Mysteries logo had begun to fray.

"He wanted to tell you that your dad's greatest regret in life was not being there for his kids. That was told to him in confidence, but he felt like your dad would have wanted you to know. He thought, in time, that Eddie would have come to tell you that himself—he wanted to make amends."

I wondered if my dad had come up with that on his own, or if he'd had to fill out a worksheet for the twelve-step program and when it came to listing regrets he'd checked off all the most common ones. At Dad's funeral, I was surprised when the priest said that "Amazing Grace" was my father's favorite song. It made me wonder if there was a part of my father that I hadn't known, if he had sought grace and redemption, and found it. I later learned from my mother that it was all part of the prepaid funeral plan Granddad had forced both of them to complete years before. It asked which hymn you wanted played at your funeral, and when my dad said he didn't care, the planner defaulted to the most popular one. The same with the poem printed on the program, which I'd seen on so many others, at so many funerals, that it offered no comfort: *Do not stand at my grave and weep. I am not there; I do not sleep.* I knew most of it by heart.

Josh smiled apologetically. "I hate to do this, but I have to run. I agreed to meet up with a group of people from the website. I'd cancel, but it was already arranged, and some of them traveled—"

"It's all right," I said. "We're all finished here." I was disappointed, though. I had thought he might want to stay and talk. I wanted to tell him about Heaney, but it could wait for another time.

Josh walked away with his head down and his hands in his pockets. A pair of volunteers from the historical society stopped by to sweep for stragglers and escort them out, and once the door closed behind them, I blew out all the candles and sank down onto the stairs, completely drained. I wanted to strip off my uncomfortable clothes and fall into bed, to sleep without remembering my dreams. Before I could work up the energy to climb the stairs, I heard a soft knocking at the door and went to open it, thinking that someone had left a jacket behind, or maybe Josh or Lauren had decided to come back.

"Hi, Arden." Heaney stood on the porch with a bundle cradled in one arm, just beyond the sallow glow of the porch light.

"I don't think it's a good idea for you to be here," I said.

He sighed. "I am so sorry, I can't say it enough times. I know you want me gone, but before I go, there's something I have to tell you, something you deserve to know." He handed me the bundle he'd been holding. It was a stack of envelopes with my name in each upper-left corner. They were all addressed to my sisters at 635 Grand Avenue. My letters to Violet and Tabitha, the ones I had mailed to Arrowood. I remembered the one I had inexplicably found in my room upstairs, and wondered if he had lost it there, if he had lain in my bed and read all those letters, all my private confessions, over the years. I felt like I might throw up.

"I want you to understand why I did what I did," Heaney said. "I should have told you sooner, but I promised I wouldn't."

"Promised who?"

"Eddie. Your dad."

At my back I felt the warmth and brightness of the house with its Christmas decorations and candles and the lingering scent of cinnamon and apples. It was false, all of it, the illusion of cheer in an empty house. I looked at Heaney's anguished face, and beyond, into the black, frigid night.

"Can I please come in?" he asked.

I didn't move from the doorway. I couldn't take my eyes off the letters, my handwriting evolving from block print to sloppy cursive. The envelopes were well worn, the edges soft; they had all been opened, the letters unfolded and refolded over and over, the contents examined again and again.

"You read my letters."

"Yes," he said. "I was just curious, at first, why you were writing to them, sending letters here. And then you started writing about your mother, how she was doing, how she was struggling. You wrote about your father. His gambling problems, the scams he was running. And I got to know you. I know what you want more than anything else. And I see it now, what it's done to you, all this time, not knowing. I can help you." Heaney cleared his throat. "I know where the twins are."

The wind sucked at the chimneys, howling softly, embers snapping. Heaney's words jumbled in my head, as though he spoke a foreign language and parts of speech needed to be rearranged, verbs properly conjugated before they could be translated into something sensible. "What do you mean, you know where they are?"

"They . . . their remains. I know where they're buried."

Frost spread through my veins, my chest, crystallized in the hollows of my heart. "You . . . ?"

He shook his head. "No! No. I had nothing to do with it. I found them."

I took a step backward and forced myself to breathe. "If you know, and you had nothing to do with it, then why didn't you say something sooner? Why didn't you call the police?"

His eyelid twitched and fluttered in a series of tiny spasms. "Your father paid me not to. He made me promise I'd never tell anyone, especially not you, and I thought maybe it was better that way, that you and your mother could still think they were alive."

"My dad? Is that how you got his watch, the one you said you bought? He gave it to you as payment?"

"Yes, but that wasn't enough. Eddie got away with whatever he wanted, his whole life. He ruined things for me. He hurt your mother. I know he hurt you, too. He scammed people for a living. I wanted him to pay, for once. He didn't have the money, though, or at least that's what he said—but he knew a way to skim off the trust. He knew how to do it so I wouldn't get caught."

I understood, in a way. I had some idea how he felt, missing out on the life he had wanted, the one he thought he deserved. He'd been a surrogate son to my grandparents, practically living in the house, hoping to marry my mother. In his eyes, my father had robbed him of that, and he wanted to get some of it back. But he had taken it to grotesque lengths.

He watched me uneasily. "I'm not proud of it, Arden. At the time, I was only thinking about getting back at Eddie."

I wondered if Heaney was making the whole thing up, though part of me thought he might be telling the truth. "Did he tell you what happened to them?"

"No. I don't know."

"Where are they? How did you find them?"

"I'll explain everything." He hesitated, his hand slipping out of his pocket and pushing his staticky hair back from his forehead. "If you agree not to turn me in for stealing from the trust. You haven't talked to the lawyer yet, have you?"

I started to shake my head, and then stopped, not sure I should tell him anything. I had left a message for the lawyer to call me, but I hadn't mentioned Heaney.

"I'd pay back the money if I could," he continued, "but I can't. So this is how I'll pay you. I'll show you where they are, and you won't have to see me ever again, and that'll be the end of it. Do we have a deal?"

I didn't plan to let him get away with robbing the trust, but I would have told him anything to find out where my sisters were. "Okay," I said. "Deal. Tell me where they are."

"I'll show you. Get your coat, we can go now."

"Now? You expect me to go somewhere with you, alone, in the dark? Why not wait until morning?"

He exhaled with force, his breath fogging up in the cold. "There's nothing left for me here, after this. I'm leaving town tonight. If you want to know, this is your only chance."

"At least tell me where we're going," I hedged. If I could get enough information out of him, maybe I could find them on my own.

"Out on the river," he said.

He had a cabin on Little Belle Isle; that would be the obvious place to look. The island could be searched with cadaver dogs. Unless I was wrong. There were other islands. Other hiding places.

"I want to bring someone with me," I said.

Heaney sighed. His gaze shifted to either side of the porch and then back to me. "Fine, but we need to get going."

I hadn't expected him to agree to it, but if he was willing to let Josh come along, it was possible that he was telling the truth, that he was going to take me to the twins.

"Let me call him. I'll grab my phone." I turned away from the door and walked two steps before Heaney slammed into me from behind.

The gravel parking lot next to the marina was empty except for Heaney's truck, and only two other boats nestled at the covered dock. They would have to be hauled out for storage soon, before the river began to freeze. I lay on the bench seat in Heaney's Bayliner, a boat similar in style to the *Ruby Slipper*, my wrists and ankles bound and my head throbbing where it had smacked into the floor back at Arrowood. The late November wind burrowed under my clothes. There was nothing around for miles, as far as I could tell, but the moonlit river and the harvested fields and the narrow farm road that had brought us here. Heaney had kindly taken the rag out of my mouth, because now it didn't matter if I screamed.

I shivered as Heaney untied the last rope that tethered the boat to the dock, fear scuttling up my spine like a leggy insect. He pumped the throttle, flipped a switch, turned the key, and then eased us out of the slip and into the current. Maybe ten or fifteen minutes passed before the boat slowed, and when I craned my neck I could see part of Little Belle, a dark void on the gleaming water. My hands and face were freezing, the beginnings of an earache tunneling inside my already aching skull.

Heaney pulled up close to the dock and secured one of the ropes, and then he hauled me up over his shoulder and climbed out. There were no other boats here, no lights, no people. It was quiet except for the wind sifting through the weeds and the leafless trees. Like most of the river islands, it was abandoned for the winter. The only way out was in Heaney's boat, and the keys were in his pocket.

Heaney carried me down a dirt path into the trees and then gently set me on my feet. My legs buckled and I fell to my knees. I was still woozy. He knelt down beside me. "Do you think you can walk if I untie your ankles?"

I clenched my teeth and nodded. He cut the cord with a pocket-knife and pulled a flashlight out of his coat pocket. He kept one hand around my wrist as we walked, and held the flashlight with the other.

The woods thinned and we came to a stilted cabin with a deck on the upper level, the lower level enclosed with weathered plywood. A padlock hung on the door beneath the deck.

"Did your dad ever tell you he had a place out here?" Heaney asked, holding the light under his arm as he dug out his keys.

He hadn't. Another secret kept. I supposed the cabin was Heaney's now, like so many other things that had been my father's.

Once inside, Heaney shined the light around. We were in a win-dowless storage area beneath the cabin. Half the floor was concrete, the rest dirt. A rusted chest freezer sat along one wall next to a genera-tor, the shelves above it crowded with fishing poles, tackle boxes, nets, and coolers.

He set the flashlight down on top of the freezer, illuminating the door and a set of steps leading up. I wondered if this lower level of the cabin flooded every spring when the rains came and the river rose, if water saturated the dirt floor and turned it to mud.

"We could go upstairs," Heaney said. "It's more comfortable up there. I've got an oil lamp." I slumped to the floor. My nose wouldn't stop running and I wiped it on my coat sleeve. Heaney hesitated at the foot of the stairs, eyeing a shovel that leaned in the corner, his brows knitting together.

My throat was too dry, and it was hard to swallow. "Can you untie my hands?" I asked. "My wrists hurt." He hesitated, thinking about it, and then got out his knife and sliced through the cord. We both knew that there was nowhere for me to go, whether or not my hands were free.

"Why did you bring me here?"

He shook his head. "I didn't know what else to do. I knew you wouldn't just forget about the trust. If I let you go, I'd lose everything, and I didn't want to go through that again." He rubbed his palm over the back of his neck. "I always thought I'd have kids, you know? A family. Your mother and I. She'd promised we would someday. I still thought we'd end up together, even after she met Eddie. I figured if I was patient, she'd get sick of the way he treated her and come back to me. She did come to me, a few times, when she found out he was cheating on her with Julia. I offered to take care of Eddie for her, but she didn't want me to. She was just leading me on, trying to get back at him, make him jealous."

He smiled bleakly. "I envied your dad, how everything came so easy for him. He didn't appreciate what he had. I almost felt like I'd traded places with him there toward the end—I had nearly everything he'd let go of. Including you." He took a deep breath. "I wish we could put things back how they were, but I don't think we can ever go back."

Moonlight showed through a gap between the door and the frame. The door wasn't locked, and I wondered if I might be able to push past him and get out, if there was any chance I could outrun him. Still, I wouldn't have the boat key. Maybe, though, if I had enough of a head start, I could untie the boat and let it drift into the channel, escaping the island and leaving Heaney stranded.

I carefully rose to my feet, unsteady. "We *can* go back," I said, knowing what a lie it was. As much as I longed to live in it, the past was dead space, flat and airless. We couldn't go back. Each breath dragged us forward into a raw, new moment in time. "I forgive you. It's just money. It doesn't matter. Let's go back home. We can work this out."

He pressed his palms to his temples. "I need to think for a minute."

"Do you really know where Violet and Tabitha are?" I asked, taking a step toward him. "Or did you just make that up to get me here?"

He nodded slowly, looking weary and distracted, his shoulders sinking as he exhaled. "Back when I first started working at Arrowood, about ten years ago, there was a problem with the boiler down in the basement, just like I told you. I had to replace some pipes, and that's how I found the hidden room under the laundry. Only it wasn't empty when I opened it up. There was a tiny sliver of tarp sticking up out of the ground—wouldn't have seen it if I hadn't looked close. I had a bad feeling, and it didn't take much work to find what was under there. I knew what it meant, that the girls were there, buried in the house, and I realized I finally had a chance to put Eddie in his place. I got ahold of him, and sure enough, he was willing to pay a price to keep it quiet."

Was that when my father had called Julia Ferris to borrow money? He had told her it was for an investment, and in a way it was. An investment in Heaney's silence. I glanced furtively at the door, and the shovel next to it, and Heaney moved closer.

"Let's go back now," I said.

"And call it even."

"Yes."

He chuckled. "I know it doesn't work that way."

"People will notice if I'm not back. They'll figure out what happened."

He shook his head. "Are you sure? I was thinking. Your arm, those scars—that was no accident. I'm not the only one who's noticed. People talk. Whoever comes looking for you'll find Arrowood locked up tight, no sign of a struggle. They'll see all those sad letters you wrote to your sisters. Maybe they'll think you just couldn't take it, being back here—the twins' birthday coming up, the holidays, and you all alone in that empty house thinking about everything you lost. They might wonder if you walked down to the river and threw yourself in."

"No. They'll think it was someone I knew. Someone with a key to the house."

He took another step, closing the gap between us, and I lunged for the shovel. Heaney smashed his fist into the side of my head. I crumpled to the floor, pain vibrating through my jaw and down my spine, as though he'd knocked something out of alignment. I'd never been struck like that before. When I looked up at him, he was rubbing his knuckles, a dazed expression on his face as though he wasn't sure what he had done.

"I'm sorry," he breathed. "I didn't want to hurt you."

I touched my head where he'd hit me, a hard knot already rising beneath the skin. Heaney kept his eyes on me as he backed up to the door and pushed it all the way shut. I curled onto my side, whimpering. It was difficult to focus with the bright pain scything through my skull. Each breath hurt my chest. I thought of the pictures that would be shown on the news along with the story of my disappearance, my expression grim and unsmiling, just as I'd wanted.

He didn't know it, but Heaney had guessed the truth about my scars. Maybe he knew me better than anyone, after all, from reading and rereading all my personal letters, my darkest, most private thoughts. I hadn't told anyone what had really happened the night I broke into Dr. Endicott's house. After I had shattered the window and accidentally sliced up my arm, I had stood there, holding the poem, watching my blood drip down onto the floor. In that moment, it struck me how wrong it felt to be there. I had never belonged at Dr. Endicott's, or in my apartment, or at the house Mom shared with Gary, or in any of the temporary homes my father had dragged us to. I'd felt at home in only one place, a place I thought I couldn't go back to. For years, I didn't care if I died, which was not the same as being suicidal. I had never slipped over the threshold of wanting to kill myself. In that moment, though, in Dr. Endicott's basement, living suddenly became unbearable. I had picked up a shard of glass, gouged it into my flesh, and cut deeper, deeper, following the vein.

Heaney nervously rummaged around the shelves, dropping things into a pile. I spied a clump of tangled fishing line. He hadn't brought me here with a clear plan; whatever he was doing, he hadn't thought it all the way through. He only knew that we had passed the point where it would be possible for both of us to leave the island. I tried to remember the prayer to Saint Jude, the patron saint of lost causes, whose help would often arrive at the eleventh hour, but instead, Madame Yvonne's words hovered in my mind. I hadn't paid much attention to what she'd said about the Wheel of Fortune card, which had seemed the least important one at the time, though it resonated now. *The Wheel of Fortune is unpredictable. It's a turning point. Everything rests on the way the Wheel turns, and your reaction to it. You can't choose your fate, but you can choose how to respond.* The wheel had spun and landed me here with Heaney, but that wasn't supposed to be the end. It was meant to be a crossroads. I had to make a choice.

Heaney had his back to me, as though he was no longer worried that I'd try to get away. He squatted down to pick up the items he'd gathered, and I lurched forward, knocking the flashlight back behind the freezer, nearly blacking out the room.

"Goddamnit!" Heaney hissed. In the moments before our eyes could adjust to the darkness, I ran blindly in the direction of the door. Heaney barreled into me and knocked me back against the stairs, and I heard the shovel clatter to the floor. My head was swimming. He grabbed at my legs, grunting, and I kicked as hard as I could, clipping him in the face. I squirmed backward, but he caught me at the knees as I tried to get up. My fingers scrabbled over the concrete seeking the shovel, and I latched on to it as Heaney yanked me toward him. I struggled, unable to wrench my legs away, and I knew it would be harder to fight if he managed to straddle me and pin me down. Time had run out, and I had no leverage to swing the shovel, so I clutched its metal head in my hands and smashed it into Heaney as hard as I could.

He howled and I struck him again, feeling his grip loosen as he recoiled and tried to grab the shovel from me. I scrambled to my feet and started swinging, the blade coming down on him over and over, until he quit fighting, and then I swung again. I would not be the girl who only hit hard enough to gain a head start. I had to be sure that I could beat him to the boat.

When I stopped, the room was still, and I was dizzy. I had screamed my throat raw, and my ears were ringing. Heaney made a gurgling noise, and I knew that he was breathing. I wanted to get out of the cabin and away from him, but first I had to kneel down and dig through his pockets to retrieve the keys, expecting at any moment that he might reach out and grab me. I staggered out into the night, taking the shovel with me, and ran down the dirt path until it emerged from the woods. Lights glittered over on the mainland, signs of life beyond the empty fields. I jogged to the end of the dock, sweating despite the cold, and untied the boat with shaking hands. I used the shovel to push off and then heaved it out into the channel.

The boat drifted lazily into the current and I fumbled the key into the ignition, twisting hard and begging it to start. The engine cranked but didn't turn. I tried to focus, to remember what Heaney had done, but instead I thought of my father, of all the times I had sat on his lap as he drove the *Ruby Slipper*. He'd position my hands on the wheel and the throttle and place his hands on top of mine so that I could help him drive. I could hear his voice as clearly now as if he spoke over the water. *Nothing to it, kid. Just like that.*

My breath puffed out in white clouds, and low waves slapped the sides of the boat as Little Belle gradually slid past. I told myself that there was no need to panic. I was safer in the boat, away from the island, away from Heaney. This time, I pumped the throttle before turning the key, and the engine rumbled. I eased the shift lever forward and steered the boat toward shore.

I worried that I would miss the unlit marina, so I edged the Bayliner as close to land as I dared and moved at a crawl. When it finally came into view, I did my best to maneuver toward the dock, but as I focused all my effort on steering, I neglected to pull back on the throttle and rammed into the slip. I leaned out and clawed at the dock, grabbing hold of a cleat and pulling myself out without bothering to tie up the boat.

My fingers were numb, and I kept dropping the keys as I fumbled my way into Heaney's truck. Once inside, I locked the doors and huddled in the driver's seat, my breath shushing in and out, my entire body shaking. I drove down the gravel road in what I hoped was the right direction, glancing obsessively in the rearview mirror, as though Heaney might appear at any moment in the darkness behind me.

Was it true that he'd found the twins' remains in the basement room and blackmailed my father? He had told me those things thinking that I wouldn't leave the island, so there was no reason for him to lie. What would it mean, if I found my sisters there? That I had been terribly wrong about so many things. That my father had known they were dead all along, and he knew who had killed them. It would be one answer out of countless questions, the end of one kind of grief and the start of another.

I parked Heaney's truck down the block from Arrowood and used his keys to let myself in through the laundry room. The house still smelled faintly of apple pie, thanks to Mrs. Ferris's candles. The first thing I did was run hot water in the laundry sink to thaw out my trembling hands, and then I found my phone and dialed 911.

"There's been an accident on Little Belle Isle," I said. "A man attacked me—his name is Dick Heaney. I fought him off, and I think I might have hurt him. It was self-defense." I hung up before the operator could ask me any questions. I knew I would have to go to the station and talk to the police—and it probably wouldn't look good that I hadn't done so right away—but it would have to wait.

From the utility closet, I retrieved one of the trowels that Heaney and I had used to plant flower bulbs. I tossed it down the hole into the hidden room and climbed down after it, lighting the way with my phone. I knew where to dig, in the far corner where the water dripped down the wall. I knelt and ran my hands over the smooth dirt floor, the cold slowly seeping through my clothing, into my skin, chilling my knees and fingertips. I nosed the trowel into the hard ground and scraped up a furrow of earth. I continued, dissecting the floor in careful layers, both fearful and hopeful that something would surface.

Cold sweat tracked down my scalp as I uncovered the eroded edge of a thin plastic tarp. I dropped the trowel and dug with my bare hands, my fingernails clawing the dirt until I exposed a broad swath of the plastic. It lay in tatters, disintegrating as I tried to peel it away. At first I thought there was nothing beneath it, but as I felt around, my hand touched something solid in the dirt, a dome like a turtle shell. One, and then another. Two small skulls. I closed my eyes, unwilling to see.

When I was hospitalized after my accident, a nurse had started an IV antibiotic that I was unknowingly allergic to. I'd felt a sharp pain in the back of my hand where the needle bit in, and a tingling in my arm as the drug flowed into my veins. There was an icy sensation as it reached my heart and fluttered across my chest, my blood pressure plummeting and the edges of my vision turning black and curling up like a photograph that had been set on fire. I was going into shock. I felt the same way now, the ice in my chest, the overwhelming urge to vomit.

My sisters were here, in this hidden room. For all the years I'd waited for them, they had lain side by side in the dark, cold earth. They had not grown up. They had not left this house. They had been here, beneath us, until my father took my mother and me away from Arrowood and left the twins behind. I had finally found them, what remained of my beautiful sisters. I withdrew my hand from the smooth curve of bone, and as I got to my feet, I noticed a small object that had been dislodged from the dirt. A button. I slipped it into my skirt pocket, then climbed out of the hole, my limbs weak, my fingers struggling to grip the rungs and haul myself up. I gathered my things and hurried out the door.

CHAPTER 19

Once the adrenaline wore off, I felt the full extent of my injuries. I stopped at a Break Time in Cedar Rapids and bought their entire supply of tiny packets of Advil. The fluorescent lights buzzed like angry hornets in the otherwise silent store, and the guy behind the register eyed me warily as he rang up my coffee and pills and beef jerky, setting my change on the counter to avoid contact with my filthy, outstretched hand.

I locked myself in the restroom, soaking paper towels in the sink and scrubbing at the dirt that streaked my face and caked my fingernails. There was a cut on my forehead. My hair was tangled and my eyes bloodshot, the side of my face where Heaney had struck me swollen and beginning to bruise. I looked like I'd clawed my way out of a grave.

Back in the car, I tore open two foil packets of Advil and washed the pills down with scorched coffee. I checked the map, the red and blue highways branching out like a network of arteries and veins, and continued north, toward Minnesota, the road stretching into darkness beyond my headlights. If Heaney was telling the truth, my father had known that the twins were buried in the basement of Arrowood. If my father knew, there was a chance my mother knew, too, and she was the only one left alive who could tell me what had really happened.

The sun rose as I neared Rochester, revealing a slab of low gray clouds. I exited the highway and wove through a labyrinth of suburban streets to reach the upscale subdivision where Mom and Gary lived. Their house sat at the end of a cul-de-sac, the yard edged with spindly, perfectly spaced maples that had been planted when the house was built five years before. It would take five more years for them to grow above the roofline. Not a single dead leaf blemished the lawn; Gary paid a service to suck them all up every fall, to apply mulch to precisely delineated areas, to exterminate every last dandelion. Like most homes in the neighborhood, the brick ranch's most prominent architectural feature was a protruding three-car garage. Inside, every surface, from walls to floors to counters to woodwork, was a neutral shade of brown. No hundred-year-old wallpaper, no stained-glass windows, no ceilings clad in decorative pressed tin. It was exactly what my mother had longed for, a house with no history. She had wanted to start someplace fresh, with no reminders of the past.

It was just shy of eight when I rang the bell. An enormous wreath hung on the front door, with little pinecones spelling out GIVE THANKS.

When the door opened, my mother stood there in her velour robe and slippers, confusion twisting her face.

"Arden? Dear Lord! What are you doing here? What happened to you?"

After making me take off my filthy boots, she led me into the living room, which, like the rest of the house, was decorated to Gary's taste. Or maybe it was my mother's taste, too, now that she was Gary's wife. Fake flowers. Puffy La-Z-Boy recliners. An assortment of pillows and plaques instructing you to COUNT YOUR BLESSINGS and PRAISE THE LORD and LIVE, LAUGH, LOVE.

"Sit down," she said, grabbing the phone off the coffee table. "Were you in an accident? Gary's already left for the early service. I can call him back here."

"No," I croaked. "It's better if he's not here. I need to talk to you."

She set down the phone, her forehead wrinkling. It had been a long time since I'd seen her without the makeup and hairspray and bright clothing that I associated with her life with Gary. She looked tired and uncertain, tiny red veins marbling her nose and cheeks. I remembered her slicing through the wake of the *Ruby Slipper* on skis, never once falling. My mother, before the twins disappeared, before she knew about my father and Mrs. Ferris, before life disappointed her in too many ways, was a different person. We all were.

Garbled voices drifted in from the TV in the kitchen. The Home Shopping Network. "Well, what is it, Arden? What kind of trouble are you in now?"

On the drive up, I'd tried to figure out what to say, but now the words wouldn't come. I took the button from my pocket and held it out to her, dropping it into her palm. She stared at it for a moment, and then her hand started to shake as she realized what it was. A little button shaped like a duck, from one of the blouses Grammy had made for the twins. The blouses they'd been wearing that day.

"Where did you get that?" she asked.

"Arrowood."

One hand closed around the button and the other clamped over her mouth.

"Mom?"

She sank down onto the overstuffed couch, her eyes pinched shut.

"They're dead." I didn't want to believe the words as I spoke them, though they were undeniable as a key turning in a lock, the final click of a latch as it snaps into place.

"Arden—"

"Did you know?" I asked, my voice breaking. "That they were there, in the house, all along?"

My mother's body shuddered, like something inside her was trying to get out. Tears coursed down her face and she didn't wipe them away.

"Did you know?" I asked again. She didn't answer. Numbness spread out from my chest. My arms and legs were tingling. "Please tell me." I wanted her to say no, that she had been in the dark, like me, that she had fallen apart from the pain of not knowing, and that the news I had given her was a horrible, unbearable shock.

She looked me in the eye. "I'm sorry, Arden."

There was a lag between hearing her words and understanding. "What happened? Who . . . ?" She didn't answer, and my throat dried up, the words coming out like bits of gravel. "Was it you, or him?"

She shook her head in slow motion. "I know you're confused, but you have to know that your father and I would never have hurt the girls. We loved them so, so much. You know that." She scooted over next to me, her icy hands settling on top of mine. I didn't want her touching me, but I couldn't make myself pull away.

"What do you remember from that day, Arden?"

"You know what I remember."

"Tell me. Please."

I gritted my teeth and tried to breathe slowly. "We were playing outside," I said. "I left them for a minute, to pick dandelions in the backyard, and when I came back, they were gone. The gold car was driving away. I ran after it."

"That's right," she said. "That's what happened. But they weren't . . . they weren't in the car." She paused for a moment, studying my face. "I came out to get them. They were tired and cranky and covered in grape juice. I called for you when I brought them in, but with all the noise next door, you must not have heard."

My head buzzed and my pulse accelerated. I remembered the landscapers mowing and weed-eating at the Ferrises'. The twins' little hands, sticky, stained with juice.

"I put them in the tub, and not long after, you came running up the stairs, calling for me, hysterical. Your eyes got so wide when you saw the twins. You told me about them disappearing, about seeing them in the gold car. It was just a mistake. Then the phone rang, and I asked you to keep an eye on your sisters for one minute while I answered it. It was Eddie, telling me he'd be late getting home. I knew he was with her—with Julia—and I was furious. I'd found out earlier that morning that he'd drained our savings account without telling me."

My mother had been livid at the bank that day, though I hadn't known why. My sisters and I were more concerned with the Tootsie Pops we'd received from the teller.

"I hollered for you to drain the tub and get towels for the twins, and then I went into the bedroom to talk to your father. I didn't want to let him off the phone until he agreed to come home and explain what he'd done with our money, and I didn't want you girls to hear us fighting. You heard me yelling anyway and got worried and came to check on me. I told you to stay with your sisters, get them dried off, that I'd be right out."

I'd heard those words plenty of times from my mother back then, that she'd be right there, that she'd get out of bed or fix us lunch or play Candy Land or unstrap the twins from their high chairs. Instead, I'd hear the rattle of her pill bottles and find her sitting wherever we'd left her, staring at the wall.

"I don't know how long I was on the phone. When I opened the door, you were still there, in the hallway. You'd fallen asleep on the floor, waiting for me. You'd been sick the night before, remember? You'd been up late. You were tired and feverish. I hurried back to the bathroom to look for the twins, and right away I saw the water. You hadn't drained it out like I'd asked you to. It was spilling over the sides of the tub, and there were mounds of bubbles. When I left you with the girls, the water was only a few inches deep. I always hated those old claw-foot tubs—they're too deep, too slippery. There's nothing to grab hold of."

I scrunched my eyes shut and folded myself over so my head rested on my knees, struggling to dredge up a memory that wasn't there. Every single time the twins took a bath, they begged for more Mr. Bubble. You had to add water to make it foam, but my mother was always the one to do it; I hadn't been allowed. Had I not listened when my mother told me to drain the tub, or had I not heard? Was it possible that I had wanted to please the twins, that I'd given in to a request for more bubbles, and in doing so caused them to drown? I couldn't remember. When I tried to return to that day in my mind, I still saw the gold car, the one that had obsessed me for nearly twenty years, the one I now knew had nothing to do with my sisters after all.

"It was too late. I took them out of the water and held them. It was the worst moment of my life, and it didn't feel real. Your father came home and tried to blame me—he accused me of drowning them to punish him somehow. Deep down, though, he knew it wasn't true. He felt guilty because he should have been there. If he'd been home, if we hadn't been fighting, it wouldn't have happened."

My mother kept talking, her voice blending in with the chatter from the TV. The truth was still seeping in, curdling inside me. I should have known, should have felt it. All the water in the house, leaking, dripping, overflowing. They'd been trying to tell me and I hadn't understood. They had drowned.

"You heard us and woke up, and came running down the hall. Your father and I were both crying, and you said, 'What's wrong, Daddy?' and he said, 'The twins are gone.' Your face just crumpled. You told him all about the gold car that had driven away with them. You said you had a dream that it hadn't really happened, that they were home safe in the bath, and you wished you hadn't woken up. He told you it was a fever dream."

Like a trail of gasoline ignited by a flame, it zipped back to me. The dream I had, that the twins were home safe after all, the dream that had felt so real that I often replayed it in my mind to feel again that deep sense of relief, if only for a moment—it wasn't a dream but a memory.

I sat up, and my mother let go of my hands. She was staring at the wall, at an amateurish painting of a shepherd with a lamb. The perspective was off, the figures out of proportion. It was signed in block letters, GARY.

"I took you to our bedroom and put on a movie and told you to rest," she continued. "Your father and I both agreed. We dressed Violet and Tabitha in the clothes they'd been wearing that day, and we buried them in the basement, in a hidden place that nobody knew about, where they wouldn't be found."

I imagined my parents rushing to dress them, grabbing a little white shirt off the floor, a button becoming wedged behind one of the tub's clawed feet.

"It was the hardest thing either of us had ever done. Grammy came over to get you, and we called the police. We told them what you had seen, and when they talked to you, you told the same story, too. You weren't lying—you were scared and confused and your mind was just filling in the blanks, trying to come up with something that made sense."

I remembered, all those years ago, how she had stopped washing our clothes, how I had dug through my overflowing hamper each morning to get dressed for school. She had avoided the laundry room, knowing what lay beneath the floor. She had never again helped me with a bath, in the claw-foot tub or any other.

"It was Heaney who told me," I said. "He found them. He claimed Dad paid him to keep quiet." I didn't tell her what Heaney had done, and what I had done to him. I wondered if he was still on the island, if he was still alive.

My mother sighed. Her face was dry; she was done crying. "Arden, I was stuck, like you, for a long time," she said, her voice soft. "It doesn't get you anywhere. Like it or not, you've got to find a way to move on."

"Why didn't you tell me? Why didn't you tell the police?"

"Nothing could change what had happened, so what did it matter?"

"What about Singer? You let him take the blame, watched his life get torn apart when you knew he was innocent?"

"We didn't mean for that to happen. We didn't know if there really was a gold car, or if they'd find it. There was no evidence against him, no charges filed. He was never even arrested."

"You could have told the truth," I said. "That it was an accident, that they drowned in the tub."

"Then what?" she said, her eyes searching mine. "Would you have been better off knowing that? That you were responsible? We were trying to protect you. What do you think would have happened if we'd told the truth? You could have been taken away from us. We might have been prosecuted. And none of that would bring them back!"

My mother spoke as though she bore no responsibility, as though all the blame fell to me. She claimed she'd hidden the truth to protect me, but surely she didn't believe that. She'd been protecting herself; she never should have left us alone. Yet I did feel responsible.

I had only been a child myself, but I had known better than to leave them in the bath. Even at eight years old I had been my sisters' fail-safe, compensating for our parents' inattention. I made snacks for them when they were hungry. Kept them from falling down the stairs. Turned off the stove when Mom left the gas burning all day. I had promised to watch over Violet and Tabitha, to keep them safe, and I had failed. I didn't know how I could live with that.

Would it have been any different, any better, had I known the truth from the beginning? If everyone had?

"Arden!" my mother shrieked as I fled out the door, clutching my muddy boots. "Come back here!"

Snow had started to fall while I was in the house, and the windshield was coated with downy flakes. I started the car and stomped on the gas, my hands shaking on the steering wheel and tears blurring my vision. I caught a glimpse of my mother in the rearview mirror, her mouth wide open, still yelling, though I could no longer hear her. I switched off the ringer on my phone in case she tried to call.

I drove past the outskirts of town and pulled over on an empty stretch of road. Weeds rustled around me in the bitter wind as I bent over and retched. My legs were too weak to carry me back to the car, so I crawled up the slope above the ditch and rolled onto my back. The sky was pale, nearly colorless, the snowflakes blowing in every direction, like those in a shaken snow globe. I lay there, the cold working into me from the ground below and the wind above, until the low whine of an approaching semi urged me up. I didn't want anyone stopping to see if I needed help.

After crossing into Iowa, I parked at a Flying J truck stop in Waterloo and slept in my car with the doors locked and the engine running. When I woke, stiff and hungry, it was well past lunchtime, and I decided to go inside and eat at the restaurant. I sat alone in a red vinyl booth that could have easily held six people, and ordered the lumberjack breakfast. I couldn't remember ever being so thirsty, and the waitress nodded, unfazed, when I requested four drinks: coffee, orange juice, water, Coke.

While I waited for my food to arrive, I pulled out my phone and checked my messages. My mom had called and left a voicemail, which I didn't listen to. Mrs. Ferris had called to remind me to fill out the feedback survey on the open house. There was a flurry of increasingly concerned texts from Ben. *Mom says there's a police car in front of Arrowood . . . everything okay? Hey, if you can, text back and let us know if you're all right, if you need anything. Mom went over to talk to the cops and they wouldn't tell her anything . . . we're all getting worried. I called Lauren and she said she hasn't heard from you, either. Where are you??*

I texted back and told him that there had been a family emergency and I'd had to drive to my mom's unexpectedly. He replied immediately to ask what had happened, and I stared at the blinking cursor, not sure how to respond.

I opened a packet of Advil and swallowed the pills with juice. Another text popped up on my phone as the waitress delivered a platter loaded with pancakes, bacon, hash browns, and scrambled eggs. The message was from Josh. *Where are you? Call me ASAP. They're looking for you.*

The closer I got to Keokuk, the more worried I grew about what would happen upon my return. Had the police figured out that I was the one who had called 911 about Heaney, or had they only gone to my house because Heaney worked there, and his truck was parked nearby? Had he been found alive and taken into custody? What if the police hadn't taken the call seriously, and hadn't sent anyone to Little Belle Isle? Heaney could have called someone to come get him, and he could be looking for me. I didn't regret what I had done to him, though I knew there might be consequences. I was thinking of the woman who went to trial for kicking her attacker in the head more times than were necessary to escape. I had used a shovel. I would tell the truth, that something inside me had shifted, and I had chosen to survive.

I would tell the police, too, about the twins. No one knew the full extent of what had happened except for my mother and me, and I could choose to keep it that way, but after a lifetime of secrets and lies and unanswered questions, I didn't want to hide anything. And there was another reason: Harold Singer deserved to have his name cleared, even if it was far too late to undo the damage that had been done.

I couldn't bring myself to listen to the message my mother had left. I knew she would want me to leave the past buried, and I doubted there was any way to prove, or disprove, her story after all this time. If it was deemed to be an accident, that would likely be the end of it, as the statute of limitations would have run out on anything short of murder, though maybe they would find a way to hold her responsible for all the time and money wasted searching for the twins. There would be news coverage, for sure. There always was when a cold case got cracked, especially one involving missing children. It wouldn't take long, though, for other stories to push it out of the spotlight. Every day, kids disappeared, families were murdered, women escaped from locked rooms after years of indescribable torment. The demise of the Arrowood twins wouldn't hold anyone's attention for long, at least not outside of Keokuk.

It was past dark when I exited the highway at Fort Madison and drove through town to Josh's apartment. I knocked, hoping that he was home. The door opened, and his face flooded with relief.

"Thank God," he said, throwing his arms around me before I could say anything. It hurt my ribs, but I hugged him back. He let go and stared at me with disbelief. "You're okay. Mostly okay," he corrected, taking in my appearance. "Come in. Everyone's been looking for you."

Files were spread out over the coffee table and stacked on the floor, and the apartment smelled like Chinese takeout. He offered me a carton of fried rice. "Are you hungry?" I shook my head. "Here, let me make room." He cleared papers from the couch so I could sit, and fetched me a glass of water.

Josh sat on the floor across from me. "How badly are you hurt?" he asked. "They found blood at the cabin on the island, but neither of you were there—"

"I'm all right," I said. The blood must have been Heaney's. I hadn't been able to tell, in the dark, how badly he was injured. Not badly enough that he couldn't get away, apparently. "I'm just a little banged up."

"I heard on my police scanner last night that officers were dispatched to Little Belle Isle to search for a wounded assault suspect. You know how my ears perk up at things like that." He shot me an apologetic glance. "I don't know all the details, but my cousin Randy called me a few hours ago, when they figured out it was you who made the 911 call. They still hadn't located Heaney. I got ahold of your friend Ben, and asked if he'd heard from you. He said you'd gone to your mom's. Then he warned me to leave you alone, and wouldn't tell me anything else."

"Don't take it personally," I said. "He didn't have anything else to tell."

"He was worried about you. We both were." He was silent for a moment, watching me. "Anyway, when you didn't call, I was hoping it was because you didn't feel like talking to me, and not because Heaney had done something to you."

"I needed time to think." I'd spent my last hours in the car running through the movie in my head. The gold car. The door slamming. My dream about the twins being safe at home. The memories I was looking for weren't there, any lost footage long since swept from the cutting room floor. I couldn't remember pouring the Mr. Bubble or twisting the handles to fill the tub, though that didn't mean it hadn't happened.

If my mother was lying, I would never know, any more than I would recall the truth.

I sipped my water and set it back down. "You said people were looking for me?"

"Yeah. I mean, not like hunting you down. You're not in trouble, that I know of. The police just want to talk to you and find out what happened, make sure you're okay." He thumbed through the stack of folders on the coffee table between us. "I don't understand why Heaney would want to hurt you. What was going on? Why were the two of you out on the river at night? You don't have to tell me if you don't want to, but—what happened, Arden?"

I'd decided, well before I pulled off the highway, that Josh would be the first one I'd tell. I explained what had happened with Heaney, and tried to hold myself together as I told him what I'd found in the basement. The tarp, the two small skulls. The conversation with my mother. When I finished, Josh got up off the floor and came to sit next to me, carefully wrapping first one arm and then the other around my stiff shoulders.

"It wasn't your fault," he murmured, his voice low and soothing, his head tilted against mine. "You know that, right? You were just a kid. She never should have put you in that situation."

Everything I'd been holding back came bursting out, and I wailed into his chest until my throat burned and my tears finally began to slow. I let myself relax against him, let him hold me, and tried to think of nothing more than the intake of breath, the contraction of my heart, the merest elements necessary to survive. When I was ready, I pulled away. "Will you go with me to the police station?"

"I'll go wherever you want," he said. "You shouldn't go anywhere alone, not until they find Heaney."

"Do they think he got off the island? I took his boat, and I didn't see any others at the dock."

"I don't know." He shrugged. "There could have been other boats stored somewhere on the island, I guess. And it's possible that he's still there, but you'd think there'd only be so many places to hide. All I know is that they checked the buildings, and they didn't find him, only that small amount of blood at the cabin."

"Were you surprised?" I asked. "That it wasn't my blood? That I got away?" It had surprised me, the strength of my desire to survive.

"No." He shook his head, and the faintest smile crossed his lips. "Not at all. You're stronger than you think you are." The smile faded. Josh squeezed my hands in his. "They'll find him."

I nodded, and we sat there together in silence until I stopped shaking.

"What's it like?" he asked. "To finally know?"

I couldn't explain what it was like to have an answer that wasn't the one I wanted, to know the real reason I had been left behind. Closure, as I had imagined it, did not exist. I couldn't cauterize my wounds as my mother had done. Closure for me meant moving forward with a cathedral of loss inside my chest. I was no longer waiting for the twins. They were with me because I remembered them, and that had to be enough. What I had done as my eight-year-old self I would have to learn to forgive, though I couldn't fathom how I might begin to do that. My guilt was a hole that gaped wider with each passing moment.

We locked up the apartment and I left my car behind, riding in Josh's van to Keokuk, where we walked into the station together.

CHAPTER 20

I stayed at Josh's place, wearing his flannel pajamas, eating pizza delivered from Sorrento's down the street. He clicked away on his laptop, trying to keep up with the message boards on Midwest Mysteries, while I sat in a chair near the bay window looking out to the street below, where a police car would periodically cruise by. Now that the mystery of the twins' disappearance had been resolved, Josh had abandoned his book about the Arrowoods. There were other stories to write, he said, ones that still needed endings. He'd leave the Arrowood story to me.

A week after Heaney attacked me on Little Belle Isle, I received the call that his body had washed up at the dam, though my wait wasn't over until the autopsy results came back and I learned that he had drowned. I went limp with relief. It wasn't known whether he had drowned accidentally, while swimming back to the mainland in the frigid current, or if he'd taken his own life. Either way, Heaney had walked to shore and entered the water on his own, and there was no indication that the injuries I'd inflicted with the shovel had led to his death.

There was no such relief when it came to the twins. I still couldn't reconcile what I had done. It consumed my waking thoughts and my nightmares as I struggled to understand how I could have turned on the water and left them to die.

I'd barely spoken to my mother since the day I drove up to see her in Minnesota, though I finally listened to the message she had left on my phone after I ran out of her house. She had begged me not to tell anyone about the twins. She feared that she would lose the new life she'd built with Gary, the second chance she'd been given when she was born again. I had doubted from the beginning that my mother was a true believer, certain that she'd embraced faith and forgiveness in only the most self-serving ways, but she clung to Gary and his church, finding strength in them, and they stood by her, unwavering.

Josh had gone to see Singer, who had charged him twice his former rate, claiming he was being courted for interviews by *Inside Edition* and *Dr. Phil*. When Josh asked how it felt to be cleared of any involvement in the twins' disappearance, Singer had said, "Too little, too late," with a few choice curse words thrown in. I wrote him a letter, though I didn't hear back, so I couldn't be sure he read it. He had hinted to Josh that he was considering a lawsuit, though he hadn't figured out on what grounds. I hadn't meant to falsely accuse anyone. It was one more thing that I couldn't undo, that I would have to learn to live with.

Once we knew that Heaney was gone, I returned to Arrowood. The twins were gone, too, their remains sent off for forensic examination before they could be released to me and buried in the Catholic cemetery. I kept the doors of the laundry room and bathroom closed, unable to look at the hole in the floor, or at the claw-foot tub. I tried not to see the news, either, but the story was everywhere, and traffic on Midwest Mysteries hit an all-time high. A lot of people were disturbed by the way my parents had lied to cover up the twins' deaths, and plenty doubted that it was an accident. What made it slightly less painful were the individuals who offered their condolences, strangers who had been haunted by the case and were sorry to learn that my sisters had died.

I was overwhelmed by the reactions in Keokuk. People from the community reached out to me, sending cards, offering prayers, filling my refrigerator with casseroles and homemade pies. Ben came over on my first night back, bringing takeout from Sonic, and we sat together on the leather sofa in the drawing room, talking late into the night, no tension between us, no awkwardness, nothing left unsaid. It felt just like the old days, when we were friends who could tell each other anything.

A few days after my return, Mrs. Ferris stopped by with an enormous arrangement of snapdragons, lilies, and gladiolus that probably weighed more than she did. After setting the bouquet down on the hall table, she enfolded me in an unexpected hug. "I'm so sorry," she murmured, before letting me go.

"Wait here," I said. "I have something of yours." She stood next to the flowers, a quizzical look on her face, and waited as I went to the study and returned with a folder.

"Medical records," I said. "I found them in Granddad's things. I shouldn't have read them, but I did. I had no idea you'd lost a child."

Mrs. Ferris stared at the folder, her eyes losing focus. "That was a long time ago."

"I overheard you talking to my dad once, at my parents' last Christmas party. You told him you hadn't forgiven him. Was it something to do with this?"

She frowned. "I lost a baby. It had nothing to do with your father."

"What was it, then, that you said he had to make up to you?"

She smiled wanly. "I was angry with your father because he had pulled me back in. Eddie and I were together off and on for a long time, but I put a stop to it completely when your mother was pregnant with the twins. I didn't think I could live with myself anymore. Eddie had a way, though, of weakening my resolve. That's what I was saying at the party—I hadn't forgiven him for dragging me back to him. I hadn't forgiven myself, either. We were both to blame, after all."

"You said before that the two of you weren't in love."

"It's true, we weren't. I was. But not him." She squeezed my hand, her bony fingers warm and strong.

"I want to talk about something else," she said. "The work you sent me by accident, those hundred pages you wrote about your family— I shared it with the others at the historical society. I hope you don't mind. I was a bit shocked, actually, after you seemed to be struggling so much with the profile. We've been looking for someone to write a new edition of *Legendary Keokuk Homes*, with more of a focus on the families and the stories behind the houses—something we could sell to all the tourists we're hoping to bring in. I think you'd be perfect for it. We'd pay you, of course. Not much, but I'll see what we can work out."

I had never expected that Mrs. Ferris would be the one to hand me such a lifeline. I thanked her, and she gave me a bittersweet smile.

"I'm truly sorry for everything," she said. "I still wonder what would have happened if I hadn't gone to meet your father in the carriage house that day."

"It still could have happened. If Dad hadn't called Mom and gotten into a fight on the phone, she wouldn't have left me alone with them in the bathroom. But maybe something else would have distracted her."

Mrs. Ferris's forehead creased. "Hmm. She said they were fighting on the phone?"

"Yeah. He called to say he'd be late, and she wanted him to come home. She was angry about him taking money out of their savings account."

She shook her head. "She might be remembering wrong. I don't think he called her that afternoon. At least, not while he and I were together. There's no phone line in the carriage house."

I shrugged. "Maybe he called on his cell."

"Arden, it was 1994. He didn't have a cellphone. None of us did." Her voice had sharpened.

"He could have called from somewhere else, after he left?"

Her lips pressed into a tight seam, fine lines feathering out around her mouth. She nodded slowly. "It's possible. I thought he went straight home, but maybe he didn't. I don't really know. Not that any of it matters now, I suppose."

Memory, as I knew better than most, was not reliable, the truth a shadow that reshaped itself over time. Maybe Mrs. Ferris was wrong about the phone call, and maybe she wasn't. Maybe Mom believed every word she had told me. Maybe her version of that terrible afternoon played in her head like an endless film, the same as my version played in mine. Maybe, to her, it was true. Even if it wasn't.

"Do you think she drowned them?" I asked. Mrs. Ferris appeared frozen for a moment, her mouth slightly ajar, eyes unblinking. Then her gaze drifted toward the staircase, to the second floor, where the twins had died.

"It's hard to imagine that anyone could do that and try to lay the blame on an eight-year-old child."

She hadn't said no.

I thought back to all the water in the house, the leak in the bathtub that led me to the button, the flood in the laundry room that took me down to the basement and the hidden room, the dripping faucet on the third floor, where I had found Mom's medical records.

I imagined my mother in a daze of pills, angry at my father, about the money, about the affair, about her life not turning out as she'd planned. I imagined her filling the tub and watching my sisters slip below the surface. Trying to decide if she could do the same to me, if she could hold me down and still pass it off as an accident. My father coming home before she could find out. Mom hadn't wanted me to come back to Arrowood, or to talk to Josh Kyle about his book. Maybe she had been worried about what I might find, what I might remember.

I had always had a vivid memory of the twins safe in the bathtub that afternoon, though my father had said it was a fever dream. But the other things my mother said—that she had left me alone with them, that I had overfilled the tub—brought no glimmer of recognition. I couldn't recall the smell of the bubble bath, the feel of the metal handle twisting in my palm, the screech of the faucet. I didn't remember any of it. Could that mean that it hadn't actually happened, that my mother had made it all up to cover up her crime? The fortune-teller had told me to trust myself, that the truth would come from within. I didn't believe that I had drowned my sisters. I believed that my mother had done it.

I called her as soon as Mrs. Ferris left, my heart hollowing out like the dark mouth of a cave as the phone rang and rang, dread seeping in. Finally the answering machine picked up, my mother's recorded voice artificially giddy. *You've reached the Swansons! Please leave a message! Have a blessed day!*

"Mom," I said. "It's Arden. I have some questions about what you told me." I wasn't sure how much to say on the machine. I wanted her to call me back.

There was a clicking sound, followed by Gary's voice grating in my ear. "Arden? It's Gary." As if I couldn't tell. "I know you're dealing with a lot right now, and I want you to know your mother and I are both praying for you."

"Is she there? I need to talk to her." I could hear faint television voices in the background.

"Your mother has suffered greatly for many years," he said, "and now she's finally giving it all up to the Lord and letting herself be healed. I hope you'll be able to find peace in our Savior as well."

"Did you know?" I asked. "Before this all came out, did she tell you? What did she say?"

"We're praying for you, Arden," Gary continued, deaf to my questions. "We're praying real hard."

She had fooled him, too.

Lauren was the one who suggested selling Arrowood and buying the Sister House. *We could live there together*, she said. *I can rent the upstairs for summers and holidays until I move back. It could be a Sister House again.* Not newlyweds, not widows, and not exactly sisters, though close enough. Two women starting out.

I hoped that Granddad would have understood. I was grateful that he had given me the house—I never would have found the twins if he hadn't—but I couldn't live there anymore. I'd thought that coming home would fix me, but it wasn't Arrowood that I had been longing for. I'd been drawn back to this dying town at the convergence of two rivers, the place where I had been born, where the Arrowoods had lived for one hundred and sixty years. The place where I had once been whole and might one day be whole again.

The lawyer explained that it would take some time to get Arrowood on the market and find the right buyer, but there was nothing standing in the way of selling it. Courtney offered to guide me through the process of buying the Sister House from the bank, which I could get started on right away, and Ben promised to help with the restoration, to repair the porch and cabinets and floors, to piece it all back together.

It was one of those deceitful winter days, so bright and sunny that you're convinced of its warmth until you step outside and feel the wind's teeth. I had spent the past few months sitting by the radiator in Granddad's office, working on *Legendary Keokuk Homes* and finishing my long-neglected thesis while frost encased the windows and the river froze and snow blew into dunes around the house. The snow was gone now, and days like this made it seem like spring was a possibility.

Mrs. Ferris had come by earlier in the morning to let me know that I was a shoo-in for the teaching position I'd applied for at the Catholic school, thanks in part to the stellar reference she had provided. It didn't hurt, she added, that the school's gymnasium had been a generous gift from my grandparents and bore the Arrowood name.

Now, my coat buttoned up to my neck in the chilly house, I waited, watching out the window for Josh to pull into the driveway. Staked into the dead grass along the sidewalk out front, a red and white Sutlive Real Estate sign shuddered in the wind. Courtney had stood in last month's melting snow in her high heels and pounded the sign firmly into the ground with a mallet. In the flower beds surrounding the porch, squirrels dug up the bulbs Heaney and I had planted before they had a chance to bloom.

Josh took my hand as I climbed into the van and pressed his lips against my cold fingers. He looked worried. "Are you sure you're ready?"

I attempted a smile to reassure him that I was, and he leaned across the console to kiss me, his fingertips trailing along my jawbone, my skin warming in the wake of his touch. We drove through the quiet streets, past the abandoned elementary school and the Sister House, away from the new Walmart and the old factories, to the edge of town, the good side of the Catholic cemetery.

Josh parked at the top of the hill, on the gravel drive. I wanted to see the new headstone on my own, and he understood. He squeezed my hand and released it, and I looked back, halfway down the hill, to see him waiting in the biting wind, there if I needed him. On the slope beneath the sycamore trees, I traced my name on the stones of the three other Ardens. I had somehow outlived them all, and I hoped that I had a long way to go before the time came to join them. I would be the fourth Arden Arrowood to lie on the hill, and the last.

My father's grave was nearly a year old, the ground smooth and covered with bleached winter grass. I thought of the panicked moments as I'd drifted downriver in Heaney's boat, Dad's voice calm and clear in my head. He never got a chance to make amends, but I hoped he knew that I had forgiven him, that a part of him would always be with me.

Next to Dad's grave lay a mound of bare dirt with a new granite marker, flanked by two marble angels. ARROWOOD, read the chiseled block letters. Beneath that, VIOLET ANN & TABITHA GRACE, DECEMBER 12, 1992–SEPTEMBER 3, 1994. For my sisters, who had been together at the beginning and the end, it was fitting to share a stone. The interment had been private, just me, and I had watched the pearl-colored casket lowered down. Though I knew now where they were, where they rested, I couldn't think of them buried in the cemetery or hidden beneath the house; I couldn't picture them tucked into the earth. They existed for me as they always had, in memory.

I had brought along one of Singer's photographs that I'd stolen from Josh, the one of me with the twins on the day they went missing, and I bent to place it on my sisters' grave. It was an accidental gift from Singer, that he had captured this moment, Violet and Tabitha as I would always remember them: laughing beneath the mimosa tree in the front yard of Arrowood, clover crowns in their hair, matching white shirts with yellow buttons shaped like ducks—and me, watching over them, smiling, no hint of the darkness to come.

Before turning to go, I closed my eyes and whispered a prayer to the burning saints, that they might watch over us all, the lost, the found, the living, and the dead, and light our way home, wherever that might be.

ACKNOWLEDGMENTS

Thank you, as always, to my family—the Runges, McHughs, Gilpins, Gipsons, and Berners—and especially Brent, Harper, and Piper.

Huge thanks to all the people who helped bring this book into the world. I'm grateful for the opportunity to work with the exceptionally kind and gifted Cindy Spiegel and the fabulous folks at Spiegel & Grau and Penguin Random House, including Annie Chagnot, Beth Pearson, Jennifer Prior, Elizabeth Eno, Sandra Sjursen, Julie Grau, and publicist extraordinaire Maria Braeckel. In the U.K., the wonderful Selina Walker at Century Arrow, and Judith Murray at Greene & Heaton. And, of course, my hardworking agent, Sally Wofford-Girand.

Much love to my dear Beasties: Ann Breidenbach, Nina Furstenau, Jennifer Gravley, Jill Orr, and Allison Smythe.

Many thanks to Veronica Runge, Lisa Gilpin, Diane Berner, Ellen Runge, Jessica Kirby-Runge, Barb and Bill McHugh, Paula Parker, Elizabeth Anderson, Hilary Sorio, Angie Sloop, Sally Mackey, Thomas Jacobs, Ryan Gerling, Dan Sophie, Nicole Coates, Melinda Jenne, Emily Williams, Amy Messner, Julie Hague, Sarah Norden, Liz Lea, Mary Atkinson, Angela Scott, Taisia Gordon, Adonica Coleman, and Martha McKim. Long overdue thanks to Helen Breedlove and Janice

Blisard—I've never forgotten what you taught me. I'm also incredibly grateful to all the librarians, book clubs, booksellers, writers, and readers who have supported me along the way.

I owe a great debt to the cities of Fort Madison and Keokuk, Iowa, my first homes. I took liberties in my portrayal of Keokuk and the surrounding area, though many of the landmarks mentioned in the book are real. Special thanks to the Samuel F. Miller House and Museum, the Lee County, Iowa Historical Society, and *Tales of Early Keokuk Homes* by Raymond E. Garrison for providing inspiration, and thank you to Diane and Kevin Berner, whose historic Second Empire home inspired aspects of the Arrowood house.

To my grandparents, Floyd and Telka Silvers, thank you for giving us a place to call home. I wish that we could all be together again in the little white house.

ABOUT THE AUTHOR

LAURA MCHUGH is the author of *The Weight of Blood*, winner of an International Thriller Writers award and a Silver Falchion Award for best first novel. *The Weight of Blood* was named a best book of the year by *Book-Page*, *The Kansas City Star*, and the *Sunday Times*, and was nominated for an Alex Award, a Barry Award, and a Goodreads Choice Award. McHugh lives in Missouri with her husband and children.

Facebook.com/lauramchughauthor
@LauraSMcHugh

ABOUT THE TYPE

This book was set in Electra, a typeface designed for Linotype by renowned type designer W. A. Dwiggins (1880–1956). Electra is a fluid typeface, avoiding the contrasts of thick and thin strokes that are prevalent in most modern typefaces.

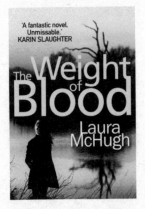